PAY-DAY

The car slid forward and disappeared round
the corner of the Phoenicia. Latimer watched
it go and then turned back into the Criterion.
His heart had started to beat unpleasantly
and he realized now that he had invited her
for a drink largely in order to postpone this
moment. In Oxford it had seemed so
straightforward, so logical: if Angus,
masquerading as Dr Steven Latimer, had
installed himself in Room 509 of the Criterion
Hotel in Beirut, the simplest way, surely, for
the real Steven Latimer to deal with the situation
was to go straight to the Criterion and ask for
his key. . . . But here in Beirut a dozen valid
objections at once presented themselves.
He hesitated.

Pay-Day

Helena Osborne

CORONET BOOKS
Hodder Paperbacks Ltd., London

Copyright © 1972 by Helena Osborne
First published 1972 by Hodder and Stoughton Limited
Coronet edition 1975

Printed and bound in Great Britain for
Coronet Books, Hodder Paperbacks Ltd,
St. Paul's House, Warwick Lane,
London, EC4P 4AH
By Hunt Barnard Printing Ltd,
Aylesbury, Bucks.

ISBN 0 340 19676 9

I
PANJEH

The man on the stretcher said suddenly, 'Holy Saint Patrick'. His eyes were shut and his hair and clothes were soaked through with salt water and oil, but the only visible sign of injury was a thin trickle of dried blood thick with flies down one side of his face.

Dr. Latimer said, 'So you're from Ireland, are you?' He leaned down and lifted the man's hand, feeling for the pulse. The fishermen who had carried the stretcher up from the harbour pressed forward with an excited babble of Arabic: it was the first sign of life that the man had given. They started to describe the explosion to each other yet again, flinging out their arms to indicate the eruption of water and débris, their voices rising higher and higher. Latimer pushed them out of the way and called to his assistant, a young Kuwaiti called Rifai. Together they lifted the man out of the fierce sun, across the broad verandah and into a narrow white-washed room containing only a strip of palm-frond matting and an iron bed. From similar rooms on either side came the smell of meat cooking in rancid butter as the relatives of other patients prepared the midday meal. Latimer and the young Kuwaiti laid the man down on the bed and Latimer flicked an electric switch on the wall. A decrepit fan hanging from the ceiling creaked into motion and slow eddies of the stifling air began to move above the bed.

'You're certainly a long way from Dublin – or perhaps you're from the west? I visited Ireland once, it's a beautiful place. So green. All that marvellous rain.' Latimer spoke soothingly – on the off-chance that the man could still hear and understand him – but all the time his hands were moving, cutting away the remains of the blue cotton shirt and trousers, sponging down the blood-stained face with swabs of cotton-wool, feeling gently along the bruised limbs for signs of injury. The man on the bed said nothing more but when Latimer's hands reached his pelvis he groaned piercingly, and for a moment his eyes flickered open. The fishermen, who had clustered tightly round the open door – just as the flies had clustered on the dried blood – groaned loudly in sympathy and excitement.

Latimer said gently, 'All right then, Paddy, you're all right,' and the eyes dropped shut again. Latimer gestured briefly and Rifai began to prepare an injection. The group of spectators was growing. Some of the women, harpy-faced in their bronzed leather masks, had managed to elbow their way through the tightly-packed mass and were squatting down on the floor only a few feet from the bed.

Latimer and Rifai worked on. The wounded man must be somewhere in his forties, Latimer thought. The face was lined and very brown, as were his hands and forearms, but the rest of his body was white like a child's.

After ten minutes Latimer straightened up. He nodded at Rifai and started to say something but stopped as a mechanical clattering became suddenly audible. At first it sounded like a child running a wooden stick along a railing and for a moment Latimer was puzzled. But then the volume of sound increased sharply and behind the clatter he could hear the beat of a powerful engine. The sound became deafening, directly overhead, and from all over the hospital building came screams of fear. The women squatting on the floor started to wail, covering their heads with their black draperies, and the men clustering round the door jostled backwards into the room, forgetting in their alarm all about the man on the bed. Latimer cursed at them in Arabic, elbowing his way through the crush.

The helicopter was just settling itself down on the bare patch of earth in front of the hospital, the wind of its rotor blades driving out a stinging curtain of dust and sand. The vast crowd that had been waiting tirelessly in the hot sun for Latimer to begin his surgery was streaming away in a mill-race of black-and-white draperies, the men's dark red turbans bobbing along like débris on the tide. Latimer, shielding his face with one arm, swore under his breath. It was the Ruler's helicopter. Not that the Ruler himself ever travelled in it – a helicopter at take-off and landing presents far too static and obvious a target – but he used it to bring in asparagus and strawberries from Bahrein, and his household and staff used it for shooting ibex and for joy-riding. More recently the Defence Force had used it once or twice for potting at guerrillas in the mountains of the interior.

Latimer looked at it with loathing. A Westland Lynx couldn't cost less than a quarter of a million. With a tenth of that sum he could have built and equipped a proper operating theatre. With only one thousandth he could have bought an air-cooler for the existing one . . . But it was too late now even to think of such things.

Major Dickens came running towards him across the beaten earth, bent double to avoid the whirling rotor blades, one hand clutching the binoculars slung round his neck. He was wearing a khaki shirt and shorts and on his head a *kafir* and *agal* – the characteristic Arab headdress of black-and-white checked cloth held in place with a double circlet of black rope. A gilt badge was pinned jauntily, slightly askew, to the black cords at the front of his head. He looked like something off a recruiting poster. This was no accident – Dickens saw life in poster terms. He liked to think of himself as lean, fit and bronzed, leading a man's life, leading men. It was still a mystery to him that the British army should have declined to extend his short service commission and even his present title, 'Commander of the Panjeh Defence Force', failed to console him. He was described officially as a 'contract officer'. Latimer called him a mercenary.

Now he came smartly to attention with a salute that was ostensibly humorous, but which also masked considerable un-

7

certainty: in his nine months on the island he had failed altogether to get on to terms with Latimer, and he had no idea why. In Dickens' eyes, as the two white men in the place he and Latimer should have been allies and cronies, drinking companions probably, and certainly the recipients of each other's complaints about the Ruler's eccentricities. As it was, Latimer's unvarying reserve and his grim contempt for the Defence Force and its methods had defeated Dickens entirely.

Now he said boyishly, 'A patient for you, Doc!' As an afterthought he nodded curtly at Rifai.

Latimer started to raise his arms towards heaven, converting the gesture at the last moment to rake both hands back through his straight, greying hair.

'Could you not,' he said, controlling his voice so rigidly that he sounded hardly more than ironic, 'could you not have put that unnecessary machine down somewhat farther away from my hospital?' Abruptly he twisted up his crumpled, expressive face into an almost heraldic representation of anger. 'How the hell do you expect us to teach these people even the rudiments of hygiene when you use your wonders of modern science to drive dust and filfth into their faces as they lie in bed?'

Dickens recoiled slightly. 'Oh . . . oh, sorry. Yes, I didn't think of that. But actually, it's a very urgent case. His Highness himself has sent him.' Dickens would far rather have said 'Old Salad Oil has sent him' but Latimer's manner discouraged familiarity, even on so eminently humorous a topic as that of His Highness Sheikh Saladin bin Abdul Rahman, Ruler of Panjeh.

The helicopter's engine coughed and died and the rotor blades slowed till they were individually visible. Two privates of the Defence Force were struggling to get a stretcher out of the cabin. With sudden misgiving Latimer said, 'Who's he sending me this time? One of the women?'

'*Oh*, no!' Dickens was full of importance, delighted with himself. 'A saboteur.'

'*Saboteur?*'

'That's right. Looks as if we've caught the man who actually did it.'

'Did what?'

'Blew up the drilling rig. We think he's one of the guerrillas from the interior. He was rowing away from the rig, towards the island, but he isn't a local man and he doesn't seem to be connected with the oil company. It's difficult to be sure, of course, because there aren't any survivors. We don't even know yet how many people there were on board.'

The rig had been serviced direct from Dubai. All stores and equipment had been flown in by helicopter and the crew, who alternated one week on the rig and one in the fleshpots of Tehran, had never been allowed even to set foot on the island. The Ruler had made this a condition when he granted the oil company permission to explore in his offshore waters.

'There's one survivor, anyway.' Latimer jerked his head reluctantly towards the room behind him. 'Some fishermen picked him out of the sea. One of the drillers, I should think. An Irishman.'

'Really? Can I talk to him?'

'You'd be wasting your time. He's unconscious . . . and he won't live long.'

Dickens looked suddenly alarmed. 'Well now, look here, that's just what's *not* got to happen to *this* bloke.' He gestured towards the stretcher, which had been finally manoeuvred out of the helicopter and was resting on the ground. 'The Ruler's absolutely adamant about that . . . Absolutely adamant,' he repeated, liking the sound of it.

Latimer said conversationally, 'A lot will depend on whether the Almighty is adamant, too.'

'Yes, yes of course,' Dickens said hastily, 'but I mean he's really *got* to be kept alive, for a few days at least. And conscious.' He glanced at Latimer with sudden nervousness. 'To – to answer questions.' He had serious reservations about the interrogation techniques that the Ruler was likely to employ but had forgotten them in the euphoria of actually catching one of the guerrillas. Now it occurred to him, too late, that after three years on the island Latimer would certainly know all about the Ruler's methods; the fort was clearly visible from where they were standing, hanging on its cliff above the harbour. Dickens glanced at it uneasily.

Latimer screwed up his eyes behind his glasses as though he

were peering into strong sunlight. 'What's the matter with him?'

Dickens said eagerly, 'Only a bullet wound. Really. In the shoulder. Shot while trying to escape. His Highness thinks you should take the bullet out – and stop the bleeding.'

'Does he now.'

Despite the heat, the stretcher that the soldiers were carrying towards them was wholly covered with a thick blanket. They carried it awkwardly, hampered by the submachine-guns slung over their shoulders. Conscious of the crowd of spectators, Latimer signalled to Dickens and the stretcher was carried along to the far end of the verandah and set down in his own small office. When the soldiers had gone Latimer shut the door and drew a curtain across the window. Dickens, who had followed with Rifai, said brightly, 'Well, you won't be needing me any more now, so –'

'Stay here.' Latimer bent down and turned back the blanket. Then he drew it off altogether and stood holding it. He said slowly, 'He's only a boy.'

'Yes, quite a young chap. Well –'

Latimer replaced the blanket over the figure on the stretcher but left the face uncovered. 'His Highness knows perfectly well,' he said levelly, 'that I am not prepared under any circumstances to operate on a man whose legs are in irons.'

Dickens started to bluster. 'This fellow's dangerous, you know. Don't forget I'm responsible for internal security. I have a duty to His Highness. This man's a saboteur. He's killed dozens of men – the whole crew of the rig – and the rig itself must have cost thousands. Millions of pounds, probably.'

'Maybe.'

Dickens tried a subtler approach. 'He's bleeding pretty fast, you know. Losing a lot of blood. He can't last long like this –'

'I can see that.'

'Well, don't you think –'

Latimer lost his temper. He did it quite deliberately, as a tried and reliable means of dealing with Dickens. 'Get out!' he roared. 'Get out of here and take this poor bugger with you. I won't put a finger on him and nor will anybody else

10

till you get those bloody great irons off his legs.'

But Dickens, surprisingly, stood his ground: he'd had an idea. 'You're off pretty soon, aren't you?' he asked cleverly. 'I don't suppose Dr. Riffy would mind operating – '

Latimer said dangerously, 'As you very well know, Dickens, I'm sacked as from tomorrow at noon. I leave on the afternoon plane . . . But today *I'm still here.* So go on. Get out. You can leave him here but you go straight back and tell His Highness to send a blacksmith. Straight away. Go on.'

Dickens found that he had retreated right out on to the verandah, into the dense, interested mass of Arabs. He pulled himself up sharply and tried to rescue some dignity. 'Very well,' he said grudgingly, 'but I'll have to leave these guards with him.'

Raising his voice, he clipped out a series of commands to the two men. Then he doubled off smartly towards the plane, shouting up at the pilot, a Pakistani officer on contract like himself, to start the engine. The pilot stared back unimpressed and put a leisurely hand forward to the controls. 'Hurry up! It's urgent!' shouted Dickens. 'We'll go straight back to the palace!'

He scrambled happily on board, panting, reflecting with satisfaction that by tomorrow night Latimer would have left Panjeh for good. The pilot, continuing methodically with his take-off routines, raised a grave hand in greeting to Latimer, motionless on the verandah. Latimer grinned and waved back.

Spewing out its baggage of sand the helicopter inched off the ground. The screams of alarm from the spectators this time were mere routine and Latimer turned back to the prisoner. Obedient to Dickens' order the guards were standing one on either side of the stretcher and with their equipment seemed to fill the narrow room entirely. Latimer pushed them out on to the verandah, overruling their objections forcefully. He also sent Rifai off on an errand to the dispensary. Then he leaned down to the stretcher. He removed the blood-stained pad that had been strapped to the boy's shoulder and started to examine the wound. The boy opened his eyes and tried to smile. He was wearing European clothes – a khaki bush jacket of faintly military flavour and khaki trousers, but he had the fine bones of the Arab. There was a short curly beard round the line of his jaw.

He made a faint sound – but not a sound of pain. Latimer said hastily in Arabic, 'Don't tell me anything. Don't say *anything.*'

The boy smiled more broadly. He said, 'You're Dr. Latimer?'

'Yes, but don't talk to me. You're far better to say nothing at all.'

The boy laughed, and then winced from the pain. He said softly, 'Down with British imperialism in the Gulf! Long live the Popular Front for the Liberation of Penjeh!'

Without stopping what he was doing Latimer said slowly, 'So you're one of those, are you . . . ? Well, don't imagine that I've any sympathy with you. I don't like terrorism.'

'Maybe not, but you support our aims, don't you? – that's why you're getting the sack.'

Latimer corrected him calmly, probing the wound, 'The Ruler has decided not to renew my contract.'

The boy laughed again, and gasped at the pain. 'Stay another week and we'll be in power, today was only the start. In exactly a week's time – '

'Don't *tell* me,' Latimer repeated urgently. He wondered if the boy had the slightest idea of what was going to happen to him once Saladin had got him into the fort for 'interrogation'. He said angrily, 'I've not the slightest sympathy for you. There's a man dying along the corridor here, from the rig you blew up today. You've as good as killed him.'

With sudden seriousness the boy said, 'Don't worry, I shall be killed too.'

The island was the last, most westerly tip of the mountain range of Muscat and Oman, separated from the mainland by only five miles of shallow sea. The inhabitants were Arabs but it was Persian seamen who had named the island – Panjeh, the five fingers – from the five rocky promontories that thrust themselves out from the northern shore. The coast on all sides of the island was harsh and forbidding; but high up in the interior there were springs and green oases, patches of cultiva-

12

tion and huge flocks of sheep and goats. In these inland areas the guerrillas now moved freely, carrying with them what little equipment they had, living off the land and matching Saladin himself in brutality towards any tribesmen or villagers who refused to help them. No one knew how many they were, or for certain how long they had been there: when they murdered three of his palace guards and distributed leaflets in the town Saladin appealed to Britain for help against 'this well-established, thousand-strong, Chinese-trained and Chinese-equipped army', but once his Defence Force had got a British Commander and some new British equipment, and the guerrillas had stayed quiet for a couple of months, Saladin recovered his nerve and started to talk about 'scattered handfuls of ragged desperadoes'. The other Sheikhs of the Trucial Coast, by contrast – rulers of some of the smallest and richest kingdoms in the world – continued to behave like chickens at the sight of a fox. They had been alarmed ten years before when guerrillas first appeared in Dhofar, in the extreme south of the Sultanate of Muscat, but that had been a thousand miles away, on the far side of the Empty Quarter of Arabia. Panjeh was right on their doorsteps. With one voice they implored Saladin to beg for the return of British forces to the Gulf. But Saladin preferred to go his own way, as he always had done. He was prepared to make use of the British if there was no alternative, but he never liked to be too publicly involved with them – and never to have too great a cause for gratitude.

Twenty-five years earlier he had been the ambitious younger brother of the much-respected ruling Sheikh, Hassan, and had longed to make himself Sheikh, to make himself Ruler of Panjeh. But the blood of a murdered brother cries to heaven for revenge . . . and so Saladin had merely lamed and blinded Hassan and his two other brothers and had turned them out to live and very soon to die in the dusty lanes beside the harbour. In Saladin's book this didn't count as murder. The British had been appalled and sickened, though powerless to interfere, and Saladin had continued for twenty years to believe that they would welcome any chance to displace him. He was always afraid that they might exact too high a price for their help –

that they might succeed in deposing him. And just at this moment he was more than ever determined to stay put.

Panjeh had always been a poor relation on the Coast, an oil-less sheikhdom. But now, though the fact hadn't yet got into the newspapers, oil had been discovered in Panjeh's offshore waters, a vast deposit: Panjeh was about to join the club. Saladin was about to become one of the richest men in the world.

Steven Latimer wasn't really sorry to be leaving. Throughout his time in Panjeh he had been haunted by hopelessness and failure and now he was content to capitulate. His decision to become a doctor had been taken when he was already grown up, in a mood of revulsion from violence – in the first shock of having seen a man murdered. He was already twenty-three when he started his training, and within two years he discovered that he had made a bad mistake: he had no real liking for the work. But he had persisted, had completed his training and had gone into private practice – chiefly because his wife Felicity, an American, had insisted. But he always felt himself an impostor. He had found with dismay that many people he met – his patients, his friends, even his family – were determined to regard doctors as intrinsically *better* than themselves, as paying with lives of self-sacrifice, a debt for society as a whole ... To Latimer, who had been impelled into medicine by a grim sense of obligation and who was now installed in a profitable London practice, this was doubly ironic.

But a few years later he felt free to leave England; his wife had died and he took the Panjeh job thankfully when it was offered because there, he thought, there was a need. The need was undoubted, as he quickly found, and he could have worked for twenty-five hours out of the twenty-four, dealing with endemic disease alone. But even in Panjeh violence was inescapable. Soon after his arrival the guerrilla attacks began and from then on the casualties and the atrocities mounted. He was sickened by the methods of both sides: patching up the victims of Saladin's 'interrogations', rescuing what he could of those whom the guerrillas had chosen to use as examples ... Change must come in Panjeh, the fact was obvious, and it was

14

impossible not to sympathise with the rebels' professed aims – an end to tyranny, a new life for the Panjehi – but their actions ceaselessly contradicted everything they stood for.

There seemed to be no obvious middle way, and Latimer found himself sometimes thinking about Haider bin Hassan, Saladin's nephew and the son of that Sheikh Hassan whom Saladin had deposed and murdered. He had been at school in England when his father was murdered and Latimer had met him a few years later, at Oxford. For a time they had been friends. Haider already had all his plans ready for avenging his father and uncles and himself assuming power. He would then, he had decided, rule on the enlightened principles of his father, Hassan, but with further innovations – better schools, hospitals, roads . . . He talked about becoming Ruler of Panjeh with confidence, almost with indifference, as though he were the acknowledged heir apparent: it was simply an event that was going to take place quite soon. He had powerful friends in Britain, he implied, who would give him all the help he needed . . . but in the meantime there was the far more pressing task of turning himself into the perfect simulacrum of an English undergraduate – punting, drinking beer, campaigning for election to the Union committee . . . Ten years later Latimer met him again, briefly, in the States. Haider's confidence was undimmed, but he had transferred his hopes of support from the shadowy corridors of British power to that shining hope of the Arab world – Nasser's Egypt, and Britain had become the arch-villain. Latimer had no idea what had happened to him now, and his occasional, half-hearted attempts to get in touch were all unsuccessful. Sometimes he had a depressing vision of a little group of exiles, in Cairo perhaps, sinking down into an unreal world of empty hopes and unfulfilled promises . . . That was probably the best that could have happened to Haider bin Hassan – who might have been an enlightened, a modern Ruler of Panjeh.

2
LONDON

1

'Dr. Latimer. Good morning.'

She stepped out of the small crowd waiting outside the customs and stood solidly in his way. She was well past middle age and made no attempt to look less, but her plump, upright figure sparked with vitality.

Latimer said politely, 'Good morning.' He had hardly slept on the plane and as always when he was tired his eyes had begun to water. He blinked and looked at her more closely but the result was still the same: he had never seen her in his life before.

'I am Alice Wedderburn.'

'Oh . . . yes?' He shifted his case to the other hand and an Arab family, emerging through the swing doors behind him, jostled him painfully to one side.

'Well, we had better move,' she said briskly. 'We're only in the way here.'

'Yes, but – ' But she had already gone, moving with surprising speed towards the exit.

Unwillingly Latimer let himself be swept along in the same

direction, his head turned over his shoulder, searching the crowd that had been waiting.

'Are you expecting somebody to meet you?'

'Not expecting, really.' Her question dispelled the flicker of fantasy that had accompanied him on the flight. 'Just hoping.' It was six months since he had been in London on his last brief leave and for a girl in her twenties that can be a long time.

'That's all right then. I've got a car. We can talk on the way in.' She stumped out through the automatic doors and across the pavement, and halted beside a red Mini, parked in defiance of every possible regulation immediately outside the terminal. She wrestled briefly with the lock of the boot and the lid swung open.

Trailing after her, Latimer shivered as the fresh air hit him. Four hours ago he had been in Beirut and two days before that in Panjeh: a fine English October morning felt like the South Pole.

'Come along.'

Latimer put his suitcase down on to the pavement. 'I'm very sorry,' he said hesitantly, 'but I'm afraid there must have been some mistake.' Dickens would hardly have recognised him: except in the context of his profession, Latimer had always been diffident and considerate, easily bullied. 'My name *is* Latimer but I don't think we've actually met and –'

'Of course we haven't met. But please don't argue. As you must realise, I am Margaret's mother. I was rung up from Beirut last night and told that you would be on this plane. I naturally wanted to see you . . . It was Luc Duquair who rang.'

Duquair . . . the name meant nothing. He had only changed planes in Beirut and had spoken to no one. Could Duquair perhaps be somebody connected with the airline?

He said non-committally, 'Ah – ', but his uncertainty disarmed him and when she made a further impatient gesture he put his case obediently into the boot, closed the lid and climbed into the car beside her.

She ground the little car sharply through its gears and shot away into the traffic, driving with a fierce concentration that at first left no room for conversation. Latimer glanced at her cautiously. Wedderburn, she had said her name was. Alice

17

Wedderburn. The name meant nothing to him. But equally, she was clearly *somebody*. Her profile was craggy and impressive and her white hair was brushed straight back to disappear under a curious hat of great distinction.

He said foolishly, feeling his way, 'It's very good of you to come and meet me like this.'

The corners of her mouth slid momentarily back in what was certainly amusement. 'Well, I don't have much to do in the mornings now. Since I stopped being a magistrate. I gave it up two years ago, you know. I wasn't really sorry. My granddaughters had started behaving in a way that I would have said meant they were in need of care and control – but everyone else seemed to think it was perfectly normal . . . After all,' her tone altered slightly, 'even fifteen years ago public standards of behaviour and morality were very different from those that obtain today.' For a moment her eyes flicked sideways and to his astonishment Latimer caught a look of great meaning.

'No, no,' she said a moment later, answering some remark that he hadn't made, 'things were simply moving too fast for me.' She accelerated sharply, as though to disprove the admission, and the little car shot down into the exit tunnel like a rabbit into its burrow.

She didn't speak again until she had settled the car firmly in the centre lane of the motorway leading in to central London. Then she said at once, 'Now we can talk.' But it was clear right away that the talking was going to come from her. And it was clear too that she had long considered what to say and how to say it. It came out as an entirely formal statement. 'I have remained silent all these years, Dr. Latimer, only at my daughter's request. I have often wondered whether it was a wise course – whether you would not perhaps have gained the impression that her family did not care about Margaret and her happiness. Or you might perhaps have thought that, having no father or brother, she was helpless and unprotected. I do assure you, most seriously, that this was not and is not the case.'

She paused, but Latimer was too astonished to speak.

'Now, however, that you are following her to Beirut and have already started to pester her again I feel obliged to tell you – '

Latimer said loudly, 'I haven't the faintest idea what you're talking about.'

She said with irritation, 'Don't interrupt. I don't expect you to agree with what I say. A man who behaves as you have done is not likely to admit it. Nor is he likely to be influenced by reproaches or appeals from me. To have left her in peace all these years and then to reappear just when at last she has a chance of real happiness – of marriage, perhaps, and a proper family life . . . It was her fiancé, Luc Duquair, who warned us that you were going to Beirut and that you had already started to pester her again. I must admit that in my old-fashioned way I would have expected better from a man in your career, a physician . . . but I am *not* going to appeal to you. I am simply warning you that if you persist in this behaviour I, and the rest of Margaret's family, will pursue you with every legal and private remedy open to us.'

She had stopped talking but Latimer continued to gaze at her: she was in earnest all right . . . But was she sane? He glanced quickly out of the window for reassurance. Beyond the grey rim of the motorway was a solid wedge of new houses, a playing field with goal posts, a narrow overgrown stream and then, just as the motorway lifted itself on to a flyover, one of those uncared-for fields that you find around London, with three or four tousled ponies . . . He took off his spectacles and polished them carefully. Then he turned back towards her and spoke with all the conviction he could muster.

'Mrs. Wedderburn, you must believe – '

As he spoke she jerked round to look at him and the car veered widely to the left. Startled, he put a hand to the wheel, but she had already recovered herself and the car was back under control.

'Go on,' she said quietly.

He started again, less forcibly. 'Please. You have really got to believe me. I don't know in the very least what you are talking about. As far as I know I have never even met your daughter. Until I saw you this morning I had never even heard your name, or hers. Quite frankly, you must have got the wrong man.'

She glanced at him quickly. 'But your name is Steve Latimer?'

'Well, it's Steven.'

'And you were at Oxford in the early 1950s reading Arabic? And then you went to the States and trained to become a doctor? You got married in 1964 and your wife died five years ago?'

He said 'Yes,' helplessly, to every question and her mouth hardened. 'And now you are proposing to go and live in the Lebanon for six months . . . *to write a book*.' She made it sound like loitering with intent.

Latimer said 'Yes' again, and was annoyed at the defensiveness of his own tone.

'And why should you, a doctor of medicine, suddenly take it into your head to *write*?'

'It's what everybody does in the Middle East, when they've been sacked.'

'Do they? But why Beirut? Why not London?'

'Libraries,' he said brusquely, 'and climate.' Did he really have to go on for ever being polite?

'Mmm.'

Latimer suddenly found himself angry. 'Now, listen. You clearly have a certain amount of information about me, but it could all have come from college registers or from – '

She said with violence, 'I know far more about you than you will ever believe. I've taken care to know *everything* – your friends, your professional standing . . . '

'Well, you've certainly slipped up on my recent activities.'

'No . . . You've been staying in the Criterion Hotel in Beirut.'

Startled, he said, 'But that just isn't true.'

'Room 509,' she said implacably, and was silent.

They had reached the end of the motorway now and Latimer began seriously to consider escape – but his suitcase was still in the boot.

Suddenly she said, in the calm reasonable tone with which she had started, 'I don't believe in coincidence, Dr. Latimer. And I don't believe in mysteries. You don't deny that you are planning to live in Beirut for the next few months. There can hardly be two people of identical name, background and appearance going to Beirut at this time.'

'Appearance – ' he said slowly. 'Yes, how did you know what I looked like?'

She stopped the car carefully at some lights before answering. Then turning to look at him closely, quite without embarrassment, she said, 'I recognised you at once, of course, from Margaret's description. But it is true that at close range you are not quite – what I had expected.' Almost as an afterthought she opened her bag, took out a pair of severe black-rimmed spectacles, put them on and looked hard into his face. Then, without comment, she returned them to her bag.

The lights changed and the line of cars moved forward. More hesitantly she said, 'I know you were young at the time, Dr. Latimer, but you weren't a child. She *was*, really – really not more than a child. But she has had to suffer since as a grown-up. It has altered her whole life, you know. It's altered her – character, too. She was a very sensitive girl – and she still is, *very* sensitive.'

Latimer listened with new astonishment. This was unmistakably sincere emotion – and for a second he felt a spasm of pity for the unknown girl, the ruined life.

'I was prepared – ' she was almost arguing now, seeking at all costs to be reasonable, 'I was prepared to forget the past altogether, but I *cannot* accept that her life should again be ruined.' Abruptly her voice resumed its coldness. 'Are you now prepared to give me an undertaking that you will cease to molest my daughter?'

'Oh, for heaven's sake!' He flung up his hands in irritation. 'I've *told* you that it's all nonsense. I really can't even discuss it.'

'I must warn you that other members of my family, my son-in-law in particular, that's Anna's – my other daughter's husband – are not inclined to be so open-minded as myself.'

'Will you drop me here? I'll walk.' The car had stopped again at some lights and he started to fumble with the door handle.

'No, Dr. Latimer, I want to show you something. Something that you ought to know exists.' While he hesitated the lights changed and the car shot forward again. From the Earls Court Road she turned up the Brompton Road and so into the

21

Boltons, following a complicated route with the confidence of long practice. She didn't speak again.

When at last she drew up they were outside a large Victorian block of flats, down by the river.

'Come with me.' She led the way without looking behind her and, reluctantly – curiously – he followed. They creaked slowly up to the third floor in an ancient lift with mirrors while she rummaged in her bag for a latch-key. The front door of the flat was covered with brass, all in a state of brilliant polish – knocker, door-knob and letterbox. The flat inside gave the same impression of applied energy. Carpets and furniture were worn but good, and every object was fiercely in its place. There was one exception, however. In the drawing-room a large photograph album lay open on a table by the window.

She stood back to let him go forward by himself. There was only one photograph on the open page. It was a snapshot, taken out of doors during a picnic. A thermos was clearly visible, and a tartan rug spread out on the ground; and in the background there were some ill-focused bushes and a hillside covered with pine trees. The photograph showed a young man and a girl, sitting together on the rug. At least, the girl was sitting on the rug, laughing, and she was holding out an arm to the young man who was just sitting down beside her. He must have set the time-switch on the camera and then run back to get into the photograph – but not quite quickly enough. The angle of the girl's face made it difficult to be sure, and the out-of-date clothes were distracting, but it looked as though she had been extremely pretty, and very young. Her hair was short and it curled up at the back of her head and round her face; and the arm she was holding out to the young man was slim and graceful. Yes, the girl looked attractive and charming and gay.

And the young man . . . Latimer peered more closely, cursing his own poor eyesight and the instant of movement that had left the young man's image in the photograph as a mere blur of arms and legs. Flannel trousers, dark hair, horn-rimmed spectacles . . . it was no use denying it: the young man could perfectly well have been himself.

2

It was nearly two a.m. the following morning before Latimer finally caught up with Patsy, in a discothèque in the Fulham road with black plastic decor and overwhelming amplification. If it hadn't been for Mrs. Wedderburn he probably wouldn't have bothered: Patsy hadn't come to meet him at the airport and he would just have left it at that. But Mrs. Wedderburn's confident identification of him as a Don Juan – as a *pesterer* of women – had, on reflection, cheered him enormously. He would go and find Patsy.

She came in with a young man in pink velvet trousers and her face lit up when Latimer touched her on the shoulder.

'Didn't know you were back!' she screamed, sinking down at his table and waving the pink trousers away. She was a long straight girl with a lot of long straight hair. He was never sure how much he liked her, but she certainly roused powerful emotions.

Now he shouted against the blare of the music, 'I sent you the time of my plane.'

'*What?*'

'I said, "Don't worry, another bird met me."'

'Oh, that was nice.' He could never decide whether she was really obtuse or just very cool. Still, on his last leave, in April, she had been extremely friendly.

He said, 'I thought about you a lot during the summer. In Panjeh.' It was the truth.

'Did you?' She seemed surprised. 'Are you on leave again now?'

'No, I've finished with Panjeh. I got the sack.'

'Oh – ' It clearly happened more often in Patsy's world than in his own and she was unimpressed. 'So you're back for good.' She didn't sound very elated.

He said patiently, 'No, I'm going to Beirut for six months. To write a book . . . Don't you remember?' They had met originally when Latimer was discussing terms for the book with Patsy's employer, the publisher Tim Kellett. 'One of the

23

reasons I'm in London is to collect my advance.'

But she had turned away to look at pink trousers dancing with another girl and her face was hidden by the curtain of her hair. Alpha for unmemorability – that seemed to be Latimer's mark today. Then he thought of Mrs. Wedderburn – and her daughter: *she* had remembered him, it seemed. Or somebody just like him.

The music was momentarily less deafening. Latimer said, 'Would you recognise a photograph of yourself taken fifteen years ago?'

'*Fifteen years* ago?' Patsy looked round, astonished, suspecting mockery.

'No, I suppose not . . . too much hair even then, I expect.' He laughed, and the lines on his face were swallowed up in creases of amusement.

Patsy, watching him, smiled suddenly. 'I missed you terribly,' she said.

'Nonsense.' He put a hand round the back of her neck, under the hair, and she moved her head against it. 'You'd forgotten all about me. What reminded you?'

'The top of your head . . . the way it goes back when you smile.'

'Ah . . . and I do card tricks too.'

'Don't laugh.'

'I'm not.'

He moved his hand down on to her shoulder and she turned her head round to kiss him. 'Did you really think about me in Panjeh?' Gently she started to rub the tip of her nose backwards and forwards across his cheek and Latimer sat still and looked at the dancers. A few minutes later she said, 'And did you miss me?' She drew a finger slowly down the line of his forehead and nose, skipping lightly over the spectacles. 'Did you?'

Latimer cleared his throat. He said brusquely, 'Can we go? Can I take you home?'

This was the moment he always hated. He had never got used to offering or accepting bed as he would a cup of coffee – but that was how it seemed to be now, with the young. He had grown up in a convention that had seemed satisfactory enough at the time, though looking back it occurred to him now that there had been an extraordinary amount of planning and hiding, of leaving flats with a crowd and slipping back later by himself, of muffled giggling. At a distance of fifteen years it all seemed very childish, very innocent. And once he had met Felicity, of course, he had married her just as soon as she would agree to have him. The great revolution had taken place somewhere in the years when they were married and he hadn't even noticed, and when his marriage stopped he had simply woken up one day in an unfamiliar moral climate – one that didn't really suit him.

Now he waited with a mixture of embarrassment and impatience for what Patsy would say. But he needn't have bothered. She said at once, 'Well . . . not really,' and indicated pink trousers, who had reappeared beside their table and was standing, loose-limbed, in an expectant sort of way.

Wearily Latimer observed that he suffered no great burst of jealousy . . . he didn't in fact mind very much. And that was another difficulty. He was a romantic. He was always falling half in love with tall fair confident girls and pursuing them with all the conviction of a stronger emotion – but by the time they had been to bed together a few times his burst of romantic feeling would be over. He hated to acknowledge the fact.

Now, against his will, he said, 'Tomorrow?'

'Tomorrow?' Suddenly she giggled. 'You must come to our Speeding.'

'*Speeding?*'

'God-speeding. Tomorrow. Twelve noon.'

Pink trousers was making disjointed Come-on-and-dance gestures. Patsy said, 'Do come, Steven . . . say you will?'

Pink trousers jerked again, more violently, and Patsy said 'O.K.?' She smeared a kiss across the side of Latimer's face and smiled – with just a trace of embarrassment. Pink trousers had got hold of her hand and was sidling off into the crush.

Latimer nodded without speaking and she smiled again, more happily. 'By the way, we've moved,' she said, and let herself be pulled away into the crowd of dancers.

It really *was* a relief, he told himself firmly, paying off the taxi: he was tired as hell and there was a lot to do next day. He no longer had a flat in London and had taken a room at a cheap hotel behind Victoria. He had been going there for years, ever since he used to travel backwards and forwards for the school holidays to Cairo, where his father had been in business. The name of the hotel had altered once or twice but the only other change was that over the years the smell of boiling cabbage on the stairs had given way to the smell of curry . . . and that would do very well, he thought, enjoying his own little joke as he took his key from the board and started on the long climb to Room 38, as a microcosmic social history of Pimlico in the period under review . . .

The stairs were steep and he paused after the third flight and leant against the wall. If ever you can honestly say that you don't care for anybody at all, he thought suddenly, then you can't ever be hurt – and that means you're not really alive any more.

Self-pity . . . Latimer clenched his teeth and started up the final flight of stairs. His footsteps echoed curiously in the narrow staircase and as he reached the turn he had a sudden clear conviction that someone besides himself was listening to them.

He toiled up the last few steps and the man detached himself from the shadows and stood directly under the light.

'You don't know me,' he said unnecessarily. He was short and plump, with flat, prematurely white hair and a weak face. 'But you saw my mother-in-law this morning.'

'Oh, come in, come in.' Latimer wrestled with the lock and pushed open the door of his room. 'Come one, come all.' He put on the light and walked in, throwing his coat down on to the bed. 'Have you come to show me some more photographs?'

The man followed slowly and stood just inside the door. Turning to face him, Latimer was forced to register how rich he looked, with a suit that even at three in the morning was uncreased, and a heavy tie still neatly knotted. Feeling by contrast crumpled and unwashed, Latimer took off his jacket and started to pull at his tie. The man said nothing. He was perfectly composed, but with a curious undercurrent of irresolution and embarrassment. It occurred to Latimer suddenly

26

that he must have come to apologise for his mother-in-law's behaviour.

'I'm sorry,' Latimer said, 'I shouldn't have spoken like that.' Then, struck by an idea, he added, 'How did you find me?'

'Through the airline . . . ' The man advanced slowly into the room. With unnecessary loudness he said, 'I have come to tell you to keep away from my sister-in-law, Margaret.'

'Oh, for Christ's sake – ' Latimer stood still, trying to summon up enough energy to get him to go away.

'I am her only male relative, you know,' the man went on earnestly. 'I don't want you to think that I make a practice of this sort of thing, forcing myself on a man's privacy at three in the morning, and particularly somebody who – well, a *doctor*, like yourself . . . But you have really left us no choice. Margaret is most unhappy, *most* unhappy, you know. She's a very – *sensitive* girl, and I feel responsible for her. She's my sister-in-law. Her sister,' he explained carefully, as though to a mental defective, 'is my wife, Anna.'

Latimer said nothing. The man went on, 'I understand from my mother-in-law that you have refused to give an understanding to cease to molest Margaret.'

Latimer started to speak but the man talked straight on. ' – and I have come therefore to tell you not to go to Beirut.'

'To *tell* me?'

The man nodded gravely. 'Until you will give us this understanding, we do not wish you to be in the same town as Margaret.'

'You must be mad.'

'I warn you, most sincerely. The consequences will be most unpleasant for you, *most* unpleasant . . . '

Latimer said, 'Go to hell.'

For a moment the man seemed at a loss. Then, 'You have left me no *choice*,' he repeated. Slowly, he raised his right forearm and equally slowly curled up the fingers. Latimer looked in some surprise at the resulting fist, and then the man hit him with considerable force just below the left eye.

27

3

The duck peered doubtfully at Latimer's shoe and then, having examined the ground under the bench he was sitting on, retired across the concrete path and launched herself into the lake with a brief quack of irritation at having wasted so much of her time. The drake, who had been less hopeful in the first place, stretched his green neck and tucked his head back into his wing feathers.

Latimer squinted at his watch. The Speeding – whatever that proved to be – was due to start in ten minutes, and after that there was a train to catch to Oxford. But he still felt reluctant to move. St. James's Park was warm, golden and empty – and above all the Wedderburn connection wouldn't know where he was. Tenderly he put a hand to his left cheek. The eye was almost completely closed and the cut below it smarted as he touched it.

He had got past wondering why all this was happening by about 5 a.m. Since then he had been concerned chiefly with what, if anything, he ought to do about it. Mrs. Wedderburn might have been a harmless – if well-informed – lunatic, but the son-in-law was certainly sane . . .

He shifted his position on the bench, recrossing his legs, and the slight movement sent shafts of pain up through his cheek into the top of his head. His face was far more painful now than it had been at the moment when the man hit him. 'You have left me no choice,' he had said, and then – *crash*. He had looked fairly astonished as he did it. 'You have left me no choice – '

A poodle, very white and fluffy and secure in the knowledge that he couldn't get at them, was prancing up and down at the edge of the water barking furiously at the ducks. A woman in a camel-hair coat whistled twice at him and then, with a sigh of resignation sank down on to the seat beside Latimer. 'Oh, Lord, what a nuisance these animals are.' Her voice was warm and attractive.

Cautiously he turned his head and squinted at her. She

smiled, ignoring his swollen face, and turned away again to look at the dog. She was somewhere in her thirties, with a pale skin and honey-coloured hair massed fashionably at the back of her head.

Latimer said, 'Did you follow me?'

Her face swung round again. 'Yes, I did . . . Am I so like my mother?'

'You're like her about the mouth. But it was the voice mainly . . . So you're Anna.'

'Yes.'

'If you're going to hit me I'd rather you took your rings off first.'

She laughed at that, spreading out her hands and looking at the big diamonds as though she hadn't noticed them for some time. 'No. No, I've come to apologise. About my husband. He's far too impulsive . . . My mother thinks there may have been some mistake.'

'Oh . . . does she? Why?'

'It was something you said to her, apparently. Something you called her.'

'*Called* her? I was most polite.'

'You called her Mrs. Wedderburn.'

'Well, she said that was what her name was.'

'Did she? Steve, listen to me – '

'I don't mind, you know, but nobody actually calls me Steve.'

'Well, Steven, then – Dr. Latimer – whatever you like . . . I would awfully like to get this business cleared up. If you're the wrong person we must of course apologise – and frankly, I find it difficult – we *all* find it difficult to believe that somebody in your position, a *doctor*, could really have behaved so appallingly. But if – if you *are* the person we think you are . . . ' She stopped altogether and tried again. 'This is a question on which we, as a family, feel very strongly.'

'So I gather.' He touched his cheek.

She said reproachfully, 'Margaret suffered terribly, you know, and has gone on suffering.'

'Are you prepared to tell me what I am supposed to have

29

done to your sister or have I got to go on drawing my own conclusions?' He was conscious of sounding petulant, and as she glanced at him coldly he started at once to apologise. Then, with a sudden revulsion, he said, 'No, I'm *not* sorry. I've been put in this absurd position three times in the last twenty-four hours. Different members of your family accuse me of pestering your sister, with dark hints of far worse in the past, but when I tell them it's nonsense, which it is — I find myself apologising for saying so. You, if I may say so, seem slightly more open to reason than your mother or husband and I wish you would hoist this in once and for all: I have never to the best of my knowledge met or even heard of your sister and I had never even heard the name Wedderburn till yesterday morning.'

He stopped because the cut under his eye had started to throb, but he could see that he had made an impression. She looked at him with interest and the beginnings of relief.

After a moment she looked away from him and began quietly, 'When she was just sixteen, in the summer after she took her "O" levels, my sister went to stay with friends in the country. At a village dance she met a young man called Steve Latimer. He looked — he looked very like you — '

'Did you meet him?'

'No, but there's that photograph my mother showed you. You must admit . . . Well, she fell in love with him, in a very big way, and he, apparently, with her. And — you've got to remember that she hadn't really met many men before — a few boys of her own age, of course, but this man was older — twenty-one or two . . . ' She stopped and tried again. 'Margaret had been very strictly brought up, you know. My mother is old-fashioned, as you will have realised, in some respects, and anyway, fifteen years ago these things just weren't accepted as freely as they are now. So that it meant a very great deal . . . ' Her voice stopped altogether.

'They went to bed together.'

'Yes.'

'Well, so I've gathered.' Latimer was irritated. 'Quite honestly, your reaction as a family seems to me disproportionate. Even fifteen years ago that sort of thing wasn't — unknown, and — '

'Margaret had a baby.' Her voice cut flatly through his own. 'My mother would have arranged an abortion for her but Margaret refused. The baby was deformed. He lived nearly eight months and then died.'

'Oh my God.'

'The baby wasn't the worst part of it, in a way. One forgets now what public opinion was like fifteen years ago. We all talk as if no one ever took seriously all that talk about – well, about moral standards and – and how girls ought to behave and that sort of thing. But they did . . . *I* did. So did Margaret. So did a lot of our generation . . . ' Her voice was almost apologetic.

Latimer said quietly, 'It was my generation too, you know.'

She stared at him, startled. Then she went on quietly, 'For Margaret to go to bed with him represented a fantastic step for her. She committed her whole personality to it. And then when he just went off – ' she gestured helplessly, 'it really was the end for her. The end . . . It's a bad joke nowadays to talk about "wronged" girls – a sort of Victorian snigger. But at that time it could still be true.' She said with great feeling, 'Margaret was deeply, deeply wronged.'

Latimer closed his eyes. These were cruelties that he could understand. He felt real distress for the unknown Margaret . . . But she was also *unreal*: she didn't exist – not in *his* life.

He said briskly, 'What happened to him, the man – do you know?'

'We heard that he'd gone to the States.'

Latimer glanced at her uneasily. He said, 'And now he's reappeared and is – *pestering* your sister?'

'Yes. Letters, telephone calls, that sort of thing. Luc rang up and told my mother.'

'Luc's the fiancé?'

'Well – ' she hesitated perceptibly, 'yes. Her fiancé.'

'What's she doing in Beirut?'

'She has a job there . . . Anyway, after the letters and the phone calls started Luc made some enquiries and found out that you were planning to go and spend six months in Beirut, so he rang up and asked my mother to – to – '

' – to cope.'

There was silence. Latimer let it run for a minute or two and then he said briskly, 'Look. I don't begin to understand any of this, and I can't prove anything to you about the letters and phone calls. But at least we can clear up the earlier part. Fifteen years ago I was in California and I can prove it quite easily.'

'You were?' He could see that she was pleased.

'Yes, I was. I was doing my medical training at a college called Westmoreland near Los Angeles. When exactly did this happen?'

'Well, let's think. Margaret left school in – One keeps saying fifteen years, but really of course it's more . . . much more.'

Apprehension gripped at his stomach so violently that he felt momentarily sick. But Anna didn't notice.

' . . . she was born in 1940, so it must have been – 1956. *Much* more than fifteen years, come to think of it. Poor Margaret . . .'

Latimer said deliberately, 'Which month in 1956?' – but he didn't really need to be told.

'Which? Well, I know we all went to Venice together that summer – I was already married. That must have been in July. Then she went to Scotland for a bit, most of August, I think. So that makes it –'

'September 1956.'

'That's right. And you were –' she smiled – 'safely in California.'

'No. No . . .' He could hear his voice as though it belonged to somebody else – dry and academic. 'That was before I went to California. Just before.'

'Where were you then?'

After a moment she repeated, more sharply, 'Where were you?'

He said, 'I was doing a job.'

'Where?'

'I can't tell you.'

'*Where?*'

He repeated, 'I can't tell you. I'm sorry.'

At once her irritation erupted. 'Oh, don't be so absurd. You don't expect me to believe that?'

Latimer sighed briefly and started to recite, surprised at how easily the details came back. 'I spent September 1956 staying at a house in the New Forest, a big early Georgian house with four or five rooms downstairs and eight bedrooms. It was a sort of reading party. There were seven of us, three from Oxford University and four from Durham. We were all specialising in Middle Eastern problems. I had just finished my degree in Arabic and I was working on a paper about fifteenth-century Egypt. In the mornings we worked and in the afternoons we played tennis or went for walks. We didn't mix much with the village or the people around about because we were all working pretty hard. The address was Barton House, Barton Minor, near Burley, Hampshire. The telephone number was Barton 74.'

As he spoke her face, which had been creased with worry and suspicion, started to relax, and by the time he'd finished it was quite smooth and without expression.

She said, 'I see . . . that's that then. Margaret's friends lived at Burley. Well, I must say I'm disappointed. My mother will be sorry too.'

She stood up and whistled to the dog. 'At least you were honest.' Then she walked away along the edge of the lake with her hands in the pockets of her coat. She didn't look back.

Latimer just went on sitting there, thinking about what he had said. It was odd that after all those years of deliberate forgetting he had still got every detail correct – even down to the telephone number. He realised suddenly that he had never really believed before that Barton House – or Barton, or Burley – existed. But evidently they did. He found himself wondering whether it was pretty country round there – it had looked rather nice in the photograph of the picnic. He had always wanted to go to the New Forest.

And suddenly he saw what the truth must be, and an explosion of anger and fear annihilated for a moment all sight and hearing, all power of movement . . . Angus. Once again, it must be Angus.

4

WEDDERBURN, Lady Alice Emily, J.P., O.B.E., 1969. Chairman, Inner London Magistrates Court 1952–67. *b.* 21 April 1910; *yr. d.* of 4th Earl of Crarae, K.T. (*d.* 1943) *m.* 1935 Sir David Wedderburn Bart; two *d. Educ.*: privately and at the Sorbonne. Member of official Advisory Committee on Refugee Relief (S.E. Region) 1938–44. J.P. 1945. Member of Royal Commission on Juvenile Delinquency, 1959–61. Hon. Fellow Girton College, Cambridge, 1967. Governor of Chatsworth School for Girls. Member of Governing Body Floyd Centre for Technical Education for Girls, Gosport. *Recreation*: music. *Address*: 75 Elizabeth Mansions, S.W.3.

So all her life she had been 'Lady Alice'; and after her marriage even those who didn't know would have called her Lady Wedderburn. No one anywhere, ever, would have called her 'Mrs. Wedderburn'. More especially, if he, Latimer, had ever known anything about her at all, *he* wouldn't have called her that. It was just the sort of tenuous but significant clue that someone as intelligent as herself would pick up. It had been enough to make her doubt seriously whether she had got the right person.

Latimer shrugged, still gazing at the page. Well, it didn't matter: every suspicion that any member of that family had ever harboured about him would now be fully confirmed.

He closed *Who's Who* and took it back to the girl at the desk. She was a milk-coffee negress with a smooth face transmitting a non-stop programme of disdain. It was clear that all the clients of the reference library had failed – each, no doubt, in his own individual way – to measure up to her standards.

Her eyes rested, briefly, on Latimer's disfigured cheek. *Some people will try anything*, her expression said, *to gain attention*. Still, it was something to be visible: without a bruised face she probably wouldn't have seen him at all.

In an elaborate whisper Latimer said, 'Thanks. Lovely weather we're having.'

Her expression didn't change but – almost imperceptibly – she nodded. He flashed her a brilliant smile and walked away, his shoes squelching on the noise-resisting floor. At the door he turned and waved. She didn't move but one of the long milky hands folded on the counter in front of her quivered.

5

In talking about his decision to abandon medicine for six months and write a book, Latimer generally managed to imply that the book was to be about his experiences in Panjeh. But this wasn't so. Nearly twenty years after the start of his medical training he was deliberately giving himself a holiday: he was going back to his earliest enthusiasm, Middle-Eastern history.

Tim Kellett was the brains and working parts of the Barbizon Press, a small highbrow concern specialising in books about international affairs and about the Middle East in particular. He liked Latimer and had agreed to finance in advance *An Examination of the Interaction of Christian and Islamic Thought in Lebanon in the late Eighteenth and early Nineteenth Centuries.* It wasn't a title calculated to top the bestseller lists for very long and in the circumstances Tim's financial terms were more than generous.

When Latimer had last visited them, on leave in the previous April, the Barbizon Press had occupied two narrow basement rooms in Bedford Square, and its total staff, apart from Tim himself, had consisted of Patsy and one typist. Their new address, extracted that morning from directory enquiries, was a number in Half Moon Street, very central and monied and not at all the sort of area in which Latimer would have expected to find them. And even when he got to Half Moon Street, already half an hour late for the Speeding, he walked past the building twice because he simply couldn't believe it. Barbizon's new offices turned out to be a vast block of green-tinted glass held together with strips of stainless steel.

Tim was standing just inside the plate-glass front doors, backed by dark green carpet as far as the eye could reach. A dense crowd of people was visible through green glass doors to the right and there was a lot of sprightly and incongruous music coming through the loudspeaker system.

'I'm not waiting for you,' Tim said kindly as they shook hands. He was ten years Latimer's junior but had never made him feel it. '*Well* – ' he peered at Latimer's face with interest. 'Back to the swinging life, I see. What happened?'

'Oh, I'm all right, but what happened to *you*? Have your books started making a profit?'

'Heavens no, nothing so shaming. No, we've been taken over. It's the smart thing these days. Look – '

He waved a hand at some discreet gold lettering on a green marble wall beside the lifts.

TRADE WINDS FOUNDATION FOR INTERNATIONAL UNDERSTANDING and underneath, in smaller letters,

> *Trade Winds – Barbizon Press*
> *Trade Winds Educational Books*
> *Trade Winds Television Features*

Latimer read it all twice and then he said, 'Yes, but what does it *mean*?'

'Well,' Tim glanced briefly over his shoulder, but except for a receptionist several carpet miles away the foyer was empty. 'Well, primarily it means more money, folding stuff, for publishing more and better books by distinguished authors like Dr. Latimer.'

'Splendid. And – ?'

'Well, secondly . . . secondly, it means more money, too.' He laughed without much conviction. 'We were nearly broke this summer and his offer was just too good to turn down. He's – ' he glanced over his shoulder again, a gesture so alien to him that Latimer thought for a moment he was joking, ' – a nut really. Name of Cordwainer. But a rich nut, and the terms are okay. Unlimited financial support but no editorial inter-ference – absolutely none.' His tone was defensive.

'What's the catch? The nut?'

Tim laughed again, harshly. 'Well, yes. He's all right, but he's extinct, really – a dodo. He's setting out to be a philanthro-pist, a sort of nineteenth-century iron-master who's made his pile and wants to set the world to rights.' Tim was happier now – theorising. 'He's had the hell of life and he knows what abroad is really like. But even so he goes on maintaining that the world can be put right by feelings of brotherhood.' Latimer's attention had wandered. He had succeeded at last in identifying the music coming over the loudspeaker system. It was what used to be called a country dance – sprightly, innocent tunes with suggestive titles. Latimer hadn't heard this one since he was at prep school and it was ludicrously at odds with the green glass modernity.

'He ought to have been a missionary, really. That's the life that would really have suited Master Cordwainer.'

'Gathering Peascods' – that was it. The girl at the desk called in a silvery but carrying voice, 'Mr. Kellett! Mr. Cordwainer to speak to you.' She was holding out a white telephone receiver.

Tim sprang towards the desk. 'Yes, Chairman . . . no, not yet. Yes, I will . . . Yes, I'll be here. Yes . . . Yes . . . Yes . . . Yes, Chairman.'

He put down the phone and came slowly back across the green carpet. 'All right – that's the effect he has on me.' He spoke sourly. 'It's ridiculous really. There's no earthly reason why we should be helping with this absurd exhibition at all – ' he jerked his head towards the glass doors, 'but there's nobody else. That's the trouble. He'll take on any crackpot who's got an idea about world peace but there isn't an administrator in the place . . . You'd better go in – ' He was so depressed that Latimer felt ashamed – as though he had surprised Tim in a compromising situation. 'The Minister's arriving any minute and underneath, in smaller letters,

'Minister?'

'Well, he's only a Minister of State, really – '

'Right – ' But he hesitated. 'Tim – '

'What? – Your *money*!' Tim threw up his arms in a pantomime of dismay. 'Oh God, Steven, I'm sorry. This man's got me tied. Listen, I can't do *anything* today, you can see that, but why don't we lunch? Tomorrow? Marvellous . . . I'll give you the cheque for the advance then.'

Latimer said awkwardly, 'Thanks, that's tremendous . . . That'll be extremely useful. Vital, in fact. Thanks.'

Tim Kellett smiled with satisfaction and pleasure. 'No, no,

37

I'm delighted. It'll be a most valuable book, I'm sure.'

There was a loud hum from the bank of lifts beside them and his face changed again. Latimer said hastily, 'I'm gone,' and went like a rabbit towards the green glass doors.

Tim shouted after him, 'Patsy's inside.'

The crowd wasn't in fact as dense as it had looked from outside. This was because about a dozen people were standing just inside the door, waiting, presumably, for the Minister. Two or three of them were probably journalists – there was one bored-looking figure in sagging tweeds and two very young ones – but the others were mostly middle-aged ladies in tidy woollen dresses and one or two men with beards. The noise of the country dances on the loudspeaker system was deafening. Taking a glass from the tray offered to him Latimer pushed his way through the crowd.

A big open area had been broken up with pale blue canvas screens and on these had been hung a small exhibition of paintings. The first one he looked at showed a black and white cat sitting on a circular rag rug of elaborate design in front of a table covered with a patterned velvet cloth on which rested a brass lamp and an aspidistra in a decorated pottery bowl. It was painted in glossy oils. There was no attempt at perspective or proportion and the colours were crude. But the objects were solid and well-drawn and the whole thing had a certain charm.

The next one was in the same sort of style but showed a field full of black and white cows with a wooden fence round it and a farmhouse with a red roof. A quick look suggested that the rest were on similar lines. Latimer went to look for Patsy.

He found her crouched on the floor behind a screen at the far end of the room, struggling with a tape-recorder.

'Hi.'

'This bloody thing,' she said without looking round, 'I think it must be the wrong size of tape.'

Latimer leaned against the screen and watched her long back with pleasure. 'Is this where all that extraordinary music is coming from?'

'All right, all right – ' She was immediately defensive and he realised that he had got into the middle of an old argument. 'What music would *you* have for English primitives?'

38

'Primitives?'

'That's what they call people who pretend they can't paint when they can.' She sounded irritable. 'They're supposed to look at an object and put it straight on paper, like a child. It's called having undistorted vision. Simple country people who've never had a lesson and never seen a painting and –'

'Not even Matisse?'

She laughed at that and overbalanced, sitting down sharply on the carpeted floor. Then she glanced up at him and her expression changed.

'*Steven*! What on earth have you done to your face?'

'Well –'

'I say – ' A red-veined face with bags under the eyes had appeared round the end of the screen. 'Are you by any chance the guardian angel?' It was the journalist in tweeds. He sidled round the screen, peering down at Patsy with his poached-egg eyes. 'There's always a guardian angel at an affair like this. Have I found her?' He looked with interest from Patsy to Latimer, taking in the bruise on Latimer's face with an extra lift of his exaggerated eyebrows.

'What do you mean?' Patsy stood up and dusted off her skirt.

'My dear,' his manner was confidential, 'anyone as pretty as you are must realise that an old campaigner cannot be fobbed off with – with this stuff.' He pointed to the glass in Latimer's hand. 'There must be a bottle of Scotch somewhere and I can tell just from looking at you that you're the one who knows where it is.' He paused. 'What *is* it, by the way?'

Latimer sipped at it and made a face.

'It's mead,' Patsy said wearily. 'And it wasn't my idea and no, there isn't any Scotch. Mr. Cordwainer wanted something in keeping with English rural life.'

'Scotch,' said the journalist promptly. 'What could possibly be *more* in keeping with English rural life.'

'*Patsy* – ' Tim Kellett shot round the screen. 'For Christ's sake, the Minister is here.'

Patsy crouched again over the tape-recorder and 'Gathering Peascods' ceased abruptly. A moment later a new tape began very softly – Bach, this time, something gentle on a harpsichord.

Patsy stood up. 'Undistorted vision,' she said. 'Mr. Cordwainer's own special choice.'

Tim had disappeared again and now the journalist drifted away too. 'Back in half a mo' . . . '

Latimer put his head round the screen – and withdrew it at once as he caught sight of the ministerial party a couple of yards away. It was clearly the Minister in the lead, a stocky man with a brown moustache and a blue and white striped shirt. Immediately behind him came a white-haired man in a dark suit, behind him Tim, and behind Tim a couple of smooth young men who looked like private secretaries. The Minister must have had military experience: he was dealing with the paintings as with a parade of veterans, moving briskly along the ranks, pausing occasionally to notice a campaign medal or ask a pertinent question.

The whole party was immediately on the other side of the screen now. Latimer felt his heart beating unpleasantly and Patsy, watching him, began to grin: it was like hide-and-seek.

'Oh, I like that one. I like that one very much.' The party had halted exactly opposite the place where they were standing, separated from them only by a few inches and a couple of thicknesses of canvas.

'Looks like a large white to me. Not quite the right shape, of course – but that's called artistic licence, isn't it? What?' There was a titter of polite laughter. 'But they oughtn't to leave the whole litter with her like that, you know. They're vicious brutes. I used to breed them myself and we were always losing litters – the sow would eat them. Her own litter. Just like that. Vicious brutes.'

There had been some whispering during his last remarks and now another man's voice said, 'This is one of Mrs. Winthrop's paintings, Minister. Fortunately she is here today and I've just asked someone to fetch her.'

Latimer put his mouth to Patsy's ear and whispered, *'Cordwainer?'* – even though he knew the answer.

She nodded, grinning, wagging her head up and down like a toy dog in the rear window of a car.

There was movement on the far side of the screen, some scattered 'How-do-you-do's' and then the Minister's voice once again. 'Now tell me, Mrs. Winsop, do you always leave the whole litter with the sow like that? I think its dangerous, myself.'

A high woman's voice said, 'Oh, but Minister, it wasn't *my* pig. I live in Wimbledon. I just saw the pig and its babies in a photograph in *The Times*.'

'Oh ... oh well, I see.' He was clearly disappointed. 'Well, thank you Mrs. Winsop. Perhaps I should have a look at the rest of the pictures?'

Cordwainer's voice said, 'The microphone is just over here, Minister, so perhaps – ?' and the Minister's voice, 'Yes, of course, by all means.'

There was some more shuffling, a squeal of static from the microphone, and then Cordwainer's voice boomed eerily all round the room.

'Ladies and Gentlemen, it is a great honour for me to be able to welcome here this morning –'

Latimer leaned his head towards Patsy's and whispered, 'When did he take Tim over?'

She shrugged. 'Couple of months, I suppose. But we only moved in here last week. Why?'

'... the Minister of State for the Arts and Sciences ...'

'Has the Foundation been going on long? – this Trade Winds thing?'

'About a year I think, but I don't really know.'

'Ah – er – Ladies and Gentlemen – ' The rustle of the Minister's notes, amplified, almost drowned his voice. 'I am very happy to be here today.'

Patsy started to narrate a complicated saga about Tim's office furniture, and behind her whisper Latimer heard in snatches the Minister ploughing gallantly through his prepared speech.

' ... this imaginative project ... showing the world ... Britain's pre-eminence in the field of the Arts – generosity of private patrons the support of Art through the ages ... this extremely interesting collection now setting out on its world

41

tour . . . message of peace . . . undoubtedly great success . . . privilege . . . God-speed.'

There was a thin round of applause and then Cordwainer was speaking again. Patsy had reached the climax of her story and Latimer didn't hear how he started but by the time she had finished he was talking about the aims of his Foundation. He had a good speaking voice and an easy flow of words – or perhaps he had merely had plenty of practice with this particular speech.

'Everywhere that we look in the world today we see conflict – conflict between opposing ideologies, between rich and poor, between men with black skins and men with white skins, between commercial rivals. Conflict may take many different forms but always at the root of conflict there lies fear – fear and ignorance. Fear and ignorance remain the keynotes of popular attitudes to international politics despite the almost incredible growth over the last half-century of methods of mass-communication.'

The journalist in tweeds reappeared, crab-wise, round the screen. He nodded to Latimer, murmuring, 'Just soak it in. That's best,' and with a glance of reproach at Patsy, sat down on the floor with his back against the wall and closed his eyes.

'Indeed, often it seems as though easier communication has served only to increase mistrust. The problem, I think, is that politicians, broadcasters and journalists use words that may be comprehensible to the intelligence of an ordinary man – but they do not speak to his heart.' The journalist gave a little snuffle of amusement but kept his eyes shut.

Patsy mouthed, 'You've got to hand it to him. Up to this point it's perfectly O.K. Of its kind.'

Latimer nodded, gloomily. 'What *exactly* is the extent of his control over Barbizon?'

'Well – ' Patsy was impatient. 'I've told you. He owns them, I think.'

'But Tim can publish what he likes?'

'I suppose – '

'It is to break down these barriers of ignorance, fear and mistrust that the Trade Winds Foundation has been set up. As you may be aware, we are already offering scholarships to

42

students from abroad, but this is the first time that we have been able to arrange for an exhibition of this kind to go overseas. It is a project for which I, personally, have the strongest hopes. Words appeal to the intelligence, but the visual arts appeal directly to the heart. Much sophisticated visual art is, however, difficult for people of alien culture – or of no culture – to comprehend because it has its own history and conventions, its own language almost.'

Patsy whispered, 'This is where he goes off the rails.'

'But the paintings that we have gathered together for this exhibition are the work of men and women who are not – and I know they will forgive me if I put it in this way – who are not *artists* in the popular sense of the word at all. They are all untaught – or, rather, *self*-taught – and their record of the impact that nature makes of them – '

Patsy was bored by this, and she was a girl who recognised only one certain cure for boredom. Leaning forward so that her mouth was up against Latimer's ear, she murmured, 'They all went to the Slade, every single one of them.' Then she kissed him on the neck. Latimer jumped slightly, and they both looked down at the journalist – but his eyes were still shut. Patsy suppressed a giggle and put an arm up on to Latimer's shoulder. His heart sank. In Patsy's book there was no close season for this sort of thing, and if he was stuffy about it she was quite capable of starting a noisy argument.

Cordwainer was saying, ' – the tranquillity of this undistorted vision of the world around us – '

'His peroration – ' Patsy murmured, putting her other arm round Latimer's neck. She was almost exactly his own height and her eyes were on a level with his as her face came towards him. There was a lot of clapping going on on the far side of the screen but the journalist's mouth hung open and he was apparently asleep. Resignedly, Latimer took off his spectacles and started to kiss her in earnest.

So that when the man came round the end of the screen Latimer saw him at first only as a grey blur over Patsy's shoulder. He didn't hurry to retrieve his glasses because he already knew what Cordwainer looked like – and he thought he could guess fairly accurately at his expression. But in fact when

43

he finally got his glasses on again Cordwainer looked even more astonished than Latimer had expected. But then, Latimer had seen this confrontation coming – in some form or another – for quite a long time and the surprise had already gone out of it for him.

Patsy was scarlet with laughter and embarrassment, but Latimer didn't see how any initiative of his could help. He did nothing.

Then Cordwainer took a grip and suddenly everything was very brisk and calm and ordinary-seeming.

'Excuse me,' he said smoothly. 'I came to find *you*, Miss Ashby. To ask you to put something a little more spirited on the tape-recorder. To speed the departers, you know.'

'Yes, certainly, Mr. Cordwainer.' Patsy obliterated herself over the tape-recorder and at the sound of Cordwainer's name the journalist snorted and sat up, opening his eyes. Then Tim Kellett was there, smiling with attempted confidence and saying, 'Oh, Chairman, I want you to meet Dr. Steven Latimer, who's going to write a book for us.'

Cordwainer said, 'Dr. Latimer and I have met.' He said it in such an even, pleasant way that Tim was clearly delighted and Patsy stood up slowly with an expression of relief and surprise on her face.

He smiled briefly and nodded a couple of times, and each time he nodded a gleam of light from the spotlights in the ceiling ran up and down across his flat white hair. Rich, he looked, rich; and as far as Latimer could see the knuckles of his right hand weren't even bruised.

The journalist scrambled to his feet and began asking Cordwainer questions, Patsy disappeared and Tim started to talk about lunch. Latimer said No, no thanks all the same, Tim, I've got a train to catch. To Oxford. Tim said Nicholas? Latimer said Yes. Tim said, You mustn't keep *him* waiting, Latimer said No indeed, and then they both said goodbye.

Latimer made for the door. He didn't bother to say goodbye to Cordwainer, and Cordwainer didn't say goodbye to him.

6

CORDWAINER, Charles Reginald Albert, M.B.E. 1972. M.A. (Oxon.); Director of Companies; Founder and President Trade Winds Foundation for International Understanding; *b* 11 June 1921; *es* of late Klaus Körner, Linz, Austria; *m* 1955, Anna, *ed* of late Sir David Wedderburn, Bart; One *s* two *d. Educ.* Linz Gymnasium, Tonbridge Grammar School, Worcester College, Oxford (scholar). B.A. 1949. Interned as enemy alien 1939–41. Joined British army (labour battalion) as a private, 1942. Sergeant 1943. Sergeant-major 1945. *Recreations :* flying. *Address :* Wyman's Court, nr. Henley, Berks. 347 South Eaton Place, S.W.1. *Clubs :* United Universities, Travellers, Royal Aero.

The girl at the desk had handed Latimer the *Who's Who* again without even being asked – and her expression of disdain was still in full blast. Now, however, as he approached the desk to hand the book back she exhibited unusual animation. She was preparing to speak. Latimer put the book down on the counter and prepared to listen.

'Still looking?' she asked at last, faintly, and Latimer leaned closer to hear what she was saying. 'Still looking for the name of the guy who hit you?'

Then she folded up, contorted, her head down at the level of her knees, clutching at the counter with one long milk-coffee hand but making (out of deference to library rules) no sound at all. When he got to the door and looked back she was still laughing.

7

Nicholas was waiting just outside the front door. He wore a grey overcoat and grey woollen gloves and a tartan scarf. He was clearly in a bad mood.

Latimer's heart sank. Nicholas had never concealed his indifference and for most of the time Latimer himself believed that he had disliked Nicholas from the start. But it was always so hard to be sure.

Now they shook hands and walked out into the road. It was six months since they had seen each other. Nicholas asked politely, 'When did you get back?'

'Yesterday morning. Which way do you want to go?'

'The Parks . . . You've done something to your eye.'

'Yes, it was an accident. With a cupboard door.'

'Oh. How funny.'

They turned down the land beside the school buildings and after a time Latimer asked, 'Is it all right, coming down during the week like this? From your point of view, I mean. I rang up and asked and they said it was fine but I just wondered.'

'Oh, yes, it's okay. It's only Nature today.'

'Do other parents come?'

'Not in the week. But I'm a special case.'

'Oh – isn't that rather nice?'

'Well, not really. It's because of having no mother. There are four of us. Justin's father is in prison.'

'And that makes him special?'

'Yes. And Anthony Boddington-Jones.'

'His father's in prison too?'

'No, it's his mother. She's barmy.'

'Oh I see . . . Who's the fourth?'

'Wayno. His father comes and goes so much.'

'I see.'

'Wayno scored a try on Saturday. We were playing Summerfields.'

'Were you playing too?'

'Oh no. No one else in our class was playing. Wayno's the youngest person in the Under Elevens. He's the youngest there's ever been in the Under Elevens. Mr. Williams says he'll get a Blue if he goes on like this. But his conversion wasn't a success.'

'*Conversion*?'

'Of the try. Parsons missed his kick.'

'Oh, bad luck.'

'Parsons is a bloody fool.'

They were into the Parks now and Latimer said, 'Which way? Shall we go to the pond?'

'Okay.' Nicholas shrugged. He walked stiffly, without swinging his arms, and he made no attempt to scuff through a drift of leaves beside the path.

Latimer said carefully, 'Does everyone swear at school – "bloody", and so on?'

'No much . . . ' Nicholas snuffled with amusement. 'Wayno called Matron "silly bitch" last term.'

'What happened?'

'Oh, he got the slipper . . . But Angus says "bloody" a lot.'

Ducks, Latimer thought. They had reached the pond now and the ducks were gathered near the edge, casual but watchful, ready for the bread that came with the prams. Ducks. Was he to spend the whole of the day looking at ducks while people said unexpected, incredible, inexpressibly painful things to him?

Aloud Latimer said casually, 'I didn't know you saw so much of Angus.'

'Oh yes. He comes a lot. He came – not last week but the week before, I think.'

Well, why not? Who – in nature – had a better right than Angus to come and see Nicholas? Certainly not him, Latimer. Probably.

'Daddy, in Nature we're doing trees. What's that one?'

'Elm, perhaps?' The trees in the Parks are all labelled, but unfortunately in Latin. In silence they peered at the metal plate. Latimer said decisively, 'Plane.' Nicholas nodded without interest and they walked on beside the river.

It occurred to Latimer that Nicholas had deliberately changed the subject.

'Where's Angus living now?' he asked, too quickly. 'In London still?'

'Yes, Highgate. I'm going to stay with him next holidays, to see the Post Office tower . . . but he's in Beirut at the moment.'

'*Beirut*?' Latimer stood still and stared. 'Are you sure?'

'Of course I'm sure.' His mouth was sulky and his thick

47

eyebrows were drawn down into a level line of displeasure. Angus too had thick dark eyebrows, and a similar trick of frowning when displeased . . . but you couldn't prove anything at all on evidence like that, thought Latimer tiredly. He knew, because he'd tried.

Nicholas repeated crossly, 'Of course I'm sure. That's where he was going when he came down last time.' The sulky beautiful mouth was his mother's alone – but that point at least was not in doubt. 'And he sent me a postcard. Of a ruin. Look.'

With some difficulty Nicholas took off a grey glove and burrowed under his coat. The postcard was worn at the edges from much handling and somewhat bent. It showed a view of Baalbeck – brown columns against a bright blue sky – with a group of old men in baggy black trousers and improbable peasant hats in the foreground. On the back was written, 'Very hot and sunny here. I bathe every day. Can you dive yet? You must teach me. Love from Angus.' The handwriting was neat, legible, unmistakable.

Latimer could no longer remember the moment at which he had first realised that Angus was capable of sustained malice. Rivalry, of course: they had been the only two men in their year reading Arabic and rivalry between them had been likely from the start. The contrast of their backgrounds and personalities had made it inevitable. Angus was a Highlander – the aboriginal Scot, brown and wiry and dogged as a sherpa. He had come out of a Sutherland croft and my sheer hard work had turned himself into a first-class Arabic scholar. Latimer, by comparison, had been idle and ignorant – enjoying music, reading, and pleasure – never enjoying hard work. But he had spent his childhood in Cairo, he had Arabic in his bones, and he could generally tell whether a word or a phrase was right or wrong – though Angus was more likely to know why.

Then, right at the end of their time at Oxford, they had quarrelled. Latimer had never liked Angus – he had found him pompous and sycophantic – but he had wished him no harm, and when at the end of their final term he played a trick on him, quite a mild one, he had intended no great injury. But Angus had never forgiven.

Nicholas was still looking at the postcard. 'I brought it

specially to show you,' he said reproachfully. 'We're going to use it for International Day.'

'International Day?' Latimer hastened to make amends. 'What's that? Tell me about it.'

'*International* Day?' The thick eyebrows shot up in astonishment. 'Don't you know? It's next Saturday, October the sixteenth.' He was suddenly excited. 'I'm going to dance a square dance. For America, you see. There's a Mazurka for Poland. And an Austrian dance. Wayno's doing a sword dance, by himself. That's for Scotland. And we're having pictures of places abroad. Angus can't come, but will you come instead?'

Latimer was speechless. Silently he took out his diary and found October the 16th. 'There,' he said, and wrote 'International Day, Nicholas' across the page. Nicholas beamed.

'There's the bridge!' he shouted, and started to run. It was a graceful, lighthearted bridge curving up over the Cherwell, like a detail from the willow pattern, framed in trees and bushes. Nicholas rushed up its steep side and hung over the railing. Following, Latimer looked down into the brown water. It had been green when he was up, he remembered, green and rather beautiful.

Leaning on the rail beside Nicholas, Latimer said, 'Did Angus say how long he would be in Beirut?'

'No . . . ' His feet thrust through the gaps in the railing he leaned over and dropped two twigs down on to the slow river. As soon as they touched the water he dashed to the other side of the bridge and hung over. The concrete echoed under his feet. 'It's too narrow, really,' he said in disappointment. 'It isn't wide enough for a good race . . . I ought to be getting back now. Tea's at five.'

His ebullience had gone. In silence they walked back down the steep slope of the bridge and set off across the grass towards the gate.

'That's the beech tree,' Latimer said confidently, 'a copper beech. It's called "copper" because of the colour of its leaves. Look.'

'Yes,' Nicholas said sombrely. 'I see.'

As they reached the front door of the boarding house

Latimer said, 'Shall I come again tomorrow? I could stay the night in Oxford.'

Nicholas frowned slightly. 'There's a lecture on Wild Life tomorrow. I'd like to be at that.'

'I see . . . well, I'll come down one day later in the week then.'

'All right . . . and for International Day?'

'Oh, yes. For International Day.'

8

The disorder in Peter Arden's room in college was just the same as it had always been, but sadder, somehow, dustier, like a film set abandoned but not yet broken up. The piles of books and pamphlets were still on the floor but it was plain now that they were never opened. The maps of the Middle East were still on the walls, but curling at the corners and brown with age.

And yet that couldn't be right . . . Latimer hadn't seen Arden for – nearly twenty years, but he'd read all his articles and he'd even bought his books. And they were very good. It was only his surroundings that were phoney.

Peter himself hadn't changed much in appearance either, though he now wore a baggy tweed suit and a knitted waistcoat splotched with food stains and tobacco burns. When Steven had been an undergraduate he had tended towards sandals and long cotton robes of a loosely oriental flavour.

'Scotch?' he asked, tipping bottles against the light. 'Or gin?'

'I'd rather have tea.'

'There isn't any.' Arden was irritated. 'You know perfectly well . . . you'd better have Scotch.'

Latimer held the glass in his hand and looked at Arden's chair on the other side of the fireplace. It was sagging and shabby and it held his shape even when he was out of it. There was a pipe in a bowl where the left hand would lie and a reading light and an open book . . . He's getting old, thought

Latimer, with a tiny stab of pleasure, and fat, as Arden settled himself back into the chair with a grunt.

'Well,' Arden said, 'cheers,' and waved his glass. Then, waiting till Latimer had taken a mouthful of Scotch, he added, 'To the return of the prodigal.'

He laughed immoderately as Latimer choked and reddened with anger, but then, quickly, he was serious again.

'Steven, forgive me. That was the hell of a crack. But it's been too long. Really. I can't tell you how much good it does me, just to see you again, sitting there. Here's to you, Steven. God bless.' He drank deeply and then wiped his yellowing moustache on a large red handkerchief. He repeated, 'You've stayed away too long.'

Latimer had promised himself once that never again, as long as he lived, would he allow himself to be influenced by Peter Arden, and yet now, as Arden looked at him under his spiky eyebrows, nodding his shaggy head like some genial old sage, he felt himself drawn again into the familiar field of force.

Arden had been Latimer's tutor. He had also been by far the most important thing that had happened to Latimer at Oxford, not only because of Arden's practical influence on his future, which had been immense, and disastrous, but also because of the almost hypnotic influence of Arden's personality. Latimer hadn't been alone in coming under his spell in this way, and afterwards he wasn't ashamed of it. It was just a fact. Arden was only twelve years his senior, but in terms of experience and attitude of mind he was more than a generation away. At fifteen he had run away from Charterhouse to fight in Spain – on what Latimer at least regarded as the 'wrong', the fascist, side, and thereafter, disillusioned and uprooted, had knocked about Europe as a journalist until the war came. He had then been involved in a series of secret, highly dangerous jobs in the Allied cause – jobs often hinted at in tutorials, and occasionally described in detail. As soon as the war ended he had got himself to Oxford to read Arabic, and when he had taken his degree he had been taken on at once by his own college, first as a research student and later as fellow and tutor. Even in the early nineteen-fifties he still moved in an aura of secrecy and danger, disappearing occasionally to London with the muttered apology that 'They seem to need me', returning haggard and exhausted forty-eight hours later. His colleagues in the senior common room regarded all this with unconcealed cynicism and amusement, but rejoiced in it for its undoubtedly dazzling effect on the under-graduates. He was certainly the most glamorous figure in the college in Latimer's time. He had a great shock of prematurely white hair that enhanced his extraordinary facial resemblance to the late Doctor Albert Schweitzer – a resemblance of which he was extremely proud and in the interest of which he also cultivated his bushy white moustache. In his oriental robes, mixing Bloody Marys on a Sunday morning while an ancient gramophone in the corner blared Dixieland through its gigantic horn, he had seemed to Latimer, as to many of his generation, to embody the ultimate in sophistication, in freedom from convention.

'Peter is like alcohol,' Latimer had declared in his third year, believing that he had got Arden's measure; believing too that he had shaken off the glamour of his personality. 'Fully to appreciate it you've got to know how to leave it alone.' But he had never really been able to leave it alone.

Now, in an attempt to retain his detachment, Latimer said, 'This is surely a new line, Peter. Don't tell me you've mellowed.'

But Arden knew how to hold his pose – if it was a pose – and Latimer merely sounded cheap.

'You're right, Steven, you're so right,' he agreed, sighing heavily. 'But it's just old age . . . the declension to the grave. It comes to us all,' nodding his great head, 'it comes to us all.'

He was overdoing it. Latimer did a quick calculation. 'You're not fifty-five yet.'

'No, well, that's true. But I *lived* more in my twenties and thirties than most people do in a lifetime.'

The faint note of smugness was reassuring: he hadn't changed. Latimer said, 'Living! Passing packets of marked currency to Algerian double agents in Moroccan brothels.'

'Yes, well, that was an isolated incident . . . But,' reprovingly, 'there was considerable danger involved, you know.'

'Oh yes, I know. But don't try idealising it. Not to me.'

'Don't be bitter, Steven.'

'Bitter! Of course I'm bitter. It's a bloody awful game and the way your lot play it is just too slapdash and amateur for words.'

'It's an arm of government, Steven, just like the Post Office Savings Bank.'

'No it *isn't*. You use human beings like rats in a laboratory, playing on their reflexes to get what you want. Money, fear, patriotism – you flash the signs up on a board and the rats fight each other to get into the right enclosure.'

'*Good gracious!* You must have been watching television.' He was clearly delighted – and Latimer was talking himself into a temper.

Latimer made an effort. 'Well, well. That's all in the past now. I'm growing old too, Peter. Like you.'

'That's splendid then.' Arden beamed. 'We can grow old together.' He heaved himself to his feet and reached out a hand for Latimer's glass. 'Why don't you come up for a weekend soon? I want to hear about Panjeh. There's a guest night on the sixteenth and I'd like you to meet Guthrie. He's here for a year from Princeton and – '

'*No thanks* – ' Furious with himself for giving way so quickly, Latimer said, 'I'm not here for a tearful reconciliation. I'm here because I'm being pursued – persecuted would be a better word – by a family called Wedderburn. You won't have heard of them. They accuse me of seducing one of the daughters, a girl called Margaret, in September 1956. In the New Forest.'

'September '56?'

'Yes. Of getting her pregnant and then deserting her. And then, after more than fifteen years of total neglect, of starting to pester her with letters and phone calls. She's living in Beirut now and part of my intention in going there is assumed to be the determination to – pester her some more. So far, I've been hijacked and then admonished by the mother, pleaded with by the sister and painfully struck in the face – as you can see – by the sister's husband. He's called Cordwainer. He has also cancelled my contract with Barbizon – which, unfortunately, he owns. I refused to give him an undertaking to stop *molesting* his sister-in-law, so he very sensibly acted to dry up the funds that would enable me to live in Beirut at all. So now I've got nothing to live on while I write my book . . . and no one to publish it, incidentally, once it's written.'

'But he can't do that.'

'Oh yes he can. I've never had anything in writing with Barbizon – they're not that sort of firm. And now that they belong to him he's not prepared to have them printing books by a man of provedly impure life.'

'*You?*'

'Me.'

'The man's crazy.'

'Oh, I don't know. He surprised me this morning kissing my publisher's secretary during and exhibition of English Primitives, and that, coming on top of the New Forest incident in '56 –'

Arden was watching intently, his head half turned, all set to laugh.

'No, I'm serious,' Latimer said. 'Really. He said all this to Tim Kellett, after I left London. I got a message when I took Nicholas back to the school, to ring Tim.'

Arden said slowly, 'Even if any of it were true, he can't do that. You could take him to law.'

'I don't think so. If it were true I'd probably think him justified . . . and anyway, what I *was* doing in September '56 is hardly more admirable.'

'Nonsense. You exaggerate. You always did . . . It was an excellent operation.'

'Oh, sure, excellent . . . *"Go and put Radio Cairo out of action."* Why not?'

Arden said earnestly, 'It's no use looking at it with hindsight, Steven. Things are bound to look different after fifteen years – different, and in this case, admittedly, worse.'

'It looked appalling, even at the time . . . Not even to have the foresight to get permission from the politicians before sending me in . . . !'

'I know you were upset about the way the operation ended –'

'Ended! The whole thing was appalling.'

' – but there was no alternative, you know, for me, at the

time. I *had* to withdraw you once the Cabinet turned the scheme down. It was bad luck for you that some of your friends got into trouble but from our point of view, you know, it was your childhood in Egypt that made you valuable to us. You hadn't any *other* qualifications as an agent . . . And before the operation started you'd thought it would all be rather fun – I remember your saying so.'

'Yes,' and he also remembered the quarrel they'd had when it was all over. But Peter must have forgotten. He had used the same arguments then, almost the same words. But Latimer had continued the argument, with himself, for nearly another twenty years. Now he said wearily, 'Well, anyway, can you think of any reason why I shouldn't now tell Cordwainer where I was and what I was doing in September 1956?'

Peter looked at him carefully. He said, 'You must be mad.'

'But why? It's fifteen – nearly twenty years ago.'

'Listen. You remember the Crabbe case?'

Latimer was hardly likely to have forgotten. It had happened in the same year. One of the government's other secret departments had taken on a retired naval commander, Crabbe, and put him into Portsmouth harbour in a frogman's suit to have a look at the underside of a Russian battleship. It had all happened at the time of Krushchev's and Bulganin's official visit. When Crabbe didn't come back the whole affair got out into the press.

Arden, remembering, shuddered. 'Eden had to make an apology in the House of Commons. In that section heads rolled in all directions.'

'Well, in this case there aren't any heads left to roll. They sacked me, and you, and the Chief retired. No one else either inside or outside the Department ever knew, did they?'

'No one senior. There were communications people, of course.'

'Well then. It can't harm anyone in the Department, and it's important to me. And the Egyptians already know – even if the rest of the world doesn't.'

'No, Steven, no.' Arden was suddenly decisive. 'Quite apart from the scandal, which would be appalling – *think* of the meal that the Labour Party would make of it, and abroad – at the

U.N. – quite apart from all that, this really is no moment to let something like that loose. The Egyptians are being extremely reasonable – really very *good*, actually – over the Suez Canal negotiations. There's a very good chance we'll get it open before the spring if things go on this way. But if something like that was made public they'd *have* to react . . . No, it just won't do. That month in your life has got to stay lost. I'm sorry. You'll have to find some other way of convincing Cordwainer.'

'All right then. The only other way to convince him is to tell him the facts.'

'But – '

'We needn't tell him where *I* was . . . We'll just tell him who did it.'

Aden moved uneasily and Latimer registered with sudden amusement that he already saw what was coming. Enjoying himself, Latimer said, 'Think about it, Peter. It must have been someone who knew exactly where I was and how long I'd be away, so that he could safely use my name . . . In September 1956, *exactly* how many people knew where I – me, by name Steven Latimer – was?'

'Well – ' Arden got abruptly to his feet and started to move about in the cluttered room, 'you've already said it: me, and the Chief . . . that's all at headquarters.'

Latimer prompted, '*And*?'

Arden stared at him, frowning, his big hands clutching the back of a chair. He said reluctantly, 'There must have been two or three people at Barton who knew – or guessed. Your letters used to arrive there.'

'So Barton existed?'

'Oh yes, it's one of our training centres. But the people there at that time . . . I'm trying to remember, I think they were all black except for – '

'Angus.'

'Yes, that's right.' Arden looked at him curiously. 'Angus. But – '

'Angus.'

Arden moved on uneasily, picking up a book from the desk and putting it down again. 'I've always thought it a great pity that you and Angus quarrelled.'

56

'I didn't quarrel,' Latimer said pleasantly. 'Nor did Angus, come to that. Quarrelling's not quite the word for what he did.' The cut under his eye had started to throb again and he put a hand to it. 'To steal a man's wife, cuckold him, bastardise his son, ridicule him, hold him up to public scorn – '

'Steven!'

There was silence. Arden was looking at him curiously. 'Do you *really* use words like that when – when you're thinking about it? . . . Steven, you don't think you're getting too solitary?'

Latimer made an effort. He produced the sketch for a grin and said, 'Mind you, I'm prejudiced.'

But Arden didn't smile back. He said, 'Steven . . . You, as a doctor, must surely realise that – '

'If anyone else today attributes something to me *as a doctor* I shall – ' he broke off abruptly. After a moment he said quietly, 'These Wedderburns are perfectly respectable, and sane – at least, the ones that I've met are. The girl may have been hysterical – and may be now. But it all *happened*. And you and I know that it wasn't me . . . Is there anyone else in the world besides Angus who knew where I was at that time, and who had the opportunity to do it – *as well as* the wish to get *me* into trouble?'

'But – '

'And he's in Beirut now. Nicholas told me.'

'I don't believe it,' Arden said slowly. 'You were still friends then.'

Latimer shook his head. 'Never. Never more than armed neutrality. And anyway – ' he stopped, 'anyway, by September 1956 we *weren't* friends any more.'

Arden said curiously, 'I've never known exactly what it was all about between you and Angus . . . originally, I mean . . . Something about a girl?'

'It was childish,' Latimer said wearily, 'and it was rather mean, but it wasn't – lethal. Angus had a blind date for the Commem ball. I sent a telegram in his name telling her to come on an earlier train and I went and met her at the station. I said I was Angus Bailey and I took her to the ball while he was still hanging round at the station . . . That was all. Really.'

Arden said judicially, 'I dare say it seemed a lot to him, at the time.'

'It must have done . . . He took a long time paying me back.' That business with the Wedderburn girl must have been his first attempt, thought Latimer. To Angus's literal mind it must have seemed the perfect revenge: Latimer had impersonated him, so he would impersonate Latimer – with the difference that Angus had pushed the joke through to its ultimate, logical, brutal conclusion. But then it had all gone wrong – from Angus's point of view. Nobody made a fuss, nothing happened to Latimer.

So then Angus hung on for ten years until he got another chance . . . and that *was* a success.

Latimer's voice was elaborately ironic. 'I took his partner off him, once, for an evening. He replied by taking my wife off me, for good.'

Arden shook his head slowly from side to side. 'Nobody *takes* a woman nowadays. Felicity went because she wanted to go. You ought to face the fact.'

The cut on his cheek was so painful now that Latimer's eyes suddenly smarted with the pain. 'Damn you,' he said. '*Face* it! . . . *She preferred Angus to me.* Just think about that for a minute.'

With considerable diffidence Arden said, 'I think they were very – happy together . . . in the end, you know.'

Latimer said, 'I couldn't care less.'

Arden said briskly, changing the subject, 'Well now, we'd better think up a plan of campaign.'

Latimer's eyebrows rose. 'I shall go to Beirut of course, straight away. I'd already bought my air ticket.'

'But he's in London.'

'No, Beirut. I told you.' They stared at each other in confusion.

Arden started again, determinedly. 'But you say that you saw Cordwainer this morning – '

'Cordwainer, hell. I want to see Angus. I want to see what – '

'But Steven – '

'He's in Beirut, Peter, using my name. He's in Room 509 of the Criterion Hotel.'

3
BEIRUT

1

Even at one in the morning the air was clammy, and the passengers from the plane trailing patiently into the airport building carried their jackets folded over their arms. Most of them were going on to Bombay and had been woken up from uneasy sleep in order to sit in the transit lounge for half an hour. For them Beirut was just any other airport, and they walked resentfully, their heads bent under the glare of the arc-lights. Above them, unregarded, the great dark mass of the mountains, spotted with arcs and lines of tiny lights, cut out half the sky.

Latimer was sweating before he reached the ground. He and the four other passengers leaving the plane at Beirut were penned on the steps until the last of the transit passengers had disappeared into the airport building and then a bored young man in a white shirt, his cap cocked stylishly forward over his eyes, led them across the expanse of concrete and into the arrivals hall. Brilliantly lit but deserted, its marble vistas seemed to go on for ever. It was cool and pleasant after the steamy heat outside.

Reluctantly, buttoning up their shirts, a few sloppy officials appeared from their offices, and sat down at desks behind glass screens. Health control . . . passports . . . Latimer bought a temporary visa and collected his suitcase. He carried it across several more miles of marble to the Customs and yet another official in khaki decided, finally, and after thought, not to ask him to open it. There was an atmosphere of slackness, exhaustion, indifference – and Latimer, tired already, began to feel depressed as well. He picked up his suitcase again and carried it past a group of lounging khaki figures with tommy-guns and out into an empty, brilliantly lighted hall. The air-conditioning stopped here and stifling eddies of damp air came pressing in from the black night beyond the glass doors.

Latimer turned back towards one of the lounging figures. 'Taxis?' he asked.

The man shrugged with the arm that was not supporting his tommy-gun, but he was clearly too tired to speak.

Latimer trailed out into the damp night and put his suitcase down on to the pavement. Twenty yards away the last of the other passengers, two Japanese, were climbing into the last taxi. He signalled at them feebly as the taxi swept past, but they were looking straight ahead, and the driver took no notice either.

In the airport car park there were dozens of cars in rows under the arc-lights, silent and unlighted, but no taxis. A guard with a rifle slung over his shoulder was walking up and down in the middle distance but there was nobody else in sight.

Latimer glanced at his watch. One-thirty. A deadish time. Should he wait, and hope, for a taxi? Try to telephone? Lie down on a bench and go to sleep? . . . And at that moment he saw the headlights of a car come stabbing out of the night along the motorway from the city and a moment later he heard the engine. It was a big white American car with an open top and it swung round through the car park at considerable speed, leaning over on its springs, and drew up with a squeal of brakes immediately beside him.

The girl almost fell out of the car in her eagerness. 'Oh Mr. Carmichael! Thank goodness I'm in time. I was so afraid

60

you'd have taken a taxi. I *am* a few minutes late, I know, and I was so afraid –'

Her voice was clear and agreeable, but slightly breathless now, as though she personally and not only the car had been hurrying. She was a big squashy girl in a blue chiffon dress that was marginally too tight all over. Her hair – and there was plenty of it – bounced about in plump ringlets on her shoulders. She had huge short-sighted blue eyes which she now focused unwaveringly on Latimer's face, like a spaniel, coming in rather close to him in order to do so. It was an undeniably agreeable sensation.

Latimer said with regret, 'My name's not Carmichael,' and paused, hoping absurdly for her to say, 'Oh no, of course not, I mean Latimer.' But instead she recoiled sharply. 'It's *not*? Oh, that's terrible.' She strode past him and disappeared into the airport building, and he heard her talking with animation to the lounging figures with tommy-guns. There were even a few slow replies.

When eventually she came out again she was clearly depressed and she nodded absently at Latimer as though at an old friend who has come to offer sympathy in a time of family trouble. 'You didn't see a man with a briefcase?'

'Two,' said Latimer.

'*What?*'

'Two men . . . and they both had briefcases.'

She looked at him doubtfully and moved in closer.

'They were Japanese.'

'Oh no . . . Carmichael. That couldn't be Japanese, could it?'

'I shouldn't have thought.'

She sighed, and Latimer was so close that he felt the little movement of air and the breath of scent that came with it. 'He doesn't even know where he's booked in,' she said sombrely. She turned away from him, opened the nearest door of the car and climbed in. 'That's the third one I've mucked up this week.' She frowned at the dashboard as though there were something missing, and eventually located the steering wheel on the far side of the car. She hauled herself across to it, and the blue dress twisted up to reveal a length of healthy-looking thigh. 'Next time,' she said, with gloomy triumph, 'I shall get the sack.'

She pulled the dress down again, with difficulty, nodded kindly at Latimer and started the engine. The car slid forward.

Latimer had his mouth open but hadn't actually uttered when she slammed on the brakes and the car stopped again, abruptly. Reaching forward into the shelf under the dashboard she fished out a bundle of small cards and dropped them on to the seat beside her. She chose one and held it out to Latimer, straining an arm towards him across the width of the car.

Latimer read aloud, 'Lebanon Garage. All car repairs. Automatic car wash . . .'

'Oh – no. Here, give me that one back. That must be one that somebody gave me. It should read "Jasmin Travel". Is this one right?'

Latimer looked at the new card she had given him. ' "Jasmin Travel Agency. Air, sea and bus reservations. Hotel bookings. Tours, Personal attention at all times." That it?'

She nodded seriously. 'That's it. That's us,' and the car slid forward again. But this time Latimer had a hand on the top of the door. 'I say – '

The car stopped and she looked at him in surprise.

'Do you think you could possibly give me a lift? There aren't any taxis and – '

She said doubtfully, 'Where are you staying?'

For a moment Latimer hesitated. 'I haven't booked, actually . . .' Then he said firmly, 'The Criterion. I'm at the Criterion.'

She peered at him, frowning with uncertainty. He said, 'I'm really very respectable. Honestly – ' and abruptly she smiled.

'That's all right,' she said cheerfully, 'I always carry a great big gun for emergencies.'

To Latimer's astonishment she drove very well, and fast. As they passed through the car park she had flicked out from somewhere a pair of enormous green-rimmed spectacles and with improved vision she seemed at once to become more confident, more capable. A double-track boulevard ran straight towards the city through a couple of miles of level sandy waste. The sprinklers were on along the grass strip between the two lanes, throwing up rainbows of spray under the street-lights, cooling the air and bringing the scent of grass into the car. The lights, flicking past, showed him the girl's hands on the wheel in regular, brief glimpses. They were nice hands, small and pale with the nails unvarnished. The lower part of her face, half-smiling, was lit by the glow of the dashboard. He watched her with pleasure, not bothering to talk.

Suddenly she laughed, not with amusement but with pleasure, 'I adore driving at night,' she said. The car was going faster and faster.

Latimer warned. 'The illusion of omnipotence?'

'No, just the speed. The speed.'

He looked at the speedometer, and back again at her face, smiling. Grotesque in the angled beam of the headlights an occasional hoarding was snatched past the windows but for the most part their lights showed only low sand banks on either side and the lurid green of the grass on the centre strip.

They went past a roundabout with a squeal of tyres and the car rocked on its enormous springs. Then they were into a plantation of high trees – dark, cool, arching over the road – and under the trees to the left Latimer saw suddenly a jumble of boxes and packing cases. For a moment he was puzzled, and then the quick beam of the headlights showed it to him clearly for a moment and he remembered. His elation evaporated. Shacks made of tin and cardboard, roofs held on with stones, ragged tents, windowless shelters made of petrol cans . . . History had shuffled its pack and dealt out to a whole generation of Palestinians these squalid resting places – and they'd lived in them now, with hunger and cold and the worse pains of hope, for more than twenty-five years. And abruptly Latimer was reminded of Haider bin Hassan, who had lived on hope for just as long. And now there was going to be a revolution against Saladin – which might well be successful, and to the triumphant guerrillas Haider would seem just as anachronistic, just as decadent as Saladin himself . . . Latimer, who hated insoluble problems, stirred uneasily.

The girl too sighed and he turned to look at her. But she wasn't thinking about history, or refugees.

'Nearly there,' she said, and the car began to lose speed. The rush of night air through the car slowed and at once the temperature rose again. Latimer eased himself away from the seat, his shirt wet in the small of his back. They dipped into an underpass and he blinked in the sudden brilliant lighting.

'Now, let me think – ' the girl peered forward doubtfully, talking to herself. 'Very confusing, everything's one-way.' They floated up out of the underpass and drew up at traffic lights. The sticky air closed in again through the open windows, bringing with it petrol fumes and the smell of hot rubber.

The lights changed. 'Well, let's try this.' She swung the big car across the oncoming traffic and into a side-road.

Latimer was amused. 'How long have you been here?'

'What? Oh – well, not very long, actually . . . The traffic in Beirut is frightful.'

'Yes, I know.'

'Yes . . . Oh dear.' The road turned abruptly and they were in an obvious cul-de-sac. The girl giggled slightly. 'We'll have to reverse.'

The car started to slide backwards and Latimer turned his head helpfully, if uselessly, over his shoulder. So that he didn't see the man until the beam of the torch came in through the window on the girl's side of the car.

'*Bon soir.*' The man flicked his torch into Latimer's face, and then into the girl's, and then turned it back and focused it steadily on her knees. He was in the same sort of khaki uniform as the official at the airport.

The girl launched into competent French, explaining that they had lost their way, they were looking for the Hotel Criterion, could he tell them how to get there? The policeman grunted and shifted his feet: he hadn't understood a word. The beam of the torch flickered suspiciously round the interior of the car.

Reluctantly, Latimer translated what she had said into Arabic, and at once the man become more friendly. He provided some fairly clear directions, helped the girl to back out and saluted as they drove away.

'That was lucky,' the girl said casually, accelerating. Latimer felt a curious twist of anti-climax. He had been unwilling to speak Arabic in front of her for fear of her curiosity, but instead she had simply taken it for granted. He realised suddenly and with intense irritation that he would have liked to impress her.

Directing her through the narrow streets Latimer digested this fact. It depressed him, because it was ridiculous. It was also inconvenient.

Aloud he said, 'May I know your name?'

She glanced at him with amusement, following his line of thought exactly, and he felt himself blush.

'Angela.'

'Angela . . . No surname?'

'Only for old friends.'

'Oh.' Latimer was disconcerted. Then it occurred to him that she knew nothing at all about him and he started to introduce himself, but she interrupted.

'We're there.' The car slid to a halt. On the other side of the road was the Hotel Phoenicia, a towering block, and straight ahead was the sea. Beside them was the entrance to the Hotel Criterion. It was smaller than the Phoenicia but even more modern. The canopy over the doorway was steel and plastic and the doors were sheets of glass.

A porter in elaborate fancy dress sprang forward to open the car door and Latimer clambered out obediently and took his suitcase out of the boot.

The girl smiled, watching him through the big spectacles with obvious amusement. Angela, her name was. 'Good night.' The engine was still running.

With a fair imitation of firmness Latimer said, 'Now just turn that damn thing off and come in and have a drink with me.'

Still smiling she said, 'It's far too late.'

Looking at the blue dress Latimer said, 'Are you going back to – Are you going on somewhere?'

'No-o –'

'Well, it's not too late then. Come on.'

He gestured at the porter who ran round to the car door and held out his hand for the keys. With a surprised little nod of acquiescence she turned off the engine and climbed out. The spectacles had disappeared again and the little frown of uncertainty was back. She went cautiously into the hotel, one hand held out in front of her in case of unexpected plate glass doors.

'There must be a bar in a place like this.' Latimer caught up with her and took her elbow.

She smiled gratefully. 'Downstairs, I think – '

He handed his suitcase to a porter and they picked their way down a red-carpeted staircase into darkness. Somewhere over to the right there was music of a nightclub kind and after a moment Latimer became aware of the faint red gleam ahead.

'Do you mind if I leave you for a moment?' Despite her myopia Angela's eyes had evidently adjusted more quickly than his own, and she faded from beside his shoulder before he'd had time to get his bearings. He groped his way to a washroom and then, seeing more clearly, wandered into the bar to buy some cigarettes. The only lighting was a fiery upward glow from behind a shelf of bottles against which the barman, silhouetted, moved about like a rescue worker.

Latimer bought his cigarettes and then – since there was still no sign of the girl – ordered a whisky and soda. He hoisted himself on to a bar-stool and settled down to wait, jiggling a foot in time with the music that was still faintly audible from some other room.

He sipped at the whisky and became gradually aware of a figure on the next stool. After a moment a shoulder leant against his.

The shoulder said earnestly, 'But you don't *really* accept the British government's claim to have pulled out of the Gulf?'

It was a woman's voice. English.

Latimer tried to think of a suitable reply, but before he came up with anything the pressure of the shoulder was removed. The voice continued, 'It's the grossest, most indefensible example of oppressive neo-colonialism in the world at the moment. It's worse than Vietnam.' She spoke without indignation – just stating facts, and the words were absurdly at odds with her low, rather gentle voice.

Peering into the darkness Latimer discovered with relief that she was addressing the man on her other side, a slack-looking fellow with slightly too much hair. Even as Latimer watched he finished off his drink and signalled to the barman for another in a single gesture that identified him at once as a journalist.

'All right, all right,' the man said pacifically, 'nobody pretends that the present set-up in the Persian Gulf is ideal.' His words were perfectly clear but he was enunciating with slightly too much care. 'I'm not defending the British government, heaven knows – ' he laughed at the idea with genuine amusement, 'but what do you expect them to do? They said they'd pull their forces out of the Gulf, and they did. But if the sheikhs can't, or won't, federate what can they *do*? If the British government refuses help to individual sheikhs when they're under pressure they'll just go down like ninepins.' He paid for his drink and took a long pull at it. 'Like ninepins.' A happy thought struck him. 'No – like dominoes. That's the parallel – like dominoes . . . But I suppose that's what you want,' his voice became aggrieved, 'you always say there's got to be a general shambles before we can get anywhere. Well, they're so damned inefficient that they'll probably go under anyway, with or without British help, and then you'll be happy . . . such a shambles . . . '

'You're right, of course. History's on my side.' She was laughing at him, and her voice was softer than ever, almost gruff with suppressed amusement.

The man slammed his glass down and roused himself. 'That's *not* what I meant,' he protested.

'No, I know. But it's true.' Despite the gentle voice she was clearly prepared to go on until she was acknowledged as right. Latimer began to sympathise with the other man, but he listened with pleasure to her voice. 'You see the whole problem in terms of decisions by governments, Bill, of policies, of – '

The man's head had sunk another couple of inches towards his glass and Latimer thought: You're wasting your time, my girl.

Latimer felt a touch on his arm and Angela whispered, 'You make friends so easily.'

He slipped off the stool and took her elbow. 'I need a less polemical atmosphere. Isn't there another bar?'

'Well,' she sounded doubtful, 'there's the restaurant, but the floor show's just starting . . . '

'It'll have to do.'

It was a Spanish year, apparently, in the nightclubs of the Middle East and four jolly girls with painted-on kiss-curls were stamping about on the creaking dance floor with some noodle-thin boys ten years their junior. The boys could, just conceivably, have been Spanish. The waiter gave Latimer a table against the wall, at a merciful distance from the show, and left them with two huge menus.

Angela, shuddering, thrust hers away and Latimer said innocently, 'Is the food so awful?'

'Oh *no*.' She seemed to be in pain. 'It's simply *wonderful*.'

'Aren't you hungry?'

'*Starving*.'

'Well then – ' choosing at random, Latimer said, ' – what about shrimp cocktail, spaghetti bolognese and a steak?'

She gave a little gasp. 'Oh please don't . . . Today's my yoghurt day.'

'Oh . . . but it's tomorrow now. Couldn't you – ?'

'Tomorrow's lemon juice.'

Abruptly Latimer was bored – and at once blamed himself. He knew of himself that he would always rather feel admiration, however reluctant, than pity or amusement – because the last two turned all too easily into irritation: it wasn't the girl's fault.

Gloomily, he ordered two whiskies and Angela dropped a cool hand over his own resting on the table. 'I shouldn't have come,' she said gently. 'You're terribly tired.'

Amazed, he returned the pressure of her hand and she leaned towards him so that a large curl bounced against his cheek. 'As soon as I've finished my drink I'll go home.'

'No, no,' he tried to rally, and since they were sitting on a semi-circular bench it seemed the obvious thing to put an arm round her shoulders. She leaned against him amicably and he felt her round arm flatten slightly against his own. The jolly girls drew towards a climax and stamped away into the shadows, casting brilliant smiles back over their shoulders.

Angela sighed. 'I *love* this sort of thing.'

'Flamenco?' He was touched by her enthusiasm.

'No . . . the whole nightclub *thing*. It's so unreal, such a nice change.'

68

'Is your job so dull?'

'It's not bad, but – you know – hotel bookings . . . meeting people at the airport – '

' – failing to meet people at the airport – '

She grinned. 'It gets monotonous.'

The jolly girls had been replaced by a real old pro having trouble with her flounces. She glared and stamped quite terrifyingly, mouthing to herself what might have been either ' . . . the *rat* . . . the *bastard* . . . ' or alternatively ' . . . *and* five . . . *and* six . . . ' It was impossible to tell which. It all seemed to go on for hours and though Angela was clearly still enjoying herself Latimer heard his own comments become increasingly snide. He ordered another round of drinks and then, though Angela objected, another. But even so the dancing didn't seem to improve much, and at last she said, quite kindly, 'You know, you're not really in the mood.'

It was eminently fair comment but he still felt bound to protest. 'No, no,' he said, '*you're* enjoying it. Let's stay. We'll stay.' But Angela ignored him and signalled to the waiter. The man brought the bill at once, glancing at her with what looked to Latimer suspiciously like sympathy, and he wondered suddenly whether he were drunk. But he felt quite steady as they sidled out through the darkness and headed for the stairs. What was certain, however, was that he hadn't latterly paid as much attention to Angela as she had, perhaps, expected.

'I'm sorry,' he said, as though apologising for his tiredness, 'I've had a long day.'

'*That's* all right.' She sounded surprised. But he wouldn't follow it up, Latimer promised himself. He'd say good night and that would be that.

At the foot of the stairs the journalist he had seen in the bar was leaning against a wall – it looked as though he had just been propped there. He was a bulky man and it seemed that he had no plans for moving further that night. A woman standing beside him was trying to rouse him to action. She was small and slim and Latimer was irresistibly reminded of a wren trying to shift a cuckoo.

'Come on, Bill,' she was saying encouragingly. 'Up we go. Just a few steps and then you can get into a nice taxi.' The amused gruffness of her voice identified her at once.

Bill groaned.

'Not far. Up we go.'

Latimer would have walked past them but Angela paused. Fellow-feeling, Latimer thought uncomfortably: someone *else* having trouble with their escort.

'Can I help?' He mumbled it and the English woman looked round and said sharply, 'What?' She had smooth dark hair and a pointed face. Even in the red nightclub lighting he could see that she was neither particularly young nor pretty, and she peered at him with suspicion.

He repeated, 'Can I help?' and after a moment of hesitation she said, more graciously, 'Well – yes, thanks.' Then she stood back and made a brief, rather charming gesture of handing the job over to him.

Latimer put the man's left arm over his own shoulders and clutched the bulky torso round the middle. 'Leave me alone. I'm fine,' the man said loudly several times, and he did in fact manage to take most of his own weight as they staggered up the stairs. The two women followed and Latimer heard Angela's voice once or twice. The dark woman didn't say much but clearly wasn't suffering as much from embarrassment as he would have expected. They emerged, blinking, into the strong lights of the hotel foyer and Bill remarked at once with satisfaction, '*Here* we are.'

The hall porter took one look at them and sent for a taxi. When it arrived Latimer flopped the man into the back seat and stood back to let the dark woman in beside him. She looked at him for a moment, not understanding, and then laughed. But she wasn't pleased.

'Oh no. *Not* mine . . . Bill,' she leaned in through the open door and raised her voice, 'Bill, are you listening? Ministry of Foreign Affairs at ten, then there's a pop singer arriving at one.'

'Popsie one o'clock,' said Bill obediently, and fell asleep.

She scribbled the times and places on a piece of paper and tucked it into his top pocket. Then she gave an address to the taxi-driver, paid him, removed Bill's wallet to her own bag, leaving another scribbled note in its place, and finally wrote down the taxi's number in her own notebook. She did it all calmly, as a matter of routine, and Latimer was amused and impressed. Then she banged on the taxi's roof as a signal to the driver to start and turned away. Catching Angela's eye, she smiled briefly and said, 'Must look after the colleagues.'

To Latimer she said coldly. 'Good night, and thank you.' Then she got into a second taxi and was driven away.

Angela and Latimer were left standing on the pavement. They both shrugged, and smiled, and then a porter brought her car and she slipped into the driving seat. Latimer stood beside her, looking in through the open window.

She said, 'Good night, and thank you.'

'Good night.' She looked extraordinarily pretty in the big car – but he had already decided not to follow it up.

She said, 'If I can do anything – if the Agency can do anything for you, just call us.' She scribbled a number on a bit of paper and handed it to him through the window. 'You can always reach me on this number.'

'But don't I see you again?' He leaned on the car door.

'You'll be busy – '

'So will you. What about tomorrow?'

'Tomorrow's a free day, actually. I shall go swimming.'

'Where?'

'I haven't decided . . . maybe the St. Georges.' She nodded in the direction of the sea. 'Over there.'

'Twelve o'clock? We'll swim and have some lunch. Please say "yes".'

'Well . . . okay. Yes.' She was pleased, he thought. But still the car didn't move.

Her eyes were enormous and he noticed with surprise that they were getting larger . . . Just a friendly kiss, quite brief.

He said, 'Twelve o'clock tomorrow? I shall look forward to it. Good night.'

'Good night.' The car slid forward and disappeared round the corner of the Phoenicia. Latimer watched it go and then turned back into the Criterion. His heart had started to beat unpleasantly and he realised now that he had invited her for a drink largely in order to postpone this moment. In Oxford it had seemed so straightforward, so logical: if Angus, masquerading as Dr. Steven Latimer, had installed himself in Room 509 of the Criterion Hotel in Beirut, the simplest way, surely, for the real Steven Latimer to deal with the situation was to go straight to the Criterion and ask for his key . . . But here in Beirut a dozen valid objections at once presented themselves. He hesitated.

The foyer was a shadowy region of orange carpeting broken up by masses of dark green foliage. Such light as there was – now, at three in the morning – came from spotlights mounted in the ceiling and invested random chairs or patches of carpet with an intense, wholly spurious significance . . . He could turn round even now and leave, he thought suddenly – but then he saw that he was already too late. A sleepy porter was standing by the reception desk, holding his suitcase, waiting for him. The night clerk was waiting too, a young man with a secret sorrow.

Latimer crossed slowly to the desk and said loudly, 'My key, please. Dr. Latimer. Room 509.'

The clerk was puzzled. 'You are already booked in?'

'Yes. Latimer.'

The porter looked from one to the other, uncomprehending. The clerk, frowning slightly, looked at Latimer doubtfully and then ran his finger down a list on the desk in front of him. His face cleared. 'Latimer. 509.'

He reached for the key and smiled. 'Good evening, Mr. Latimer.'

'Good evening.'

Triggered, the porter set off at once, sleep-walking, across the foyer towards the lift and Latimer followed, breathless with relief.

The lift operated quite silently and their feet made no sound on the carpets of the broad, dimly-lighted corridor on the fifth floor. Latimer followed the porter round two corners and the key jingled once in the man's hand. It was the only sound, and unexpectedly Latimer found himself beginning to enjoy the hushed, middle-of-the-night atmosphere – the secret satisfaction of being the only man awake.

A door immediately beside him flew open and Latimer jumped. A waiter with a tray of empty glasses came out through the door and over his shoulder Latimer saw, for an instant – as though in a snapshot, or a memory – the line of motionless figures in the brilliantly lighted room. It was a standard oblong hotel room with standard hotel furniture – but someone had imported some extra chairs. There must have been ten of them, pushed back into a continuous row round the white walls. The occupants of the chairs near the ends of the row wore khaki bush jackets, and one or two of them had short beards round the line of the chin. The other men wore dark suits with narrow knitted ties. But the occupant of the central chair wore a sweeping brown cloak to the ground over voluminous white robes. The white cloth covering his head and shoulders was held in place with a double circlet of gold rope. His face was bearded and at the front of his belt he wore a vast, curved, heavily-ornamented silver dagger.

Jalis . . . the Sheikh sits. Haider bin Hassan bin Abdul Rahman, pretender to the Sheikhdom of Panjeh, was holding court.

Latimer gave a gasp of surprise, and treacherous laughter grabbed him by the throat. He had last seen Haider in a pin-stripe suit, and before that in a tweed jacket with leather patches on the elbows, and before that in a red football jersey with mud on his knees . . .

Light-headed, he put out a hand to hold the door open. Loudly, in Arabic, he said, 'May God make your life long, Sheikh.'

The effect was electric. The long row of faces jerked upwards. Haider himself sprang to his feet and took two paces forward, peering out into the dimly lighted corridor.

Latimer said in English, 'Good evening, Haider.'

The other figures were getting slowly to their feet, but still Haider said nothing. His bearded face was thrust forward angrily.

'I'm sorry to startle you,' Latimer said at last, weakly, conscious of having made a fool of himself. There was silence.

Haider's face became abruptly smooth and expressionless. The heavy eyelids drooped so that the dark eyes were hidden. Drawing his cloak tightly round him he sat down again in his chair. Latimer had ceased to exist.

73

2

Room 509 was also a standard oblong box, and its decoration proclaimed the same hand as the foyer downstairs. The carpet and the counterpane were orange, the lighting fixtures beside the bed and over the writing-table stainless steel. The whole room was spotlessly clean, and empty. It might have been delivered that morning, individually packaged, vacuum-sealed in plastic, untouched by hand . . .

Null and void. Latimer said it aloud, looking around the room with astonishment and a touch of panic. He had been so sure that he would find it full of Angus's belongings – a hair-brush and comb on the dressing-table, cuff-links, hair lotion, a jacket over the back of a chair, a pile of clean laundry re-turned by the hotel on the edge of the table . . . He had seen it all so clearly that the emptiness jolted him – like the shock of anxiety with which one notices that a familiar object is missing from its place.

Making an effort, he locked the door and began methodically to search. The far end of the room from the door was all glass. He pushed aside one of the panels and stepped out on to the balcony. It was cooler now but the air still had a used-up smell. The balcony ran the full width of the room and was separated from the balconies on either side by a business-like metal grille. Immediately below was the hotel's swimming-pool, dark now and deserted, surrounded by white metal chairs and tables. Latimer stepped back into the room and locked the window.

Just beside him was a door leading, presumably, to the next-door room. He tried the handle, it was locked. He bolted it from his own side and turned to the rest of the room. He pulled back the counterpane – the bed hadn't been slept in. The bathroom yielded nothing, the writing-desk, the chest of drawers . . . nothing. The wardrobe contained a navy-blue blazer and a pair of odd trousers, a cream sports shirt and a tie – all neatly arranged on hangers. His hand shook slightly as he took them out. They were of French manufacture, bought in Beirut. They had hardly been worn. Pushing open the cupboard door so that the long mirror reflected the room, Latimer held the trousers up against himself. They were just about the right size – perhaps a shade too short. He pulled off his own jacket and put on the one from the cupboard. Just too tight across the shoulders, just too short in the sleeves. Angus...

Now there could no longer be any doubt. Latimer unlocked the door leading to the corridor, lay down on the bed and closed his eyes. He was impatient now for their meeting, anxious to get it over. Angus... he tried to concentrate all his willpower on to drawing Angus quickly into the room, from wherever he was. Come on Angus, come on... He avoided thinking in detail of what he would say, concentrated instead of the *fact* of their meeting. Across the foyer, into the lift, along the broad corridor.

But in the event his first visitor came from a different direction. The door leading through to the next-door room rattled suddenly and Haider's voice said, 'Steven? Steven, let me in... Steven?'

Latimer stood up slowly and looked at the connecting door. The handle was turning backwards and forwards. 'Steven? Are you there?'

Haider's expression when he first recognised Latimer standing in the open doorway had been one of astonishment – and something more. Dislike... or fear.

'What do you want?' Latimer said loudly, standing still in the middle of the room, 'Sheikh.'

'Oh, good heavens – ' Haider's voice slid into a giggle. 'Don't be so pompous, Steven.'

Reluctantly, Latimer stepped forward and pulled back the bolt. The door burst open and Haider, still elaborately robed, half fell into the room and flung his arms round him. 'Oh Steven, how marvellous to see you!'

Misinterpreting Latimer's expression he detached himself rapidly and put out a hand to be shaken. 'I've been away from England too long,' he said apologetically. 'One forgets.'

'Evidently... What was all that just now?'

'Oh well, for heaven's sake – ' Haider threw himself into the armchair and crossed his legs, easing the enormous dagger out of the way of his ribs, 'you can't just come barging up to me like that in public. I can't be seen hobnobbing with scum like you. Have a heart, Steven.'

'No, I suppose not . . . ' Whatever Haider's politics now, the British were bound still to be the villains . . . Latimer was suddenly appalled at what he had done. 'How stupid. I'm awfully sorry, Haider. I've been away too long, too. One – '

' – "one forgets, doesn't one"! Don't give it another thought.' He was immensely ebullient, and excited. Latimer was puzzled: Haider had always cultivated what he believed to be a British reserve and this bouncy manner was new. It was also absurdly out of keeping with his appearance.

Latimer sat down in the other armchair. 'So,' he said, wondering where to begin. He was uncomfortable with this medieval-looking stranger with Haider's eyes and voice.

'So – ' Haider echoed, smiling broadly. White teeth flashed between the dark beard and the moustache.

'So what goes on?'

'Guess.'

Trying to sound at ease, Latimer became over-genial.

'Well, judging by the fancy dress I'd say that at long last you've conned some unfortunate set of chaps into backing an attempt to get rid of your uncle and put you back in as Ruler of Panjeh.'

Haider nodded once, very slowly. His eyes were bright with amusement. 'Right so far,' he said. 'And *who*, do you suppose?'

Latimer watched him, thinking hard. 'Fairly old-fashioned chaps . . . The Saudis?'

The draperies round Haider's head moved gently from side to side. 'No.'

'The Iranians?'

Haider's tongue clicked sharply, the Arabic signal of negation.

Latimer guessed wildly. 'Kuwait?'

'*No.*'

Latimer gave up trying. 'All right then, tell me it's the C.I.A.'

Haider shook his head sorrowfully. He sighed. 'You're out of date, Steven, you know, you're terribly, terribly out of date

. . . you're thinking in terms of twenty years ago. The day of imperialism and servile puppet regimes is *over*, Steven. The day of freedom and democracy is dawning.'

Latimer stared at him. 'It *is*?' he said at last. He said slowly, 'If it weren't for the clothes – '

'Steven, the day of nationalism is past.' Haider spoke with quiet emphasis, not as one who argues a case but as one who brings the good word, and to his astonishment Latimer was reminded of the earnest young men from the Christian Union who had called on him unbidden in his first term at Oxford. 'Nationalism has played its part. Even you must be aware that since the last war it has become no more than the tool of the two super-powers. Why has Russia encouraged wars of national liberation? Why has America forced Britain to dissolve her Empire, spawning a mass of tiny, unviable units that must of necessity accept the economic domination of one power or the other? Neo-colonialism is not just a dirty word, Steven, it is the condition in which the great majority of mankind is living today.' For a moment he appeared to hesitate and then he went on, as though imparting a secret, 'Western society as it exists today cannot be reformed. It is deeply, irredeemably corrupt. All its institutions are rotten, mere engines of oppression. Western society must be swept away altogether before any kind of decent condition of life can emerge for mankind as a whole.'

He paused again, and for the first time some doubt as to how Latimer was receiving the message seemed to cross his mind. Slightly more sharply he said, 'Well? Can you disagree with any of that?'

Latimer had tried to keep his face blank but he knew that his sense of disappointment and anti-climax must be showing. Haider bin Hassan, who might have been an enlightened, a modern Ruler of Panjeh, had fallen instead for the hypnotic jargon of popular communism . . .

He said evenly, 'No . . . but you seem to forget that I've been living in Panjeh for the last three years. You also seem to forget that I'm middle-aged now. I'm forty-one.'

Haider was disconcerted. 'But that doesn't necessarily mean that my views are wrong.'

'No, but it does mean that I've had both time and opportunity to define my own attitude to all those shop-soiled ideas that you've just been trotting out.' He found suddenly that he was angry. 'It is quite simply childish to imagine that any advantage will accrue to anyone if you sweep away institutions without being damned certain that you've got something better to put in their place. The whole history of revolutionary regimes in this century suggests that new governments tend to preserve or revive the worst – never the best – features of the government they have overthrown.'

To his astonishment Haider grinned broadly. 'Got you!' he said. 'You've lost your temper.'

This was the old Haider, and Latimer relaxed. 'Sorry.' They both grinned.

'All the same,' said Latimer, 'why the fancy dress?'

'Ah! I'm glad you asked . . . We are all, I think, agreed – may I say *all*?' – his voice had become suddenly richer, heavily persuasive, and Latimer grinned, stretching himself out on the bed to listen. This was an old party piece of Haider's, an accurate and scurrilous parody of Peter Arden's tutorial manner. ' – *all* agreed, then, that in politics one must always put new wine into old bottles. No, no, don't argue. *Now*. Everyone in Panjeh knows about me. I am the only surviving son of Hassan bin Abdul Rahman, I am the eagerly-expected leader who will free them all from Saladin. And they all believe, naturally enough, that I am *like* my father, a good Arab. But Steven – and please pay attention now because I am approaching the paradox. But Steven, I am *not* a good Arab. In fact, it would probably be true to say that by their standards I am not an Arab at all any more. I lived in England for ten years, after all, I even married an English wife eventually – did you know that? I succeeded for a time in *being* English, really, and conservative opinion in Panjeh wouldn't like that . . . quite apart from my wholly unacceptable political views. However, I am undoubtedly the right sort of wine for Panjeh –'

Latimer listened unhappily. Haider clearly had no idea what conditions were like now in Panjeh. *Conservative opinion* . . . The only person allowed to have opinions at all was Saladin himself, and nothing would ever reconcile *him* to Haider.

' – undoubtedly the right wine, if only conservative opinion can be induced to grasp the fact. So, what do we do? We create – ' he patted the big dagger gently and with satisfaction, 'we create a reassuring exterior, a conservative *bottle*, as it were, to keep the conservatives happy long enough for them to get reconciled to the newness of the wine that's inside . . . In politics, Steven, one concrete example is worth five tons of theory.' His gesture included the whole of his own appearance – an appearance which, as he spoke, dropping back finally into the authentic tone and idiom of the time when he and Latimer had been friends, had seemed to Steven increasingly incongruous.

Latimer said hesitantly, 'I don't know that traditional robes will really cut much ice any more in Panjeh. I mean – '

Haider gestured dismissively, 'You're a doctor, Steven. In politics – '

With a touch of grimness Latimer said, 'Even as a doctor I saw a good deal of Panjeh's politics – and politicians.'

'Maybe, but as patients, not as fellow-politicians. Politically, you were pretty inept I hear.' He grinned briefly. 'Got yourself thrown out . . . Politics is the art of the possible, Steven. Never forget that – I never do.' He added kindly, 'You have always preferred to confine yourself to theory.'

Abruptly Latimer saw his own hands – filthy, the nails edged with black – holding a box of detonators . . . The memory was like physical pain and Latimer's face contorted. There had been precious little theory about that operation – too little. What would Haider think if he knew? Latimer looked at him curiously. Perhaps he did know – he had been with the Egyptians for years.

Haider was silent, watching Latimer's changed face with anxiety. 'Are you all right, Steven?'

Latimer made an effort, trying to remember the sort of joke they had made together. 'Nothing wrong that a stiff drink and a night out in London wouldn't put right.'

Undergraduate humour. It sounded ludicrous but Haider grinned, reassured. '*Goodness*, it's nice to see you again, Steven.'

'And you – '

'Go away now.'

'What did you say?'

'I said "Leave Beirut." Please.'

'Why?'

'For my sake. After that incident tonight they'll never believe you didn't come to Beirut specially to see me.'

' "They" being your – ah – left-wing friends?'

'That's right.'

'But why should they care whether or not I do come specially from London to see you?'

'Well –' Haider lowered his head, fiddling with the enormous dagger in his belt. 'You've got some pretty odd friends, Steven.'

For a moment Latimer really didn't understand what he meant. 'Odd friends?'

Haider glanced up from under the shadow of his *kafir*. 'Yes ... Peter Arden, for one.'

'Do you mean,' Latimer said slowly, 'that your – friends think I'm working for the British secret service?'

Haider fidgeted again. 'I don't know what they think ... But it wouldn't surprise anyone very much if you were – would it?'

'It would astonish me.'

He laughed. 'Go away, Steven. Please.'

Against all reason Latimer was hurt. He said coldly. 'Okay. I'll go.'

'Really?' Haider was immensely relieved. 'Oh, Steven –' He sprang out of the chair and embraced Latimer again. Then he stood back. 'You've got different spectacles from the ones you used to have – thinner frames. They make you look quite different.'

'Do they?' Latimer glanced at his reflection in the mirror, and quickly looked away. 'Just when everyone else in the world is getting thicker ones –'

Haider laughed uproariously. 'Trust Steven to be different.'

3

So how, in a city the size of Beirut, do you find a gentle, sensitive, deeply-wronged English girl, if all you know about her is her name and the fact that she is slim and pretty and has short curly hair? (That – and the fact that in 1956 she was seduced by a man calling himself Steve Latimer?)

Latimer lay in bed and wondered. It was past eleven o'clock and the sun was blazing through a crack in the curtains. Angus hadn't come – and Latimer had realised suddenly, waking, that he was relieved: to see Angus would solve nothing – because Angus wasn't at the heart of the problem. Instead, he must go and see Margaret Wedderburn.

He couldn't imagine now why he hadn't thought of it before. He would see her, she would acknowledge that he wasn't the Steve Latimer that she had known years ago, she would say as much to her mother and brother-in-law, Angus would be quietly outmanoeuvred and the whole problem would be solved.

Between him and Angus the account was closed and no anger on his part – no explanations even – could ever alter it. Whatever Angus was up to, Latimer would leave him alone, and the past could stay buried . . . But he would go and see Margaret Wedderburn.

But first he had to find her. He could ask the Consulate, of course – and she must have friends. Surprisingly, that thought produced at once the image of Angela, large, plump and confident – and with a sharp stab of dismay he remembered that he had said twelve o'clock, at the St. Georges . . . for a swim and lunch. He looked at his watch again. He would have to go straight there.

'I must be stark, staring mad;' he said aloud, rolling reluctantly out of bed. The early morning had always been a dangerous time for his fragile predilections. He woke each day in a state of emotional truce that gave his mind uncomfortable freedom. Now, scratching a razor across his eroded face, he recognised sourly that Angela, and his feelings about her, were part of a pattern so familiar that if he only had a graph and a slide-rule he could probably predict with accuracy the day and the hour at which he would suggest their getting into bed together. 'Would you like a cup of coffee?' He leered at himself in the mirror, flinching away from the dazzling sunlight. He hadn't the slightest desire even to see Angela, ever again.

The terrace of the Hotel St. Georges in Beirut is probably the least private place in the world to go swimming. A broad concrete pier juts out into the sea, striped with long rows of flat canvas beds in gay primary colours. On these the bikini girls recline to be admired, or else walk about absently as though in search of someone; and the young men in their irridescent trunks, torsos burnt almost black and thickly matted with hair, leap slowly up and down on the trampoline with sad concentration, and their muscles gleam in the sun. From each of the hundred balconies of the Hotel Phoenicia, a hundred yards away, visitors gaze down, and on the road at the edge of the sea there is always at any hour of the day a group of twenty or thirty passers-by gazing thoughtfully across the water at the bathers on the terrace.

There was no sign of Angela at twelve o'clock – at least Latimer didn't think there was. He had tried to imagine her in a bikini – and had failed – but there were dozens of girls about, in various states of dress and undress, all anonymous behind enormous dark glasses and all looking straight through him in his hired bathing trunks and horn-rimmed spectacles.

He sat down gloomily on one of the canvas beds and stared at the trampoline.

'Steven – '

Latimer squinted up against the sun. The man had aged a lot in the five years since they had last seen each other. His hair was grey now above the ears and under the red of recent sunburn his skin was the sickly colour of a man whose work worries him and keeps him long hours in badly ventilated offices.

Angus said pleasantly, 'I didn't expect to see you here, Steven.' Uninvited, he sat down beside Latimer on the canvas bed. 'Are you here on holiday too? It's a grand place, Beirut.'

They had met last at Felicity's funeral and Latimer couldn't believe that Angus wasn't equally conscious of the fact. But he seemed unconcerned.

'How have you been, Steven?'

Latimer tried to say something but it came out as a sort of groan. Angus said at once, as though it was the cue he had been waiting for, 'Now, Steven, we can't go on for ever feeling bitter.'

'Why ever not?'

'Steven, listen – ' He had developed a double chin since they last met and it occurred to Latimer suddenly that Angus was a man not cut out for success. Lean, thrusting, naively ambitious – as a young man he had been forgiveable. Arrived, he was repulsive.

Angus was talking away with great fluency now about bygones being bygones. They had been such friends, such *close* friends, it was wrong to destroy such friendships. They were both lonely men now and they had so much in common – he shied hastily away from that one and started instead on the subject of Nicholas. For his sake they ought to – Then, abruptly, he stopped, and stood up. Angela was standing just in front of them, smiling. Angus was smiling too, waiting to be introduced.

Angela in a bikini was, astonishingly, magnificent. There were acres of flesh, of course, but it was all an even pinky-brown and it all curved in the tense shallow curve of the earth's surface seen from a satellite. She looked like a very young Rubens goddess, sunburned.

Latimer was struck dumb.

Angela said, 'Good morning,' looking from him to Angus.

Latimer lumbered belatedly to his feet, Speaking with difficulty he said, 'Good morning. Er – this is Angus Bailey . . . Miss – er – Miss Smith.'

Then with decision, he took her arm and wheeled her round away from Angus. 'Goodbye,' he said over his shoulder.

Angus called out, 'Don't go . . . let's all have a drink . . . Steven!'

Latimer took no notice but Angela stopped. 'Shouldn't we – ?'

'Certainly not.' He tugged at her arm again and they moved on.

'Why the *secrecy*?' Angela was delighted. 'What *was* that? – why Miss *Smith*, for heaven's sake? My name's Barrington. And *why* can't I talk to that man?'

Latimer groped for some way of turning the situation into a joke. 'He's not at all the thing for you,' he said seriously. 'He's dangerous.'

But it came out more violently than he had intended and she was startled. '*Dangerous*?' she said, and to his annoyance craned her head over her shoulder to have another look.

'No, no. I'm only joking. Are we going to swim – or have a drink first?'

Angela wrinkled her nose, looking at the sea. 'Drink, please, definitely.'

Still holding her arm Latimer wheeled her round and started back towards the bar. There was no sign of Angus now.

Angela said, 'This will be known as the Plastic Age.'

His mind still on Angus, Latimer said stupidly, 'Plastic?'

'When they dig us up. Nothing destroys plastic, and it doesn't even get a nice iridescent shine on it, like Roman glass does.'

After a moment she added patiently, 'After it's been buried in the earth.'

Latimer realised at last that all this had been sparked off by the mess floating on the sea. With an effort he said, 'You think the post-nuclear museums will have bits of plastic in glass cases, labelled "1st century Pre-Bang"?'

'That's right, and Coke bottles. But mainly plastic. Now this –' they had settled themselves at a table under the awning and she pointed to a beaker holding toothpicks, ' – I can see this now, behind glass. The worst trouble, though, from *our* point of view –'

Latimer's feelings towards her had seesawed yet again. He felt himself now in direct competition with the matted torsos on the trampoline and he wanted to impress, to dazzle – but instead he was sitting there like a fool in hired bathing trunks and horn-rimmed spectacles while Angela talked relentlessly about plastic.

'It *floats*,' she was explaining, 'that's the real horror. That's what makes the pollution permanent. You throw it into the sea but it just washes up somewhere else – ' She waved a hand at the surface of the sea. 'In fifty years' time the whole Mediterranean seaboard – '

Exasperated, Latimer broke in, 'Do you enjoy Beirut?'

'Oh yes, I do!' she said at once. 'But what about *you*? How was your hotel? Have you got a nice room?'

Latimer said weakly, 'It's all right – '

'Nice people?'

Hoping to intrigue her he said, 'Very nice. Full of old friends.'

'Oh yes? . . . You knew Haider bin Hassan at Oxford, I suppose.'

Latimer said slowly, 'Yes . . . yes I did.'

She had been leaning well forward across the table, keeping him within range of her enormous short-sighted eyes, but now she blinked sharply and sank back. 'Just a minute.' She held up a hand. 'Listen.'

The loudspeaker had stopped playing pop music and a voice was speaking French. They pronounced it 'La Timère' of course, but there was no doubt about it. He was being called to the phone.

It could only be Angus . . . Latimer decided that he wouldn't even bother to take the call. But Angela said abruptly, apologetically, 'Look, I told you yesterday that today was my free day. Well, it was, but they've loaded an extra job on to me and I've got to go out to the airport after all. So I'll just say goodbye now. Thank you for the drink.' She stood up and added a smile. 'Goodbye.' And then she was gone, moving briskly away towards the changing room, a big toffee-coloured girl in a black bikini.

Latimer stood up and walked slowly over to the telephones. 'Cabin No. 2,' said the telephone girl.

The voice that said 'Dr. Latimer?' was a man's, and it had a slight foreign accent.

'Dr. Latimer. This is Luc Duquair. I should so much like to meet you. Will you come and have a drink with me this evening?'

85

Duquair . . . Margaret Wedderburn's fiancé. The voice was warm and friendly and, inevitably, Latimer remembered the other members of Margaret's family who had begun by approaching him so courteously. He put a hand to his cheek. Cordwainer was only her brother-in-law; this man was her fiancé.

He said awkwardly, 'Oh.' On the other hand, this was almost certainly the only sure way of finding Margaret herself. He said, 'Is there anything in particular you want to discuss?'

'No, no, just a chat.'

Absurdly, standing by himself holding the telephone and wearing only bathing trunks, he shrugged. 'Okay.'

Even to his own ears it sounded ungracious and he added hastily, 'It's very kind of you to ask me.' Even more absurd.

'Excellent. Seven o'clock then. Villa Haddad, Ashrafyieh. I shall expect you,' and he had rung off.

4

As Latimer crossed the hotel foyer on his way back to his room, Angus sprang up from the chair in which he had been waiting and followed. He even broke into a little run so as to get his foot into the lift door. They rode up together in silence to the fifth floor, and then Angus followed Latimer round the two turns in the corridor, waited while Latimer unlocked the door and crowded in behind him.

'You're behaving like a gangster,' Latimer said crossly.

'You used that word to describe us once before.' Angus was full of joviality.

'So it's still the Department?' They had done the room while he was out and it was null again, blank and anonymous as a sample product. Latimer drew back the curtains and hot sun slanted into the room.

'That's right . . . Steven – ' Angus became confidential. 'I'm not really here on holiday.' Angus was the only man Latimer had ever known who wore their college tie, and Latimer saw with amazement that Angus was wearing it now, with a yellow shirt and cotton trousers.

'I never for a moment thought you were.'

Angus threw himself down into the armchair and sighed deeply. 'No. I'm here on a job – and I'm baffled.' His voice was wistful and a faint trace of the Scots accent that as a young man he had suppressed so ruthlessly had been allowed to creep back into it. Honest Angus, the braw wee laddie from Scotland . . . Latimer burst out laughing. 'You're baffled, are you?'

Angus looked hurt. 'Alas, it is not a joke . . . We're worried about Panjeh and I need your advice. You've just left there, haven't you? Well, there's rumours of a coup. You remember Haider bin Hassan? Well, it looks as though someone's trying to put him in as Ruler instead of his uncle.'

Latimer said encouragingly, 'That sounds about right –'

'Ah –' Angus looked up eagerly. 'So Haider told you?'

Latimer said gently, 'What would *you* conclude, Angus, if *you* found Haider in a Beirut hotel in full fancy dress, surrounded by secret service men?'

With obvious disappointment Angus said, 'Oh –'

'But you thought I was selling him, didn't you?' With enjoyment, Latimer let himself get angry. 'Telling *you* something he'd told *me* in confidence? That's the way you and your bloody Department work.'

Angus said automatically, 'It's an arm of government, Steven, just like the Post Office Savings Bank . . . Would you be willing to tell me what Haider *did* say?'

'By all means. He said that the age of imperialism and servile puppet regimes was past. The day of freedom and democracy was dawning. He said that Western society must be swept away altogether before any kind of decent life for mankind can emerge.' He spoke with emphasis, enjoying the slow astonishment on Angus's face.

'*He* said that? *Haider* did? But that's amazing. I'm very glad you've told me this, Steven, very grateful. I appreciate your help. Really. I –'

Latimer cut in impatiently, 'What the hell does it matter? Britain's out of the Gulf. It's not your responsibility any more.'

'It's not as simple as that.' Angus spoke earnestly. 'That whole area is our responsibility. It always has been. Even now there's the oil to think of.'

'But not in Panjeh – or have they really found some?'

For a moment Angus was disconcerted. 'Yes,' he said slowly at last, 'last month, actually. It's a very big deposit, probably bigger even than Abu Dhabi . . . Didn't you know?' He was clearly surprised.

'No. There were rumours . . . but there'd been rumours ever since the rig was set up. The rig people weren't ever allowed on the island, you know.' He thought of adding 'except to die', but decided against it: Angus would think its frivolous. Angus was talking of important things, Latimer thought bitterly, oil and economics – not human lives. If Panjeh really had oil, then overnight, it had at least become worth something: the Sheikh of Abu Dhabi received two million dollars a week, just for allowing an oil company to take oil out of his territory. And the British government's concern for Panjeh would have been sharpened too. Quite apart from the high-flown sentiments about peace in the area that Angus had been feeding him there would now be a very real determination to ensure that Saladin banked his new oil money in London.

He said sarcastically, 'I'm beginning to understand your urgency.'

Angus took it straight, and nodded. 'It's urgent all right . . . ' He sighed again, deeply. 'Haider's playing a bloody funny game.'

'If it's information you want, why not ask Haider yourself what he's up to?'

Angus made a brief movement of impatience. 'He knows who I work for.'

'Well, he thinks I work for them too.'

'*Haider* does?' Latimer could almost see the careful, steady brain sifting the implications of that one.

'Yes. And that's why I've told you what he said to me. He wanted you told.'

He had hoped for an outburst of irritation, but instead Angus made only a little clicking sound of annoyance. He said reproachfully, 'Helping us would be helping your country, Steven.'

'Don't be absurd.'

There was silence. With apparent casualness Angus asked, 'And what plans do you have for your holiday, Steven? Are you here for long?'

Latimer said, 'I'm not here on holiday any more than you are. I'm here to get in touch with Margaret Wedderburn.'

A stranger would have said that Angus's face didn't move. But Latimer had seen that face in tutorials when Angus's translation of a passage of Arabic had been judged to be better than his own; he had seen Angus out dining with Felicity before he knew for certain they were sleeping together. The end of Angus's nose moved barely perceptibly to one side – a tiny, unmistakable signal of triumph.

Latimer stared, and realised suddenly that Angus must have said something. He was already on his feet, moving towards the door. Latimer said, '*What* did you say?'

Angus mumbled, 'I've got to be going.'

'Tell me about Luc Duquair.' There was no conceivable need for caution now.

'Duquair?' Angus paused reluctantly, one hand on the door-knob. 'Oil.'

'What sort of oil?'

'Anglo-French. A smallish firm, you won't have heard of it. Well, goodbye.'

'Just a minute . . . A punching man, do you think?' – he indicated his left cheek, 'or is he more likely to use something with steel in it?'

When Angus decided to look stupid there was nobody, but nobody, who could do it better. Latimer dropped the jolliness. 'All right, then. Tell me about Anglo-French.'

Angus frowned impatiently. 'They used to operate in Libya – before the coup, and they've got a few wells in Nigeria. Now they're trying to break into the Middle East. That's Duquair's job. But they're not getting anywhere. The majors – that's Shell and Texaco and the other big five – they've got a very tight hold and they're extremely jealous. If any outsider gets an oil concession in this area it'll be over their dead bodies.'

'Have Shell got the new oil in Panjeh?'

'Well, they found it, as you know, and now they're busy negotiating a new agreement to exploit it.'

'What happens if Haider gets back?'

'He'll repudiate existing agreements, set up a national company and operate it with Palestinian engineers.'

There was a short silence. Then Latimer said, 'So you knew already about Haider's – left-wing views?'

'Of course.' Angus still had his hand on his door-knob but he was less impatient to leave now. 'He hasn't exactly been making a secret of them.'

Latimer was suddenly furious. Angus knew it all, and yet had let him make himself ridiculous trying to shield Haider . . . But at least he'd dropped all pretence of friendliness – from the exact moment at which Latimer had mentioned Margaret Wedderburn.

Too angry to think, Latimer said, 'It's characteristic that your Department should be preparing to defend a reactionary like Saladin against a movement committed to progress.'

'Don't be so bloody naive, Steven. There's nothing progressive about Pufflop.'

'About *what?*'

Angus smiled thinly. 'The Popular Front for the Liberation of Panjeh. Initials P.F.L.P. . . . they're revolutionaries, Steven. And their support comes from China.'

Latimer said, '*I* know.'

'All those Chinese "advisers" in Damascus, Steven – that's what they're up to. There's a camp down in the south of Syria, financed and staffed from China, where they do nothing but train young men from the Gulf States to go back home and start revolutions. The line-up for Panjeh, Steven, is a Marxist revolutionary organisation, committed to overthrowing the present Sheikh but including in its own ranks the legitimate heir to the Sheikhdom . . . Something for everybody, in fact. Bloody clever – and quite tempting too, we realise that . . . But Saladin is the legal ruler, Steven.'

He spoke with a curious emphasis, as though he were trying to persuade Latimer of something. With sudden decision he took his hand off the door-knob and walked past Latimer to

90

the window. 'Come and look here, Steven.'

Reluctantly Latimer moved over to stand beside him. Five floors below was the hotel swimming-pool, a freehand curve of brilliant blue water set into a white expanse of marble. Only a few years ago the terrace would have been crowded with tourists – American ladies with blue-rinsed hair accompanied by slender parchment-faced husbands, sturdy British couples with bright red sunburn and sensible shoes, girls in bikinis concentrating on their suntan. Even now there were one or two obvious holiday-makers, but more conspicuous were a number of solitary men in dark suits and impenetrably dark glasses, each with a single drink and a folded newsaper on the table in front of him.

Angus said without turning his head, 'Do you see that man with the newspaper? – there, over to the right. The one by himself. He's a Russian chap. And that one, over there, by the door into the dining-room, he's the C.I.A. And the Israeli's somewhere . . . And the Egyptian. They're all here, you know.' He moved away from the window. 'Stringers, they call them in journalism, keeping an eye on things . . . Everybody's interested. This isn't a joke, Steven. Seven or eight innocent men were killed when that rig was blown up. It's a bloody dangerous situation and one that could easily turn into something very nasty.'

The curious emphasis was there in his voice again. Latimer, surprised and beginning to be annoyed, said, 'I realise that' and Angus started at once, eagerly. 'Then – '

Latimer said impatiently, 'But it's none of it anything to do with me.'

'It's to do with all of us.'

With a shock, Latimer realised that Angus really meant it. He said seriously, 'No, Angus, it's *not* to do with me. I know too much. I'm neutral. It's unfashionable, I know, but it's true. Saladin is everything that is frightful but I don't deceive myself that in practice a communist regime would be any better . . . Or indeed very different.'

Angus said obstinately, 'No one is neutral. We all have to fight for what we believe to be right.'

Latimer lost his temper. 'Oh, for heaven's sake! Your lot

wouldn't know right if you saw it. You just have a policy, and you're always prepared to trample over anything and anybody to get your way. How can you know what is *right*? Nobody knows what is right – but I'm damn sure both Saladin and the communists are wrong.'

Angus said quietly, 'I wish I could believe you,' and opened the door to leave.

Despite himself, Latimer said, 'You go to see Nicholas.' Between him and Angus all victories and defeats were merely tactical – except one. Only that morning he had decided to let the past stay buried . . . but the past *wasn't* buried and the account between them was still open, so long as Nicholas existed.

'Of course.' Angus's voice was cold.

'I didn't know that was in the contract.'

Angus flushed. He slammed the door and came back into the room. 'What contract, Steven? Just what the hell do you mean?'

What did he mean? Latimer began, self-righteously, 'Well, after all, I – '

With sudden intensity Angus said, 'Nicholas is almost certainly my son, you know that. But I'm never going to bring a paternity suit and you know that too. And yet you have chosen to live abroad for the last three years, only able to see him when you're on leave . . . I regard him as *my* son and shall bloody well continue to treat him as such. He is already my heir, and when he is older I hope he will choose to make his home with me . . . And I hope very much that you won't try to stop him if that's what he wants to do.'

Angus can't come . . . but will you come instead? Angus can't come . . .

Latimer said lightly, 'He must make his own choice, of course,' and was astonished by the pain. He turned his back on Angus, pretending to look out of the window, and began again. 'Listen, Angus – ' but the door-handle clicked once, almost inaudibly, and Angus had gone.

Latimer slammed the side of one hand against the window frame and swore childishly. Rubbing the sore fingers automatically, he stood looking down through the window at the figures round the pool. The Russian, the Israeli, the C.I.A. . . . which was which? He couldn't remember. It didn't matter. *Angus can't come* . . . He shut his eyes against the glare but behind closed eyelids went on seeing the blue pool, the sunlight dazzling off it and the white terrace spotted with black figures.

5

PANJEH SOLIDARITY MEETING

The destruction last Thursday by militants of the Popular Front for the Liberation of Panjeh of the Shell oil drilling rig has once again demonstrated the determination of the people of Panjeh to be free of Britain's oil imperialism.

Solidarity Meeting 3 p.m. today, Tuesday 12 October, Room 12B, Block H, American University of Beirut.

Britain's so-called 'withdrawal' from the Gulf at the end of 1971 has left the puppet sheikh Saladin bin Adbul Rahman supported by a mercenary army trained and equipped by Britain. In return for British support this brutal degenerate continues to protect British interests, principally oil.

The sole function of his British-equipped army is 'Internal security' – i.e. the suppression of political opposition. Hundreds are held in prison in appalling conditions. Torture is general. And yet British imperialism supports this tyrant.

The Popular Front for the Liberation of Panjeh appeals to all progressive forces to support their struggle. The P.F.L.P. is part of a worldwide movement against national and class oppression . . .

Routine stuff . . . Latimer, eating a late lunch in the hotel coffee shop and glancing through the local English-language paper for anything to distract his thoughts, read the announcement idly. This was the public, legal manifestation of the Panjeh guerrillas.

93

Long live the struggle against oppression!

Four comrades who have recently escaped from the Sheikh's prison will speak. The meeting will also be addressed – Latimer's breath stopped – *will also be addressed by Margaret Wedderburn, Beirut correspondent of the* Socialist Review.

Solidarity Meeting 3 p.m. today.

He looked at his watch. It was five to three. By five past he was there, breathing heavily, having run the whole way.

The meeting hadn't started yet but the public had arrived. Room 12B was a smallish classroom, stuffy at any time and stifling now because of the number of people crowding in and trying to find themselves seats. The organisers of the meeting had underestimated popular interest in Panjeh, it seemed . . . But then again, perhaps not. When he looked at the crowd more closely Latimer saw that a large proportion of it was made up of silent gentlemen in tight black suits and dark glasses, several of them still carrying folded copies of the *New York Times* . . . They must have moved on in a body from the Criterion pool. Their aim in every case had been to sit inconspicuously at the back or extreme side of the room, but so great was their number that the total effect was that of a black scum round the walls – or of a pudding basin lined with crust, the steak and kidney element being provided by the students who jostled in the centre of the room, shouting and waving to each other and climbing over the backs of the benches. Angus was there too, well to the side, in dark glasses.

Latimer found himself a place at the back, leaning against the wall between two of the black suits, and concentrated at first on getting his breath back. Multicoloured lozenges slid up and down over his eyeballs at every breath. He breathed carefully, slower and slower . . . but at last he could no longer escape the implications of what he had read. 'Margaret Wedderburn, Beirut correspondent of the *Socialist Review*.'

Well, and why not? Was there any reason why a gentle, sensitive, deeply-wronged girl shouldn't work as a journalist? None . . . All the same, it struck a rather different note from the one he had expected. And at once he made another connection, and cursed his slowness. The dark, efficient English woman at the Criterion last night, writing notes for her drunken colleague, organising his taxi home ... and with painful clarity Latimer remembered the expression with which she had greeted his assumption that she and the drunken journalist *belonged*. She was astonishingly like her mother – and he had missed the resemblance because at that time he was looking for a gentle, smiling, very young girl, with short hair curling up at the back of her head and round her face and a slender arm stretched out towards a young man.

A few figures had appeared now on the platform at the far end of the room – three or four students, some figures in khaki bush jackets. It's nearly twenty years, Latimer thought suddenly, she must be over thirty. The gentle, smiling, very young girl simply didn't exist any more.

Another group was climbing up on to the platform now, and she was with them. The chairman, an earnest boy in spectacles, installed her in the place of honour, on his right, and the rest of the group started to find places for themselves, adding to the general hubbub the scraping and bumping of heavy chairs. She sat down gravely and tilted her head to listen to something the chairman was saying to her, nodding briefly from time to time. She had all the composure that her mother must have shown – on the Bench, and more than ever her face resembled her mother's. She must be used to public meetings, to speeches and protests. She looked serene and confident, and her long dark hair was drawn back off her face into a knot as severe and uncompromising as her mother's curious black hat had been. But Latimer also had to acknowledge that she was the only person in the room who looked cool. She was wearing pale green and it must have cost a lot more than the earnest revolutionaries there would have approved of ... Perhaps its simplicity deceived them. So go ahead, Latimer said to himself savagely, be sorry for *that*.

'Comrades!' – the meeting had begun. He looked round, but Haider wasn't there.

It was all fairly predictable. The public language of revolutionary Marxism follows a ritual of its own, cocooning its real meaning in a blanket of jargon. The only interest for the

95

outsider lies in watching for any infinitesimal departure from the norm that might hint at a real change in policy. But it was soon clear that today there would be nothing to interest the outsider. Most of the speakers were students, and the comrades who had escaped from Panjeh were dazed and in-articulate – a little slow on the phrases about the struggle of the people of Panjeh against Western imperialism in which they had been rehearsed. Some of the black-suited gentlemen showed clear signs of boredom; some even opened their copies of the *New York Times* and started to look at yesterday's Wall Street prices. But the students were enthusiastic: they cheered the speakers, stamping with their feet at any mention of imperialism and jumping up at the end of every speech for ritual shouts of the 'Long Live ... !' type.

The chairman described a visit he had managed to make to the guerrillas in the interior of Panjeh. 'In one of the liberated areas I spoke with two comrades who had left their families in order to join the Front. Their names were Leila and Fatima. Their ages were eleven and fourteen. In the West they would be regarded as little girls. They would still be at school. But Leila and Fatima are already fighters for the cause. They are helping to prepare for the victory of the Front in Panjeh. I asked Leila about her family. "I have no family," she said. "The Front is my family. The Front has taught me literacy and Marxism." '

Cheers from the students.

'I asked her what books she read. "The thoughts of Chairman Mao," she replied.'

More cheers. The black-suited brigade listened carefully, never moving.

Then, when he had finished, Margaret Wedderburn stood up to speak. The students clapped and stamped and she waited quietly for the noise to stop before she began. Her voice was as Latimer remembered it from the previous night – gentle, and rather low – almost apologetic – but she had no difficulty in making herself heard at the back of the hall. And at the back of the hall Latimer listened with surprise. It wasn't at all a bad speech – and by comparison with what had gone before it was

96

superlative. It was brief and informative, and it led neatly on to its conclusion.

The existence of Saladin and the other Gulf sheikhs as independent rulers was an anachronism; British military power had placed a barrier round the area and behind this, insulated from normal political pressures and influences, the sheikhs had survived a hundred years past their time. And it wasn't only the *fact* of their existence that was anachronistic. The entire economic and social development of the sheikhdoms had been artificially retarded in the interests of the sheikhs and their immediate families. Until the rule of the sheikhs was removed, no sort of decent life for the people of the Gulf would be possible. The British government had been guilty not only of criminal folly in preserving these sheikhs for so long but also of gross deceit in pretending to withdraw from the Gulf while in fact continuing to shore up the futile sheikhdoms – Panjeh in particular. This help must cease. The sheikhs must go. Governments based on the welfare and development of the people of the Gulf must be established.

So far, so good, thought Latimer, glancing round at the rest of the audience with grim amusement. He, personally, agreed with every word she'd said . . . and none of it would raise even an eyebrow at any moderately liberal dinner table in London. But it was all hopelessly out of place here. No jargon, no appeal to the emotions, no cries of 'Long Live the Popular Front' . . . The students listened in gloomy silence, shuffling their feet, and barely clapped when she'd finished. And the black-suited brigade lost interest altogether. One or two even squeezed themselves round the back of the hall and tiptoed out. Clearly, they were disappointed . . .

And so was Latimer. The meeting itself had been much what he'd expected – the routine speeches, the meaningless jargon. But Margaret's speech had been on a different plane altogether. She was only too obviously clever, and well-informed, and in earnest – and she was badly out of place in that crackpot amateur set-up. It seemed a pity that she couldn't have linked herself up with a better-organised cause.

Not waiting for the last speaker he too squeezed along the back row and tiptoed out into the open air. Beyond the canopy

4   97

of shade from the pine trees there were dazzling glimpses of sea. He sat down on a bench and lit a cigarette. At least he didn't need to hide: his appearance wasn't going to cause any trouble. She had seen him the night before and hadn't connected him with 'Steve Latimer', so he could just sit and wait for her – and then perhaps he might follow her until he found a suitable opportunity for a talk. He sat and watched the door of the classroom.

When the meeting broke up she came out surrounded by a crowd of students and for a time they talked and gesticulated in a tight knot. She seemed inextricably involved. But then suddenly she had broken out of the group and was walking away alone, along a path that passed immediately in front of his bench. He dropped his eyes and gazed at his feet. Her footsteps came clicking nearer and nearer along the tarmac – click-click, click-click – and then they stopped.

Latimer left it as long as he dared before looking up, but you can't wait for ever. She was smiling, slightly.

Slimmer and shorter than Anna, and less beautiful – and disconcertingly like her mother. He smiled back. She said, 'You were quite extraordinary kind last night. Thank you so much.'

Latimer felt himself go red. The words were all right – just, and the tone of her voice was as low and gentle as ever. And yet, somehow, the implication was that he ought to be standing up and touching his cap. She smiled again, briefly, and walked on – click-click, click-click.

He jumped to his feet. 'Excuse me – I wonder if we could have a word.' She had moved so fast that he had to say it quite loudly.

She stopped and turned round, looking him up and down – and he'd never understood before just what that expression implied in terms of pained surprise. 'Perhaps some other time.' And she was off again.

He had literally to run after her – a sort of hop, skip, and jump to land in front of her, blocking her way. 'Please.' She didn't like it and made the fact plain. Hanging on to his politeness with both hands he said, 'Miss Wedderburn, I really *must* talk to you.'

This time she just said, 'No,' and stepped round him. Click-click, click-click.

He shouted after her, 'I'm Steven Latimer.'

She stopped dead, of course, and whipped round to look at him. Her face was a nasty chalk white and for a moment he thought she was going to faint. Subtle Latimer, he thought savagely, tactful Latimer.

But then she took a slow deep breath and in a small but perfectly steady voice said 'No, you are not.' Then she turned away yet again. He didn't move, but after a few steps she broke into a run.

6

Haider said sorrowfully, 'You didn't go, Steven . . . and after I asked you to.'

There was no trace of reproach – only a disconcerting echo of a schoolmaster remarking on a lapse that (while causing him personally only sorrow) was going to have appalling consequences for the boy concerned.

He was sitting in the armchair in Latimer's hotel room, still elaborately robed, but he managed to project an immediate atmosphere of well-worn leather, smoking coal fires, the cane behind the door . . . Latimer repressed a shiver. Haider had been at Stowe, he remembered.

'No,' Latimer said defiantly, 'I didn't go.' He lay down on the bed, just to show whose room it was, and closed his eyes. When he opened them again Haider was still looking at him with his schoolmaster's expression, and Latimer was struck again by the extraordinary contrast between Haider's theatrical appearance – his voluminous robes, silver-hilted dagger, hawk-of-the-desert beard – and the straightforward Englishness of his expression and conversation.

Haider said patiently, '*Why* didn't you go, Steven?'

'Because I haven't yet done the only thing I came to Beirut to do. I shan't go till I've done it.'

'And how long is that going to take?'

'I've no idea.'

'I see.' He sounded as though the whole case might have to be referred to the headmaster.

Latimer said, 'Come off it, Haider, I thought you were a pal.'

At once Haider's face crumpled. He looked as though Latimer had hit him. 'Oh but I *am!*' he said earnestly. 'You know that. It's just that all this is so *important* to me.'

Latimer started to protest, 'And what I'm doing's important too, to me' – but Haider took no notice. He leaned forward and the words came tumbling out of him. 'You've no *idea* what it feels like, after twenty-five years. We're the same age, Steven. Think how you'd feel if you'd been wanting one thing – and one thing only – since you were fifteen. Saladin *killed* my father – and my uncles – and I'm going to kill him. That's all I've ever wanted and now I'm going to get it. And at last I'm going to be Ruler of Panjeh. It's as certain as anything can be and – '

Latimer said, 'But Haider – '

Haider stopped at once. 'What?'

It took Latimer a moment to define the uneasiness that Haider's certainty roused in him. And then he remembered the painful amateurism, the almost juvenile atmosphere of the Popular Front Meeting. He said carefully, 'Your – supporters, Haider. Are you really sure they've got the organisation to do this thing?'

Haider nodded impatiently, 'Don't worry about that. Their organisation is super.'

Latimer tried again. 'You talk about being Ruler of Panjeh, but have you really thought what sort of government – what sort of *state* these people will in fact set up if their *coup* succeeds? A communist regime is – I mean – ' He stopped again, defeated. It was so obvious to him that Haider's sad, long-nourished ambitions and absurd, anachronistic draperies had no place in a Maoist commune, that he could hardly believe that Haider didn't see it too.

Haider didn't answer at once. Instead, his eyes stared and his face slowly went rigid: he might have been going into a trance. From a great distance he said, 'I – feed the air, promise-crammed. *Hamlet.*' Then his whole face broke into a broad smile and he looked at Latimer for applause.

Defeated, Latimer said, 'I get the idea.'

'It's been like that for *twenty-five years*, Steven. First it was the British – that damned Department – did you know I'd been with them? Well I was. "*Soon . . . next year . . . when the time is ripe.*" They kept me on ice for ten years, Steven, *ten years*, waiting for them. Then, after Suez, they just said it would never be any good, they'd never actually give me any military support. And Nasser was just as bad. "*Next year . . . soon . . . when the time is ripe*" – his people even used the same *phrases* as the British! And of course the time never *was* ripe. But now it is. These people have got money, and arms, and everything – and they're prepared to back me. It's all going to be *all right.*'

His confidence was absolute – and Latimer remembered sadly that it always had been. He said helplessly, 'What about Saladin's Defence Force?'

'How many men is that?'

'I'm not sure. About two hundred, I think.'

Haider said contemptuously, 'It's total complement is one hundred and fifty men, including officers . . . and there are *thousands* of Panjehi exiles living on the mainland.'

Latimer gave up. 'Okay. I expect you're right . . . for your own sake I certainly hope you are.'

'For *my* sake?' Haider's grin was always unexpected, always disarming. 'Don't you think I'd make a *good* Ruler, then?'

Latimer said slowly, remembering the hopes he had nourished about Haider, 'Well, you couldn't be worse than Saladin and you'd probably be slightly better – '

'You see! You do support me!'

Latimer laughed. 'Oh yes, of course I support you.'

But suddenly Haider was serious again. 'But you don't *really* mean it, Steven, I wish you did . . . I wish I knew *really* where you stand, politically.'

'Well, I don't know.' Latimer was taken by surprise. 'I suppose I'm fairly uninvolved.'

'You're evading the issue, Steven.' The schoolmaster tone of voice was back. 'Would you fight for me?'

'I wouldn't fight for anybody.'

Haider shrugged angrily.

Latimer said earnestly, 'Listen to me, Haider . . . From what I've seen of them here I very much doubt whether your Popular Front pals are capable of running a country properly – even something as small as Panjeh. And that's because they haven't even thought yet *how* they're going to run it.' He was reminded abruptly of his discussion with Angus only that morning, and with grim amusement heard himself using the same words. 'I'm neutral, Haider. Saladin is of course everything that is frightful, but I don't deceive myself that in practice a communist regime would be any better – or indeed very different.'

Haider said impatiently, 'You mustn't base your judgments on what you hear at solidarity meetings, Steven. That sort of thing goes down all right with the students here, but down in the Gulf they've never even heard of Mao and if they had they wouldn't want that sort of thing. They want leadership, and I can provide it. Communism is nonsense as a system of government anywhere, but particularly so in the Gulf.'

Latimer said mildly, 'The guerrillas seem to believe in it.'

'Oh yes . . . the guerrillas.' But he sounded vague.

There was a short silence. Latimer said curiously, 'Well, what *about* the guerrillas?'

Haider said impatiently, 'They're only a small group.'

'They blew up quite a large drilling rig. Only last week. And they seem to know – ' Latimer had been going to say that from what he had seen of them they seemed pretty well organised and extremely purposeful, but Haider interrupted him angrily, 'You've clearly learnt nothing about Panjeh. Like all short-term visitors you only see what you want to see.' The total injustice of the attack silenced Latimer: Haider himself hadn't set foot in any of the Gulf states since he was a boy. 'The guerrillas will never get anywhere, Steven. Surely you must realise that? Sabotage, yes. But Saladin will always have control in the town and it'll be years before they're strong enough to challenge him there. They just don't have the arms – Oh, I know all about the Chinese – and the Russians. But what they're sending is only a token, a flea-bite. The Defence

Force is armed by the *British*, Steven.'

Latimer was beginning to feel dizzy. 'But you said – '

Haider said patiently, 'You were talking about the guerrillas. I'm telling you that they'll never get anywhere. But with enough arms and money – and proper organisation – the Panjehi exiles from the coast could take over Panjeh in twelve hours.'

'But – ' Latimer stopped. Then he said slowly, 'So *your* arms aren't coming from the communists at all.'

Haider giggled and flung out his arms, flapping the sleeves of his elaborate robe. 'Why ever should the communists support *me*?'

'I give up.' Latimer was starting to feel angry in his turn. Haider had been leading him round in circles and even now he was clearly enjoying Latimer's mystification.

Haider said earnestly, 'Don't be angry, Steven. I *can't* tell you everything – you must see that. But don't worry about me. The people I'm involved with are a serious concern, I promise you. There's nothing airy-fairy or theoretical about them. They don't talk hot air about democracy or the rights of the people. They talk about power. They're professionals, Steven. And I'm a professional too, you know. I've been planning this for *twenty-five* years. And I've been trained for it, first by the British, and then by the Egyptians.' His grin appeared briefly. 'You can't ask better than that. And now at last I've got the opportunity to put it all into practice. I've got it all worked out – every last detail. The whole pay-day plan – '

'Pay-day?'

'It's the code-name,' Haider said eagerly, 'like D-Day, do you see? Pay-day stands for the invasion of Panjeh – and very suitable too.' His eyes gleamed. 'It's going to cost them the *earth* . . . The whole plan is ready and so are the arms and supplies – everything.' He was leaning right forward in his chair now, his hands gesticulating, his eyes shining . . . and Latimer could only think of Nicholas. '*I'm going to dance a square dance. For America, you see . . . Wayno's doing a sword dance.*'

'At E-hour minus one – that's Embarkation Hour, of course one hour before E-hour the forces will arrive at the rendezvous point on the mainland. We don't want them too early or we'll alarm the local authorities, but we have to have time to equip them. We ourselves – the leaders – will have got to the rendezvous point half an hour earlier, E-minus one and a half, and we'll have got all the arms ready and waiting for them. They'll embark at once. We're opting for the short sea-crossing, you see, and it shouldn't take more than half an hour. They're all small boats but very fast so they'll be able to land almost anywhere on the island – like Dunkirk in reverse. Their primary objective will be the airfield, and once they've got control of that we can fly in fresh supplies of arms and money.'

'Transport doesn't seem to bother you.'

Unexpectedly Haider laughed, 'No. Transport's no problem.'

Latimer said again, 'I see.' There was silence. 'Why are you telling me all this, Haider?'

'Why?'

'Last night you thought I was working for the British secret service.'

'But – ' Haider sounded genuinely alarmed, 'you said you weren't. You're *not*, are you?'

'No.'

Haider puffed out his breath with a little grin of relief and self-mockery. 'That's good.' But at once he was serious again. 'This is a *real* operation, Steven, and I want you to realise it. It's not a fantasy any more.'

'And – ?'

'And so you *must* go away. *Now*. Please.'

Latimer was dumbfounded. 'But what on *earth* have I got to do with it?'

'I told you last night – ' Haider had his head bent now, fiddling with the big dagger, 'if you hang around they'll only think I'm mixed up with the Department and that'll put an end to any arms or money for me. They don't trust me all that far as it is.'

Reluctantly, Latimer said, 'I don't believe you.'

Haider's head jerked up. 'You're a fool! I'm warning you for your own good. Go away!'

Latimer said sadly, 'Okay, Haider, you've warned me – '

and wondered for a moment if Haider were going to weep.

Haider said pleadingly, 'You *will* leave now, won't you? At once?'

'Not at once. But as soon as I can.'

Haider sighed and got to his feet. The movement of his robes created quite a little breeze. At the door of his room he turned. 'Steven . . . please go.'

Obstinately, Latimer shook his head.

Haider sighed. Gravely, in Arabic, he pronounced the formal farewell for those about to start on a journey, 'May Allah watch over you.' He sounded as though he meant it.

7

Luc Duquair looked almost too French to be true. His face and nose were long and narrow, his eyes pale, and his greying hair was streaked by the deep even ridges of comb-strokes running back from a high forehead. He was shortish in stature, and looked clever.

Latimer discovered all this from a photograph in the Villa Haddad – a cutting from a magazine, glazed and framed. It showed the Frenchman walking across a flat sandy space with the outline of oil storage tanks in the background, talking deferentially to an elderly Arab wearing traditional robes. The caption, in Arabic, gave a date about eight years back and referred to the opening of an oil-refining plant. Monsieur Duquair was described as manager. The lengthy titles of the elderly Arab meant nothing to Latimer. Libya, he guessed.

He had decided to arrive an hour early for his drink with Duquair. It was fairly futile defence but the best that he could think of in a hurry. He wanted if possible to talk to Duquair before Duquair had heard about Latimer's attempt to talk to Margaret after the Popular Front meeting. He also wanted to avoid any elaborate unpleasantness Duquair might be preparing for him. Casual unpleasantness he would just have to put up with.

The address in Ashrafyieh – a pleasant leafy district on a hill above the port – had suggested to Latimer a light modern villa with a patio, and a striped umbrella perhaps, and white garden furniture . . . Instead he found himself walking down a long narrow lane between two overgrown gardens towards a high blank grey wall. The trees on either side blanketed the noise of traffic from the road so that within a few yards he was conscious only of the sound of his own footsteps on gravel. The lane narrowed abruptly, passed through an open iron gate and turned at a right-angle round the corner of the house. Now there was only a blank shadowy stone passage leading straight to a heavy door, with one thickly barred window beside it.

Latimer felt a flicker of surprise and pleasure: this was a Turkish house, one of the few left in Beirut, and the forbidding approach was an intrinsic part of the design – an insistent suggestion that inside the house there was something, many things, worth protecting . . . Duquair had done pretty well for himself.

For a moment, as he waited in deep shadow while the door bell sounded far away inside the house Latimer felt as though he were ringing at the door of a prison, but the bell was answered promptly by a neat-looking maid in a blue overall who, when he asked in English for Monsieur Duquair, gestured him at once into the house without even asking his name. Then she disappeared.

The room in which she left him was small and grey with no furniture except an ornate gilt mirror, and a telephone, and no view except on to the grey passage outside. But through an inner doorway Latimer could see brilliant sunlight and an expanse of white marble. When the maid hadn't come back after two or three minutes he walked cautiously to the doorway and peered through. Still nobody came, so he stepped forward.

The brightness was disconcerting. He was in a vast hall, long and high, the far end entirely filled by a huge window of three pointed arches. The sun, shining directly in through the windows, blinded him for a moment and he stopped. Then, as his eyes adjusted themselves he moved slowly forward again. The furniture had all been grand but now was shabby, and the same was true of the tapestries hanging on the side walls and the rugs on the marble floor. But the effect was breathtaking – peaceful, dignified and harmonious. Latimer was surprised: what little Angus had told him about Anglo-French Oil hadn't suggested anything on quite such a scale. He tiptoed on down the room, stopping occasionally to listen, and taking in the photograph of Duquair which was propped up on a writing-table. Beyond the high triple window there was a line of huge cypresses and, between them, tumbling away down the hill, the curly red roofs of the old town. In the distance, down by the port, there were cranes and warehouses and beyond them the flat blue sea and the sky. Latimer stood and looked out, enjoying the view, and a voice some way behind him said, 'Please take your glasses off.'

It wasn't the sort of voice he had been expecting and for a moment he was confused. Then he turned round hastily. Shining levelly through the windows behind him, the sun lit up the length of the hall. It penetrated even to the *liwan*, an inner sanctum at the farthest end beyond a row of stone arches that cut across the hall, repeating exactly the high curves of the windows. The *liwan* was crowded with heavy sofas upholstered in brilliant silks. Latimer realised now, too late, that he had turned straight to the windows when he came in and hadn't so much as glanced that way.

In the exact centre of the end wall, looking at him down the full length of the hall, Margaret Wedderburn sat on a huge red sofa. She was wearing a long white Arab robe, heavily embroidered, and was leaning – half lying – sideways against a pile of cushions with one leg drawn up so that the foot rested on the sofa. Her dark hair was hanging loose on to her shoulders and round her face. Her expression alarmed him.

She repeated, 'Please take your glasses off.'

He obeyed, clutching them tightly in one hand, and she went on. 'Now come here.'

Latimer blundered up the hall towards her and stopped under the centre arch.

'I don't like blackmailers.'

He didn't say a word. She didn't speak again either, and they remained in silence for what felt to him like an age. Then he put his glasses on again and looked at her enquiringly.

To his astonishment she threw back her head and laughed, a pleasant sound. 'No,' she said kindly, her voice gruff with amusement just as he had remembered it, 'A blackmailer couldn't possibly look so like a tortoise peering out from its shell. Well now, what's all this about?'

So far he hadn't said a word but he was undoubtedly getting the worse of the discussion. The whole family had an extraordinary knack of putting him in the wrong. He waved his hands. 'I saw your mother in London . . .'

' – *and*?' She looked younger than at the Panjeh meeting – partly because of the hair but far more because of the malice in her eyes and round her mouth. She was enjoying herself.

' – and your sister and your brother-in-law.'

Her eyebrows went up at that. With all the conviction he could pack in Latimer said, 'My name really *is* Steven Latimer, you know.' Silence. 'You and I haven't met before but you once met somebody who called himself by my name.'

'Yes, I knew a man called Steve Latimer. But that was a long time ago.'

'And he's pestering you again now . . . I gather.'

'*Pestering me now?*' Her astonishment couldn't possibly have been faked.

Latimer said weakly, 'That's what your mother said.'

'*My mother*? Nonsense. I haven't seen Steve Latimer since the twen – since September 1956, and my mother couldn't possibly have told you anything else.'

After a moment she said, still quite kindly, 'I think you'd better go now.'

Tiredly, Latimer said, 'I assure you that's what your mother said. She said your fiancé had rung her up.'

'Who?'

They looked at each other. Latimer said carefully, 'She said that Luc Duquair had rung her up.'

'Oh, Luc . . .' She smiled, at first with some private amusement and then more broadly, with an expression of considerable satisfaction. 'No, we can rule that possibility out at once . . . It was quite a good try, *Dr. Latimer* – ' kindly sarcasm, 'but next time you must spend longer on your details.' She rose to her feet, taking her time, and said graciously, 'Goodbye.'

He shouted, 'I'm asking for *help*.' He hadn't thought about it, but it turned out to be precisely the right thing to say. Generations of committees for the relief of the needy convened themselves in her bloodstream. She looked at him with interest. 'What sort of help?'

Latimer told her. He laid it on a bit about Cordwainer and his methods of argument, and he suppressed Patsy from the story altogether, but otherwise he was fairly straightforward. He simply described his three interviews — with her mother, her brother-in-law and her sister — and Cordwainer's later cancellation of his contract.

She listened with absolute attention, a frown compressing her eyebrows and her lips, her hands deep in the pockets of her robe. And she seemed hardly to notice when he'd finished. She just went on frowning — and thinking, presumably, and then, after a few minutes, she wandered over to the wall and pressed a bell.

So he was going to be thrown out after all.

But when the maid appeared she simply said, in atrocious Arabic, 'Leila, please will you bring — ' she glanced at her watch ' — a tray of drinks.' Then she waved a hand towards one of the big red sofas and sat down herself on another.

Latimer felt an enormous flood of relief. Tea-time was past, drinks times was here, those in need of help are always also in need of sustenance . . . Quite by accident he had touched a spring that released him from her hostility and cast him instead in the sacred role of unfortunate.

Waiting for the tray to arrive, suddenly she smiled at him, and he saw with astonishment that for her too the changeover had come as a relief. Her next remark surprised him still more.

'I've suspected something like this for years,' she said conversationally. 'I kept in touch, you see, with his — ' she corrected herself, 'with *your* career. I found out which hospital you were working in, and then where you were practising. Once I even got to know one of your patients, quite deliberately, just so as to be able to talk about you. And you sounded less and less like — like *my* Latimer. He was — ' her mouth twisted, ' — even then he was a bit of a bastard.' Even *then*, Angus.

'But you never tried to see – me?'

'No . . . By the time he – you – came back from the States everything had changed. It was all seven years in the past . . . And, anyway, he was married.' She paused. '*You* were married . . . ' She stopped again and then said awkwardly, 'I'm so sorry about your wife – her death, I mean . . . I saw it in *The Times*. You must have been –'

Latimer mumbled, 'Some time ago now.'

Her eyebrows went up, but she abandoned the subject at once. 'It's funny to think,' she went on for a moment, 'that he was probably still in England, all those years, when I was thinking of him in California . . . ' She smiled suddenly. 'Who-ever he is.'

Whoever he is . . . Latimer went cold.

It must have showed in his face because she asked, quite gently, 'Do *you* know – who?'

But then the drinks arrived. They stepped civilly through the ritual of choosing and pouring gins and tonics and then, just as he was nerving himself to make some kind of answer to her question, she said – still standing by the tray, her head bent and her hair hiding her face, 'No, *don't* tell me. Not yet, anyway.'

She glanced up, apologetically, and for a moment they looked at each other without speaking. Then she said quietly, 'I want to show you something.' She put her glass down and set off down the hall, the white robe flicking across the marble behind her. She went the whole length of the room and out through the centre window on to the balcony without even looking round to see if he was following. When Latimer caught up with her she was standing at the edge of the balcony with her hands resting on the iron railing. Below them was a small paved garden, and beyond and below that, half hidden by the broad leaves of a tree, was the steep red-tiled roof of a large house. It looked as though from the garden you could jump straight down on to the curly red tiles. She said nothing for a moment, and then moved sideways along the balcony until she was standing at its extreme left-hand end. Surprised, Latimer followed and stood, like her, gazing downwards. From this point it was just possible to see that below the wall of the garden there was a narrow footpath, dividing it from the house with the red-tiled roof. The ground fell away so sharply that the footpath must have been twenty feet below the level of the garden. Margaret was gazing down with the greatest concentration at the yard or so of stony track that was all that was visible of the footpath.

Without turning her head, she said, 'Could you recognise a man standing down there?'

'I suppose so — I might. It would probably depend on the light.' The sun was right down on the horizon now, throwing a red glow up into their faces, but the footpath was in shadow. Once the sun went altogether it would be pitch dark down there.

She said hesitantly, 'I saw a man down there one evening. He looked awfully like — Steve. But I only saw him for a second. Then he looked up and saw me, and he simply shot off down the path. It was probably imagination. I hadn't even thought of Steve for — oh, for ages.'

'What was he wearing?'

'Hard to see — but spectacles, just like the ones Steve wore...'

Latimer insisted, 'But the man down there, the other night, was he wearing a navy blue blazer?'

'That sort of thing . . . but it was about this time of the evening. I couldn't really see.'

'How many times did he come?'

'Just the once.'

Latimer turned to look at her. 'And on the basis of that — that one glimpse — your fiancé telephoned your mother and — and — ' but he couldn't find words to describe the juggernaut they had released into his life.

She shook her head impatiently. 'I told you that was nonsense. Luc couldn't have told my mother.'

'But your mother said he did.' He had only to invoke that monument of integrity — surely — for Margaret to be convinced. But she shrugged. 'I don't know what my mother's up to but — ' She repeated obstinately, 'Luc *couldn't* have told her.'

'Why ever not?' She was beginning to irritate him. Then,

suddenly, he guessed. 'You mean, you didn't *tell* him you'd seen the man?'

'Well, that too . . . but – ' She hesitated, and then said carefully, 'Luc doesn't actually *know* anything about – about Steve and all that. I've never told him . . . After all, it's a very long time ago.' She sounded defensive.

Latimer was startled – and at once ashamed of himself. The idea that a fiancé should necessarily be told of such an incident was more than old-fashioned – it was Victorian. But her family, after all, had shown themselves even more old-fashioned in their views than he was . . . Latimer said hesitantly, 'It's possible, I suppose, that some member of your family might have told your fiancé – '

'Oh do stop calling him my *fiancé*!' Her irritation erupted. 'You can see perfectly well what the set-up is.'

He said apologetically, 'Your mother – '

'And she knows perfectly well too, it's just that her vocabulary doesn't run to it. Not with strangers . . . No, none of them would have told him. They don't even know him. *I've* only known him for a few months.'

Latimer said weakly, 'I don't understand . . . it's very odd.'

There was a long silence. Then she said – reluctantly, as though Latimer had asked a question and was demanding an answer, 'You see,' and her mouth twisted, 'Luc's a bit of a bastard too.'

Startled, he said, 'Then why do you bother?'

For a moment he thought that he was going to get the answer he deserved. But then she shrugged. She said calmly, 'The thing is, I find limited involvements with men the most manageable, and frankly, if you know from the start the man's a cad it's easier to limit the involvement.'

Latimer said cautiously, 'It's a point of view' – and realised with a nasty jar that it was also his own.

She was leaning out over the railings now, peering down more intently than ever into the thickening darkness. The red glow had gone from the horizon and one inadequate light had come on in the lane below. Down by the port there were dotted lines of light running busily this way and that, crossing neatly at right-angles, and in among the confusion of houses

112

immediately below them were random, warmer points of brightness. 'There's a door into this house from down there . . .' She spoke softly, as though afraid of being overheard. 'From that lane . . . But I think it's locked . . . He *could* have been coming to this house . . . if the door was open.'

Latimer felt a prickle of apprehension. After a moment he said, '*Can* it be opened?'

'I – don't know.'

'Haven't you looked?'

She was silent.

He said harshly, 'Is this your house or Duquair's?'

'Well, it's mine – at least, I rent it – but,' suddenly, 'it's awfully dark down there.'

He said as gently as he could to her profile, 'Are there any rooms down there?'

'Not really – oh,' – too casually – 'except Luc's study. He's fixed himself up a sort of workroom down there.'

'And he doesn't like your going into it.'

Even in the dark he could see that the side of her face and her neck had gone crimson, but she didn't speak. She'd never make a liar.

Latimer sighed with depression. It would have taken him an hour with a good stenographer to get down on paper all the reasons that at once occurred to him for not going down to Luc Duquair's workroom with her, for saying goodbye and leaving promptly by the front door . . . He put a hand to the cut under his left eye and sighed again. 'Why *me*?'

She turned right round to look at him. 'Because I trust you,' she said seriously. Then, at the sight of his startled face, she smiled. The outside corners of her eyes lifted and the eyes themselves glinted with amusement. Latimer stared. She said gently, apologetically, 'You forget how much I know about you.'

Latimer said, 'And you're frightened of him.' It wasn't a question and she didn't answer. Latimer said resignedly, 'All right then, where are the stairs?'

The stairs were a sort of cupboard in a corridor leading to the kitchen. As far as the door of the cupboard the floor was still marble but once inside they were on to bare concrete and the stairs themselves were enclosed in a sort of box made of ancient planks. Margaret turned a switch and a single dim light bulb went on below them, illuminating dusty suitcases and two empty whisky crates. Latimer led the way down. On every side the cellar stretched away into shadows without any sign of a wall or partition. The original house must have been enormous.

Margaret was standing just by his elbow and in the dim overhead lighting he could see only the top of her head and the dark hair falling down on to her shoulders. She raised a white sleeve and pointed and he blundered off obediently in the direction she indicated. Gradually he made out the shape of a pair of huge double doors. A second later and the darkness on either side of the doors solidified into a wall of rough-faced stone. Margaret had come pattering along immediately behind him and he turned now to look at her enquiringly, but she had reached up to take a key from a hook beside the door and was fitting it into the lock. The lock turned and she pulled open one side of the door and slipped through. Latimer heard the click of a switch and another light went on, equally dim, a few yards ahead. In front of him was a broad passageway leading straight to another pair of high doors. The doors at the far end were made of enormous planks strengthened with strips of iron, and there were iron bars set at an angle to the door with their ends in the stone floor to prevent the door being forced from the outside. The passageway leading to the doors consisted of two rows of arches with darkness beyond on either side.

'It must originally, I think, have been the stables.' She was forcing herself to speak in a normal voice, but her nervousness was obvious. She peered into the darkness beyond one of the arches. 'There are drinking troughs, things like that . . . '

'And those big doors lead out on to the footpath?'

'Yes . . . it must have been wider – a proper road – when this was being used as stables.' Her voice had diminished again into a whisper.

Latimer cleared his throat and said loudly, 'And where's his study?'

Without speaking she pointed towards the far end of the

114

passage and Latimer saw that the last arch on the right-hand side had been bricked up and a more or less modern door set into the partition. He walked forward with his heart beating unpleasantly.

Resisting the temptation to knock, he put out a hand and tried the door in the partition. The handle turned smoothly and he pushed the door open and fumbled for the light switch. He was in a small, austerely-furnished office. A desk, two chairs, a large wall-safe. That was all. Margaret peered in behind him and he heard her sigh – perhaps, in some obscure way, from disappointment.

But it was the big, outside door he had come to look at. The locks were enormous. There were two of them and they could have been almost any age. The bolts – broad, flat iron ones almost entirely covered in rust – rested firmly in their sockets. And the iron bars set into the floor and braced against the inside of the door were rusty too, unwieldy. At first glance, the fastenings of the doors looked unuseable. What was certain, however, was that they *had* been used. Recently.

Latimer turned round, glancing at his watch. Margaret had advanced a little way along the passage behind him and was standing directly under the single bulb. Her face was a mask – the forehead and cheekbones, the line of her nose and her chin white metal, her eyes and mouth black holes. Somewhere in the house above them a telephone started to ring and the mask moved slightly, a little jerk.

Latimer said loudly, 'What did you *expect* to find down here? Is that all you wanted to know? – about the door?'

The mask turned slowly from side to side. 'I don't know . . .' With visible effort, bringing her hands together to keep them steady, she said, 'I thought – I might be able to find out what *is* going on. I've heard voices once or twice when I thought he was out . . . I wanted . . . If he'd been here I'd have said I was showing you the house.'

It was so lunatic that it might just have been true. Latimer said, 'Did you know that Duquair had asked me to come here, to this house, for a drink, at seven o'clock tonight?' He heard her draw in her breath. 'It's now ten to.'

'Why didn't you *tell* me?' She had turned and was running

back along the broad passage. 'Come *on*.' She stopped at the door with a hand on the light switch. 'Do hurry. He never comes home usually till eight or nine. Oh do be *quick*.'

He caught her up, suddenly infected by her urgency. They closed the big door, she hung the key on its hook and they ran towards the staircase.

'Wait a minute.' He lurked obediently in the shadows while she pattered up the stairs ahead of him. He heard her turn the handle of the door out into the corridor, and then for a few minutes there was silence.

'Steven!' After the tension of the last ten minutes the sound of her normal voice sent shafts of alarm through him. 'It's all right! Come on up.'

He padded up the stairs and joined her. She was smiling again, almost gay. She shut the staircase door behind him and led the way back into the long hall, talking over her shoulder. Someone had turned on a few lights while they were downstairs but they didn't make much impression in the huge distances. The whole house was shadowy and – now, to Latimer – menacing.

'Luc's just rung up – Leila told me. He's going to be late . . . So that's all right.' Her relief was obvious. 'Let's have a drink.'

But the house was too intimidating – and there was no reason on earth now why he should stay. With a sudden overpowering sense of relief Latimer realised that he had at last achieved what he had come to Beirut for. He shook his head. 'I must go . . . Will you – will you write to your brother-in-law, then? Tell him that I'm *not* Steve Latimer?'

'Of course I will . . . of course.'

'Well, thank you so much then and – goodbye.' He was suddenly eager to be gone.

'Must you really go?' It was clear that she didn't want him to, but he didn't flatter himself about her reasons: the house was alarming. For a moment he wavered, but his own anxiety won. 'I'm afraid I must.'

They had got as far as the small entrance hall now and she swung open the front door on to total darkness. Then she switched on an outside light and the narrow grey passage beyond the door sprang into existence.

116

Latimer said 'Goodbye' and put out his hand, but she ignored it, peering up into his face with a half-frown of enquiry and doubt.

'Could I just – try something?' She sounded earnest, and interested – and he envisaged some experiment to do with the outside light. Instead, she raised both hands towards his face.

Despite himself he flinched, and she smiled with calm amusement. 'No, no,' she said soothingly, 'nothing like that.' Then, very gently, she put both hands round behind his neck and, standing on tiptoe and tilting her head so that some of her hair was caught between her cheek and his, kissed him slowly.

When she had finished she nodded once, with just the trace of a smile, and said, '*No.*' After a moment she added calmly, 'Do forgive me. The thing is, I don't actually remember all that clearly what Steve actually looked like . . . only what I felt about him. And just now, in that light, you looked – I wanted to be sure, that's all.' Then she put a hand on to the open door, her smile became entirely impersonal, and she said, 'Goodnight, Dr. Latimer.'

He had got to the end of the passage – as far as the corner of the lane leading up to the main road – before it occurred to him *not* to go. He turned quickly round – and she waved gaily and turned out the outside light. Then he heard the slam of the front door and the sound of a heavy lock turning twice.

He still hesitated, confused and undecided, but the house behind him was so dark, so impenetrably black, that he turned instinctively away from it. Forty yards ahead of him, at the head of the lane, the lights of the main road were brilliant and he could see the façade of an expensive-looking villa with its front door open and all its windows lit. A big car drew up and three women jumped out and started up the steps – chattering, smoothing down their dresses and touching their hair. He could just hear the high note of their voices and then a laugh from one of them . . . He felt suddenly cheerful, and free, and set off up the lane towards the light and the frivolous, noisy, normal world – and he had just time to register that the absence of lights in the lane itself was unusual before he saw them.

They were standing one on either side of the lane, pressed

117

well back against the walls, and coming from the other direction he would almost certainly have missed them altogether. As it was, their outlines were just perceptible against the lights of the main road. He was taken by surprise, and stopped before he realised what he was doing. They had been expecting him to come from the other direction, and if he had walked unconcernedly past them they might, just conceivably, have hesitated long enough for him to get to the road. But his consciousness – his immediate understanding – gave him away and as he stopped he saw the smaller of them peer towards him and give a quick signal to the other. Then they both started towards him.

Latimer turned and ran back the way he'd come, knowing it was futile even as he went. He bolted round the corner of the house into the dark passage leading to the front door, thinking only of a hiding place, of escape. But the passage, as he knew already, was as smooth, as devoid of incident as the inside of an eggshell. There was nothing but stone walls and a heavy door double locked from the inside.

But it was dark. Latimer flattened himself against a wall and as the first of them came round the corner after him and hesitated, peering into the darkness, Latimer could just see him silhouetted against the glow from the distant street lights. It was only for a second. Then the man jumped forward again and Latimer threw himself at his knees in an inept imitation of a rugger tackle. The man certainly hadn't been expecting that, and he went down over Latimer's shoulders on to the stone with a heartening crash – and just for a second Latimer was conscious of hope. But long before he himself had recovered from the impact the man had rolled over and was back on his feet. Latimer managed to land one kick as he came at him again, but the other man was very fit and young and, probably, a professional whereas Latimer – well, Latimer had never been very athletic and had long ago forgotten all that the Department had once hastily taught him about unarmed combat. The other man didn't really have much trouble with him.

Afterwards Latimer didn't remember a great deal about it. He remembered repeated blows on the side of the head as the man found his range, and one appalling kick in the stomach.

He had a vague memory of scrambling – of crawling, rather – along the stone towards the door and of reaching up to where he thought the bell must be, and of a fist with a metal guard over the knuckles knocking his arm away before he could ring. He remembered wondering why only one of them had as yet come after him and then, as his head jolted forward under a blow of scientific savagery and he curled down on to the step as an earwig curls, acknowledging that, after all, one was more than enough.

8

He knew at once where he was. He had always liked the sound of the place and in his teens had evolved some fairly elaborate daydreams about it, but he'd never, of course, actually been there. There was a scent of flowers – not strong, but pleasant – and, even closer to him, the smell of newly-watered grass. His head was in shade but a warm sun shone directly on to the rest of his body which was, however, cooled by the soft rain, hardly more than a mist, that was falling gently all round him. He was lying comfortably on one side and delicious lassitude possessed him. There was, fortunately, no need for action. Ever again.

A drop of water fell directly on to Latimer's nose and, startled, he opened one eye: he saw a spray of green leaves with a cloudless blue sky beyond. Reassured, he shut the eye again and gave himself up to reflecting how fortunate it was that he, a non-Moslem, should nevertheless have been admitted to the Moslem paradise. It must be the result, he supposed, of dying in a Moslem country – not that Lebanon was a Moslem country, of course, come to think of it, but perhaps he had died in a Moslem section of it . . . He would have to be more careful about travel in the future if accidental death in any particular country was going to result in arrival in that country's own particular version of eternity . . .

Another drop of water fell directly on to his face and he

shook his head – and was surprised and irritated by the pain. In the Moslem paradise (surely they ought to know this by now) there was no discomfort but only, on the contrary, a series of the most exquisite physical sensations: one reclined in a well-watered garden, drinking wine and eating sweetmeats and waited on by – Latimer drew his breath in sharply. For a moment he had forgotten that one of the more striking features of the Moslem paradise was the eternal presence and eternal complaisance of exquisite virgins ever miraculously renewed.

He thrust out a hand but there was nothing there but damp grass. He swung his arm back to feel behind him – and the abrupt pain in his shoulder left him nearly awake. And in the same instant a distant murmur that in his excitement he had disregarded swelled into an enormous roar that filled the sky and smashed down on top of him – passing, it seemed, directly through him – and receded again into the distance.

Its passing left him on his feet, trembling, squinting in the hot afternoon sunlight, on the grass strip in the middle of the motorway from Beirut to the airport. The airport building itself was less than half a mile ahead and immediately above his head, in big white letters on a blue ground, a huge printed notice said 'Thank you for your visit.'

Latimer knew how to take a hint. 'All right, all right,' he said aloud and, as though they were watching him, he started off at once, limping, towards the airport building.

He felt light-hearted and purposeful as he walked along – he was going back to England. England was the answer, clearly. England, home and Patsy . . .

The slope up to the airport building was getting steeper and his left knee was finding the gradient increasingly severe. He decided to give it a short rest. A taxi, screaming its horn, skidded round him and with some embarrassment he realised that he had strayed into the road. He stepped back carefully on to the grass strip and walked on. Patsy was just above his head now, a tiny, token figure – rigid – like the wax mannikins that witches are said to stick pins into. She jerked up and down in the air in time with his walking, inclined sometimes a little to the left, sometimes a little to the right.

A gentle hum sounded in the air behind him and, incautiously, he turned his head. Pain shot up through his neck and lodged behind his eyes. He stopped, gasping, and held on to a small and prickly tree. Slowly the pain in his head subsided. The noise in the air became louder and with extreme care, turning his whole body, he raised his head to have a look. A little plane was coming in to land. It was silvery and pretty in the hot sunlight, a toy, and he watched with pleasure as it swept in and disappeared behind the line of sand-dunes that cut off his view of the landing strip. But it was moving too fast for a toy, and in the moment that it disappeared the sound caught up with him and he realised that, size or no size, it had been a jet – a beautiful shiny little jet with blue markings on its silver fuselage. In the same moment its twin appeared from over his right shoulder and followed the first one in to land. And this time there was no doubt about the markings on the fuselage. TRADE WINDS FOUNDATION FOR INTER-NATIONAL UNDERSTANDING.

What a joke . . . Latimer laughed softly to himself. It had never before occurred to him to wonder *where* Cordwainer's exhibition was going to start its world tour, but here it was, with its message of undistorted vision, in Beirut . . . Undistorted vision, indeed! He huffed to himself with amusement as he started off again.

And now he was at the end of the grass strip and there was only the long concrete slope down to the airport building itself. He took a deep breath and set off carefully. Patsy had some-how got tipped on to her side now. She still jerked in time with his steps but from an uncomfortable sideways lean, like an idol tipped off its pedestal. The airport building was leaning a bit too.

He had only just got in out of the sun in time, he decided, sitting down for a moment on a marble bench in the echoing airport hall. He went carefully through the pockets of his jacket and found his air ticket in the inside one – just where it should have been. Wallet with money, keys, diary, pen, hand-kerchief – all where they ought to be. Feeling by now a bit stronger he limped across to the BOAC desk. The girl's eye-brows went up at the sight of his clothes but she booked him without comment on a flight to London leaving in an hour

121

and Latimer concluded, after a bit of thought, that the eyebrows were just an act. Perhaps she looked at everyone like that. In any case she repented eventually and gave him a nice smile as she handed his ticket back.

'Did you have a good holiday?'

He tried hard to remember. 'It was a – business trip.'

'Oh . . . ' She looked again at his clothes and then back at his face. 'And you've finished all your business?'

Latimer said slowly, 'Would you mind saying that again?'

The girl blinked. She said conclusively, 'All your business here is finished.'

Like an automaton Latimer repeated, 'All your business here is finished.'

Angela . . . It was exactly as though curtains hiding a lighted stage had whisked open. He had forgotten all about her – the very fact of her – and now as she sprang back into existence there came with her a nagging consciousness of questions that had never been answered, of business unfinished . . . A stab of anxiety. Angela. She had seemed so plausible, at first, stepping so civilly through the opening figures of their mating dance, the big blue eyes floating up towards him through the window of the car . . . But then – something . . . What was it? Something had happened. Already the effort of trying to remember was making his head burn. Something . . .

The girl behind the BOAC desk said, 'Aren't you feeling all right?'

Latimer focused with difficulty and nodded slowly. 'No, I'm fine. It's just there's something . . . I forgot.'

Haider – that was it. '*You knew Haider bin Hassan at Oxford, I suppose.*' How could she possibly have known that? She knew altogether too much, for a girl who worked in a travel agency.

'Something I forgot,' he repeated, turning away suddenly from the desk and hurrying away across the marble vistas, almost running out towards the hot afternoon sun and the taxi rank.

9

The offices of Jasmin Travel were very smart, and so was the young man behind the counter. He wore a well-pressed dark suit with a level centimetre of white handkerchief in the top pocket.

'Miss Barrington, please.'

'Excuse me?'

'Miss Barrington.'

'I am sorry . . . ' He was sincerely trying to be helpful but he was puzzled.

'The English girl.'

'English?' The young man was starting to sound stupid now and his face puckered as he realised it.

'Yes – the big English girl.' There couldn't be two.

The young man jerked his head up and backwards in negation and abruptly the truth took shape. Latimer took two deep breaths and decided to ignore it. The handkerchief in the young man's pocket had a single initial embroidered on it, in red.

There might still be some mistake. Latimer put both his hands carefully on top of the counter. 'When I arrived at Beirut airport last night,' he said elaborately, 'no, no, I'm wrong, I'm sorry, it was the night before – or before that, was it? – there were no taxis. Miss Barrington happened to be there, meeting someone else – ' He ploughed on with his narrative, determined to omit no detail. The initial embroidered on the young man's handkerchief was an A. Ahmad? Ali? Abdul-Azis? 'She very kindly gave me a lift and – '

After a time Latimer became aware that he had finished all he had to say, and a moment or two later the young man realised it too and smiled with relief: somewhere in the course of his narrative Latimer had put himself into the broad, straightforward category of Cases to be Referred Up.

'I think,' he said kindly, 'that you should see the manager. Will you wait a moment?' Abubakr? Abdullah?

He left Latimer alone with the brightly-coloured brochures – 'A Tour to the Cedars', 'Beirut's Night-Life' – and Latimer continued to ignore the truth, holding it well away from himself like an unexploded grenade. Ambrose? – perhaps the young man was a Christian. Anthony? The counter top was made of blue plastic.

The manager in his upstairs office was even smoother, with a faint whiff of hair cream and faultless French-accented English. Latimer repeated his entire story. There must be some explanation . . .

'I know a lot of extremely nice English girls,' the manager said soothingly, gazing despite himself at Latimer's clothes. 'Any of them –'

'No, *no*,' said Latimer, his thumb pressed well down on the lever. 'She works for Jasmin Travel.'

'They *all* like to work for Jasmin Travel –' The pin jerked out of the grenade. Count three.

'A large girl,' Latimer said desperately, 'very large – and blonde.'

'I understand exactly the type you want –'

Latimer jumped to his feet and started for the stairs. The manager called after him, 'Wait! Mr. Aghaghian will show you –'

But Latimer didn't wait for Mr. Aghaghian. The truth was exploding all around him and he ran down the stairs and out into the sunlight and all the trees in the public garden made little jumps of excitement – now to the left, now to the right. It hadn't been a mating dance with Angela after all, it had been a game of chess . . . just the beginning. But who was his opponent? – that was the question. Hilarity pressed up through him like a bubble and burst out into laughter. That was the question – who was he playing? Well, he would go and find out. Mr. Aghaghian came out from behind the desk to look at him curiously through the window and Latimer waved back. 'King to Queen's rook 4!' he shouted, and then laughter overcame him entirely.

10

Angela's voice said, '*Steven!*' It was far too loud and too strong for a girl whose latest admirer has merely been off the air for twenty-four hours – but he decided to let it pass.

'That's right. That's me, Latimer. The celebrated rapist. Can I see you right away?'

Her laugh was quite good – not much more than a gurgle, and not too long. 'How *are* you, Steven? You sound very cheerful.'

'Yes, I'm fine. I want to see you.'

'That would be lovely.'

'It's urgent. I'll come now.'

'No, not just now.'

'Ten minutes then.'

'*No*, Steven.'

'I think it's time for another move.'

'What did you say?'

'I said, "I think it's time for another drink." '

Her hesitation was barely noticeable. 'All right then . . . where shall we meet?'

'Where's your flat?'

'Well . . . ' This time the pause was longer. There was time for thought – even, perhaps, for consultation. 'All right, Steven . . . Immeuble Rizk, fifth floor. It's up on the Corniche, two roads back from the coast road. Come in – half an hour.'

'I'll come now.'

But in fact the taxi-driver couldn't find it and it was more than half an hour before he got to the Immeuble Rizk. In the taxi he tried to comb his hair but at the first stroke a large tuft clotted with blood came away, quite painlessly, and he decided to abandon the attempt. There was, in any case, nothing to be done about the state of his trousers and jacket.

The Immeuble Rizk stood by itself above the sea on a stony hillside strewn with refuse. In another year the bumpy track would be tarmac and there would be blocks of flats on either side, but for the moment it was alone. There were other blocks on the headland but they accentuated rather than relieved the isolation, like a graveyard in which all the plots are reserved but few as yet occupied.

Latimer took the lift to the fifth floor and rang the bell. 'You're my gorgeous girl,' he said, pushing her back into the flat and putting his arms tightly round her. She detached herself equably, and then stared at his clothes. 'But *Steven* – ' she began. She was wearing a dark voile dress today, far too tight and showing the strain at the armholes. The general effect was not good and Latimer was relieved: for what he had in mind it was better that way.

He moved quickly through into the main part of the flat. 'Nice place you've got here.'

She followed warily. The flat was appalling, an amorphous space walled with glass, carpeted in grey and dotted with dirty white sofas. The curtains on the massive windows were grey and there was a crazy paving fireplace stuck down in the centre of the room, with a rusty metal chimney disappearing up through the ceiling.

'Cosy,' he said, giving her an opening.

'Oh now, come *on*!' She was clearly relieved. 'A furnished flat is a furnished flat. I'll make it better in time . . . But the view's lovely, don't you think?' It should have been marvellous – a massive half-circle of blue Mediterranean – but in practice it was monotonous, and the glare was agonising.

Latimer said, 'Lovely . . . What about a drink?' He padded after her into the kitchen, neat as a colour supplement advertisement. 'Let me get the ice out.'

'Thanks. Scotch or gin?' There was a full bottle of each so he said, 'Gin for me, please.'

He ran the ice trays under a tap and put the wet cubes on to a plastic plate, wiping his hands on a handkerchief. Angela opened the bottle of gin and after a short search produced an opener for the six bottles of tonic that were grouped on the table. 'It's my day for normal eating and drinking,' she said with animation. 'I mustn't waste the opportunity.' They carried their drinks back into the living-room and Latimer stood by the window, squinting out at the flat desolation of sea.

When he looked round again she was watching him carefully.

There was something different, something wrong . . . He closed his eyes for a second to concentrate and Angela said, 'Are you all right, Steven?'

'I'm fine.' He opened his eyes. 'But you – ' And then it struck him. 'You can *see* me . . . Contact lenses?'

She blushed. 'You notice everything.' She tried to make it sound like a compliment.

'Well, cheers,' Latimer said quickly, and went on drinking till he'd finished the glass. 'That was very nice. What about another?'

With the merest flicker she said, 'Why not?' holding out her hand for his glass. But he ignored it and set off back towards the kitchen. 'I'll get it myself.'

He poured an inch of gin from the bottle into the sink and was filling up his glass with tonic when Angela arrived. 'I don't think you're really trying,' he said accusingly. 'Here.' He slopped some gin into the top of her glass, but she had hardly touched it and the gin overflowed on to her hand and down the front of her dress. 'Oops. Never mind. Drink it up, then, there's a good girl.'

She sucked goodnaturedly at her hand and took a pull at her drink. Even so, the smell of gin was still too strong and she glanced round the kitchen enquiringly as they started back towards the living-room.

She sat down on a sofa and started to open a tin of nuts.

'I thought you might ring up last night.' She managed to sound shy and embarrassed but her face was hidden as she leaned forward, struggling with the tin.

'Did you? Well, I thought of it too, but then I went out on the town instead. A friend took me.'

Her hands, turning the key on the tin, moved more slowly. 'I expect you have lots of interesting friends in Beirut.'

He was surprised that she should take it so fast. 'Well, yes, I do know quite a lot of people here, but unfortunately I can't introduce any of them to each other.' He laughed heartily.

'No?'

'No, they're all on different sides and working for different people and altogether – ' He stopped talking as he disappeared with his empty glass and started again as he reappeared with

127

the glass re-filled, ' – altogether it's a thoroughly uncomfortable social set-up. *However* – ' he sat himself down beside her on the sofa and put an arm along the back of it, behind her shoulders, 'in other ways my Beirut social life is looking up.'

She smiled nicely. 'It is?'

'Yes, like nobody's business.' The kiss was cool and not much more than a formality.

After a decent pause Angela said, 'When you rang up you said you wanted to see me urgently.'

'Yes. Well, there are several things I want to tell you, but that was one.'

'What was?'

'That my social life is looking up.'

She laughed, with evident disappointment, and he kissed her again. This time the kiss had a bit more conviction on both sides but it was uphill work. The back of his neck was increasingly painful, and the surroundings gave no help at all. The room was bleak and the sofa, though soft to the touch, basically unyielding – and that went for Angela too. It was like making love in the departure lounge at London Airport. For a moment Latimer considered abandoning the project altogether, but then Angela, leaning back, said, 'Tell me more about your friend. The one who took you out on the town. Who was he?'

Latimer stared at her. She was really rushing it.

He said carefully, 'I'm not quite sure of his name.'

'Was he an Arab? A friend of a friend?'

'What do you mean?' He was genuinely puzzled.

'A friend of Haider bin Hassan?'

'Oh, Haider – funny you should mention him – ' Without thinking, he jumped to his feet and pulled her up by one hand.

Waiting, rigid, for the pain in his neck and head to subside Latimer mumbled, 'I'd like – to see the rest of your flat. I'm fascinated by – other people's houses.'

'Steven, are you *really* all right?' She swam back into focus, looking worried.

'Of course I'm all right. Do show me.'

There was very little to show – two bare little bedrooms and a bathroom. Each bedroom had long fitted cupboards filling the whole of one wall, a bed, a dressing-table – and nothing else. In one of them there were a few cosmetic pots and a hand mirror on the dressing-table. Latimer walked through and out on to the little balcony beyond. From this side of the flat there was a view of the mountains, reddened by the glare of the afternoon sun. He pretended to admire it while Angela stood impatiently beside him.

After only a moment she said, 'Go on about Haider.'

Latimer was seized with irritation. She must consider him a total fool.

Their hands were resting side by side on the railing. Latimer dropped his right hand gently over her left and said, 'Come here and let me kiss you properly.'

She turned willingly enough and after a few false starts Latimer found an angle at which he could kiss her quite hard without too much pain in the back of his neck.

After a time he shuffled her sideways into the bedroom and sank cautiously on to the bed, pulling her down beside him. She was tense with impatience and annoyance and in a gentle considerate voice he said, 'Would you rather I went away?'

'Oh no.' With a perceptible effort she loosened up and started to kiss him.

They lay back on the bed and kissed for a bit and then Angela put a gentle but exploratory hand into his hair. Hastily, he reached behind her and pulled at the zip of her dress. If he'd done that to Patsy – or to anyone else for that matter – the zip would undoubtedly have stuck, but as it was it slid down smoothly and he pulled the dress gently off one shoulder. She didn't seem to mind, and for one vertiginous moment Latimer wondered whether perhaps the zip had been oiled. Perhaps he'd got the whole thing wrong.

But then he pulled the dress down a bit further and to his relief Angela said, 'No!' That was better. And when he took no notice she repeated, with a sudden edge in her voice, '*No, Steven.*' But he went on pulling and she pushed him away and sat up. He grabbed at the nearest bit of dress and she was jerked momentarily towards him. Then she struggled away and a long strip of dark voile tore sharply away from the front of her dress and remained in his hand. They both said, 'Oh', then Angela said, 'Oh dear,' and sat still, contemplating the tear. It was a moment when they both might have giggled, and relaxed – and then things would have gone on again very nicely thank you. But Latimer didn't want that. He gave it a moment and then got up on to his knees, pushed her back on to the bed and crushed himself slowly down on top of her, holding both her arms back above her head. She hadn't been expecting anything quite like that and it frightened her, he was glad to see. But not enough. With some difficulty he transferred both her wrists to his left hand and with his right started to fumble underneath the remaining bits of her dress. The pain in the back of his neck was excruciating and at one moment he thought he was going to pass out, but it seemed that his gasps were convincing. She began to fight in earnest. It couldn't be long now, he thought.

It wasn't. She made a convulsive movement with her knee. She had been carefully rehearsed and did it well, but fortunately for him he had been expecting it and moved in time. Even so the force of it rolled him over, off her, off the bed and on to the floor.

'Angus!' he roared as he landed. 'So it's *you*! Queen's pawn to K.3, Angus! *Where are you*? Come out of there!' He staggered to his feet, almost incapacitated with laughter, and tugged at the cupboard doors. The handles broke off in his hands. He put a shoulder against the lock and the wood cracked. He kicked at it – and the door of the empty cupboard swung gently open. '*Where is he*? Where is he, that lousy operator? . . . Only the British,' he said at last, sinking breathlessly down on to the bed and wiping tears of pleasure from his eyes, 'only our own dear Department would let its girls defend their virtue so efficiently at such an *early* stage.'

Associating laughter with amusement, Angela said cautiously, 'Was that a joke Steven?' Then, as he continued to laugh, she said more quietly, 'Bastard.'

She swung her long legs off the bed and stood up, and the torn remains of the dress dropped down round her ankles. She kicked them away and sat down at the dressing-table, exactly as though she were alone. Taking a brush out of a drawer she started to brush her hair.

The last gleam of laughter left him. He stood up. 'I'm off.'

Through the mirror she gave him a look that should by rights have cracked it. '*Why?*' she said.

Defeated he sat down again on the bed. He had entirely ceased to enjoy the situation and the pain in his head and neck was excruciating. 'Why did you try to make a fool of me?' He corrected himself wearily, 'Why *did* you make a fool of me?'

'You were behaving so oddly – the Department were worried. They asked us to keep an eye on you.'

Helplessly he said, 'Of what *conceivable* interest can I be to the Department?'

Through the mirror he saw her compress her lips with irritation. She put down her brush and said carefully, 'You've had the room next to Haider's booked in your name for the last two weeks –'

'That's not true!'

She ignored him ' – and there was evidence of your having used it. You were seen in Beirut on Saturday, then you flew to London and came back only two days later. We knew you had been friends with Haider years ago and we knew that you could pass as an Arab – and after all the very first thing you told Angus yesterday was that you wanted to get in touch with the Panjeh Front people. Of *course* you were of interest to us.'

The pain kept interrupting him when he tried to think – but in any case it all sounded such a hotch-potch, so ill-digested, misunderstood . . . With an effort he isolated just one of her remarks.

'What do you mean,' he said slowly, 'by *evidence* of my having used that room? It was Angus who was using it –'

She hesitated fractionally and then nodded. 'Yes of course. That's how we knew . . . Angus has been using it for – well, for keeping an eye on Haider.'

Laboriously he repeated, 'Keeping an eye on Haider.'

She said with irritation, 'Keeping an ear then . . . Don't pretend you don't understand.'

'Microphones?'

'Haider's room is probably the planning centre of the whole operation. We might hear a lot that's of interest.'

'Oh . . .'

There was silence. Released, Latimer's mind started to wander. The pain was subsiding and he felt slack and exhausted, but he couldn't stay here. With an effort he stood up and started towards the hall.

Angela said hesitantly, 'Are you going back to your room? . . . You'll find Angus there now.'

He nodded absently, half-way to the front door.

Angela said, 'Steven . . . '

The tone of her voice was explicit, and with consternation he realised what was coming. He turned reluctantly.

She said, 'Steven – you mustn't think that because of – of what happened just now that I don't like you, as *you*. There was – ' she tried a joke, 'there was nothing *personal* about it, you know. I mean – '

Latimer said stupidly, 'I know – '

'And that night, when you arrived, I was so pleased when it was – you. It might have been somebody awfully – well, somebody not nearly so nice. And I – '

'Yes, yes, of course. I know – ' Latimer was nodding stupidly, trying to make her stop. 'I understand. Really.' He'd be apologising himself in a minute. He tried to make a joke of his own. 'No offence taken.'

Angela's face lit up with relief. 'Oh Steven – ' She stood up, smiling, and despite himself Latimer recoiled. He wondered if she had really forgotten how little she had been wearing under her dark voile dress.

She said gently, advancing, 'You look terribly tired, Steven, and your clothes – Are you all right? – or have you been involved in some awful fight? Come and lie down. You look as if – '

Mesmerised, Latimer found that she already had hold of his hand. He said desperately, 'No!' and she paused for a moment but didn't stop smiling.

He mumbled, 'Terribly exhausted . . . '

She said at once, forgivingly, 'I understand.'

11

His elation had finally gone and he felt appalling, in every way. His head still ached and throbbed, and gritty, disgraceful memories of the scene with Angela came creeping in round the edges of his consciousness however hard he tried to keep them out. He wasn't cut out to take charge of situations, to take action at all . . .

Without thinking he had told the taxi to take him to the Criterion, and once there he headed automatically for the desk to get his key. He would go back to England – but not until tomorrow. For the moment he could think only of lying down, of kindly sleep . . . And if Angus was there too it just couldn't matter less.

'My *dear* Dr. Latimer – ' A figure had detached itself from a group sitting at a round table under the shade of a carnivorous-looking rubber plant, and for a moment Steven couldn't place him – though the vibrations were unpleasant. 'I'm so delighted to run into you. I *very* much want to have a word – '

Cordwainer . . . as smooth and as rich as ever. Latimer stood still and tried to absorb the implications. 'Do you know Mr. – ah – the British Council representative? and Professor Hosseini of the American University? These gentlemen are giving me most valuable advice about my exhibition. Dr. Latimer is a most distinguished physician and an expert on the Middle East.'

The exhibition . . . of course. English Primitives. Remembering abruptly, Latimer grinned – and Cordwainer, misunderstanding, smiled back at him genially. 'We really must have a word, Latimer, I owe you a most sincere apology. Also some explanations. I'm sure these gentlemen will excuse us. Can we – ? Where can we go? Can we go to your room?'

Latimer said hastily, 'No, no, not my room,' and then, as Cordwainer's eyebrows rose, he grinned again, enjoying the private joke. He said gravely, 'I've lent it to a friend of mine. Angus Bailey. I'm sure – ' he giggled suddenly, 'I'm sure he'd like to meet you.' Then, seeing Cordwainer's mystified face, he made an effort to be serious again. 'Perhaps we can talk down here?'

Cordwainer nodded gratefully. He took Latimer in a firm grip by the elbow and drew him round behind the vast promontory of green foliage. 'There has clearly been,' he said earnestly, 'the most appalling confusion and misunderstanding. I am unable to express what I – what I *feel* about this. I am so entirely ashamed that such a thing should have happened to a man of your – your standing and eminence. We have really treated you disgracefully. I am more distressed than I can possibly tell you and I do beg you to accept my most sincere apologies.'

Latimer was silent. It was the sort of apology that normally happens only in fantasies, and he was embarrassed. He heard himself muttering, 'Oh that's all right . . . really . . . as long as – ' He wanted to say ' – *as long as I get my contract renewed and my advance paid*' – but such considerations were clearly too mundane.

Then Cordwainer said, 'I telephoned Margaret as soon as I got here. She said I'd got it all wrong – an appalling mistake. I cannot repeat too often how – '

'Margaret?' Latimer said. 'Margaret?'

Cordwainer looked at him in surprise. 'My sister-in-law,' he said. 'Margaret Wedderburn.'

Margaret. Once again a dark curtain in Latimer's mind swept back . . . *Margaret*.

Cordwainer said, 'Are you all right, Latimer? You look – '

Latimer said automatically. 'I'm fine . . . ' It was all there again, suddenly. The Villa Haddad, Duquair, Margaret, the search in the dark basement – another whole layer of memory. He realised with a considerable shock that since his waking on the road to the airport he hadn't once tried to explain his injuries to himself. His thinking mind had accepted them dumbly, shying defensively away from any attempt to remember: the shadowy men in the lane, the lane, the fight in the stone passage, the savage kicks, the blows . . . Now, remembering, he flinched and closed his eyes.

'A drink,' Cordwainer was saying, 'a drink is clearly what you need.'

134

'No . . . thank you,' Latimer said slowly. 'No. There's something else I must do . . . some unfinished business.'

Margaret.

12

Margaret said gently, 'Has it occurred to you yet that you may have concussion?'

Puzzled, Latimer said, 'But in that case I'd be unconscious.' He had his eyes shut but he heard her little snort of amusement.

'Well, it's your field, not mine.' She had cut away the hair round the wound on the back of his head and now she was washing it with cotton wool dipped in water and antiseptic. 'But if you were unconscious after they hit you you ought to rest . . . ' She dabbed at the wound with a dry piece of cotton wool. 'It's not all that bad actually . . . There. Don't move. I'll put some gauze on . . . Just turn over a bit. That's it . . . now put your head back on the cushion and I'll get you a drink.'

Flat on an enormous sofa, Latimer opened his eyes cautiously and watched her go down the hall to the tray of drinks on a side-table. She was wearing black this evening, another long robe, with silver round the neck and sleeves. Her hair had been elaborately arranged and she was wearing a good deal of make-up. As she came back up the length of the hall he said accusingly, 'You're very smart.'

'I'd been out to dinner.' Her voice was full of amusement.

Jealousy grated like a match down its box and Latimer closed his eyes to hide the pain. Miserably he felt the flame catch and blaze.

She said gently, 'Here – ', handing him a glass. He raised his head cautiously and sipped. Incredulously he said, '*Orange juice*?' and, reassured, she sank down on to the far end of the long sofa and looked at him with open amusement. 'You can't drink alcohol if you've got concussion.'

'Why ever not? I've been drinking all afternoon,' though it wasn't true.

'Perhaps that's what's producing the symptoms.'

'Of concussion?'

'Of everything.'

Latimer sipped again and made a face. He said carefully, 'I don't know what you mean by symptoms but I'm stone cold sober.'

'Are you?'

'Was and am . . . Can I smoke?'

'I don't see why not – I'm not actually an expert on concussion, but *you* ought to know.'

'Well, would you – ?'

She stood up and took a cigarette out of the box.

He said carefully, 'It wasn't just a passing idea, you know. It's the reason I'm still here. Otherwise I'd be in England by this time . . . Thanks. No, sit down here.' He heaved himself over to make room and she sat beside him.

In the tone of one who has let a joke go on long enough Margaret said, 'Now be honest. Would you ever have come back to see me again – would you even have *thought* of coming back if I hadn't – I hadn't kissed you when you left last night?'

Latimer considered for a moment. 'No –'

'Well then –'

'– but that doesn't mean that I wouldn't have realised pretty soon – as soon as I got back to England, I expect – that I would have to see you again.'

Her face was perfectly friendly, but he wasn't convincing her.

With a neat change of mood she said, 'Well anyway – it isn't often that a man I've only met once before rushes into my house, kisses me passionately and then goes into a dead faint on a valuable Bokhara rug.' She made it sound gay but dismissive, the summing up of a long discussion. The next step would be a change of subject.

Latimer said quickly, 'Madame Chairman, I have a point of order.'

She grinned briefly. 'Well?'

He hesitated. 'What about a proper drink first?'

She laughed, and went to fetch it. 'You look extraordinarily pleased with yourself, lying there.'

'I feel like a pasha.'

'You look like a – delinquent.'

'Felicity used to say that. She used to say that I had a permanent look of successful guilt – but only on the apple-stealing level.'

'Apple-stealing?'

'It's what small boys steal in America, apparently . . . ' He said abruptly, 'You remind me of Felicity.'

'Oh . . . ?' Her expression was cautious.

He said rapidly, 'She was tall and fair and immoral and very beautiful and very American and very stupid – '

Margaret said conversationally, 'I see,' but her eyes had gone blank.

' – and I loved her so much that I came out in an appalling rash all over my hands and arms. It lasted for years, off and on – '

There was a pause. Margaret said crossly, '*Well*?'

'The backs of my hands are itching now. It's what reminded me.'

'Oh, good heavens!'

Hurt, Latimer said, 'You make it sound like an imposition.'

'That's exactly what it is.' It was the first time that he had seen her angry, and he was daunted. 'You just make up your mind one day to say – well, to say all that. Okay, lovely for you. Splendid. But what am *I* expected to say? "Thank you so much, sir. What an honour"?'

'You might say – whatever you feel.'

'How do I know what I feel? – I hardly know you.'

Latimer said slowly, 'This happens to you quite a lot, I suppose . . . People falling in love with you.'

'Don't be absurd. Hardly ever.'

'But when it does – ' She started to speak again but Latimer cut straight in: he'd got there now, ' – when it *does* you don't believe a word and you immediately turn off the tap of anything at all that you might have started to feel. That's right, isn't it? Isn't it? Well that's *all right*.' He sat up, immensely excited. 'That's all right, we've got time, we've got masses of – time.'

His voice stopped abruptly as his head went back on to the

pillow. Margaret said drily, 'I should think so too.' She stood up and walked slowly down to the far end of the hall, away from him. Latimer watched unhappily.

He couldn't see what she was doing but abruptly there was music – quiet soft, but filling the hall. A violin, above an orchestra . . . and a viola. Inter-twining arabesques of sound. Mozart. Latimer closed his eyes, concentrating.

When he opened his eyes again she was standing quite still, looking down at him from a couple of yards away. He said at once, briskly, 'I'm not a pile of washing-up, so don't look at me like that.'

She said, still hovering, 'I like your turn of phrase.' It was nearly a laugh.

'I must concentrate more on amusing you. Your voice goes down about an octave . . . did you know?' Seeing her face he added hastily, 'A truce to it,' and she laughed properly and sat down beside him again on the sofa.

She said, 'Don't be so sanguine. I've never yet learned to leave a subject alone. Steven – ' She stopped. 'I used to think that I was going mad,' and for a second he genuinely didn't know what she was talking about, 'but that stopped quite soon. And then, once I began to realise that it probably hadn't been *you* I wanted to know who it really was . . . But now I only want to know why. *Why* should he have done that?'

Latimer said slowly, 'Why does knowing matter so much? Can't you just – forget, put it all behind you?' The phrases sounded banal even to his own ears . . . he would have to tell her about Angus, and about the childish trick he himself had played on Angus . . .

She shook her head. 'I must know if it was something to do with *me*. If it was, it wouldn't matter how much I had changed the – the infection would still break out again, sooner or later.'

Appalled, he said, 'You mean you think there's something in *you* that precludes fidelity in others?'

She hesitated. 'Well – yes. Probably.'

'Oh good heavens – '

'*You* know why, don't you?'

'Yes I do. *Listen.*' He propped himself unsteadily on one elbow. 'It was *nothing* to do with you. It was to do with *me*.

138

It was an act of – well, of revenge. Against me. He wanted to – blacken my name, I suppose, get me into trouble generally. It might have taken quite a bit of time before I could prove to your family that I was the wrong man.'

She waited for him to say more and when nothing came shook her head slowly. 'I still can't – feel that, as a reason.'

'But – '

'No . . . It may well be the truth,' she sounded apologetic, 'but it isn't enough for me.'

The music made its final emphatic statement and ceased.

Latimer said, 'I *know* that that was the reason.'

Margaret said quietly, 'You weren't there.'

A man's voice spoke at the far end of the hall and Latimer's head jerked momentarily off the cushion. A B.B.C. voice . . . the radio. He lay back again and, to cover up his alarm, said lightly, 'I thought the music came from a gramophone.'

Margaret raised a hand. 'Just a minute. I want to hear the news.'

The news . . . So, even while he had been talking to her of love – and she had been reacting with such strong emotion – she had still remembered that she wanted to hear the news. She had turned her back on him and had walked away down the length of the hall, to turn on the radio.

He said sourly, 'I had forgotten you were such a political animal.'

She nodded without rancour, accepting the description. '*The Overseas Service of the B.B.C.* . . .'

He went on unpleasantly, 'Well at least the Mozart wasn't deliberate, then. I was afraid for a moment you were making some clever statement about counterpoint and – '

'Ssh.' Again she held up a hand.

' . . . *here is a summary of the news*.' More executions in Baghdad, continuation of the talks on the Suez canal, the Jordan-Israel cease-fire now in its second year . . . nothing much.

Then – 'There have been unconfirmed reports of fighting in Panjeh, the island sheikhdom seventy miles north of Dubai where a Shell oil rig was blown up last Thursday. Gunfire has been heard in the town and in the area of the palace, and radio

139

communication from the island has ceased. Air services have been temporarily suspended.'

'Well!' Her eyes shone with excitement. 'I wonder what's happening. Wouldn't it be *marvellous* if the guerrillas – '

'Would it?' He interrupted her at once. 'If the guerrillas took over and set up a communist regime?'

'Steven!' Her voice held real distress. 'You're not – you don't support *Saladin*?'

'Would you care?'

'But you've *lived* in Panjeh – and you were at that Solidarity Front meeting yesterday. I assumed then that you were at least – '

' – at least right-minded?'

'Well – yes.'

Latimer said wearily, 'I'm neutral' – and shut his eyes. He felt as though he had spent the whole of the last three days defending his views on Panjeh.

'But Steven – '

Latimer made a gigantic effort. 'That lot I saw you with at the meeting yesterday – do you really think they'd know how to run anything? They'd simply open the door to direct Chinese control and if you really think the Panjehi would be better off under that – '

'Now, Steven, you musn't judge too harshly. That was only a solidarity meeting – you know, students, mostly. That's not *really* the whole story – '

Certain that she would produce the straight Party line, Latimer heard with surprise the unmistakable note of doubt, of defensiveness in her voice.

'But there *are* some more impressive figures – at least there's one, a remarkable man. He seems to have all the right ideas, even though he does come from the Panjeh ruling family.'

Latimer said slowly, 'Haider bin Hassan.'

'Yes! Do you know him?'

'At Oxford – '

'He's really very good, I think. I've only heard him talk at meetings, of course, but he's excellent. I have my doubts, honestly, about the practical ability of some of the other Front people but Haider's different. He's a convinced Marxist *and* he would know how to put those concepts into practical effect.'

Latimer said doubtfully, 'You know him well?'

'Not at all. He doesn't like the press, so I've never been allowed to get near him. But he's the reason I support the Front, really. He's the only one I'd actually go and fight for. The guerrillas in Panjeh itself are a fairly primitive and inefficient lot, I think – even though they did manage to blow up that rig. But Haider is an idealist *and* a man of practical ability, I should say – '

Latimer closed his eyes and listened to Haider's earnest voice running on inside his head, drowning Margaret's words. *'Communism is nonsense as a system of government anywhere, and particularly so in the Gulf . . . The people I'm involved with are a serious concern, I promise you . . . They don't talk hot air about democracy and the rights of the people. They talk about power.'*

Was it really his job – his responsibility – to tell her?

He opened his eyes. Her head was turned away. She was looking across the hall into the distance.

He said, 'So you'd fight for Haider, would you – ?' watching the line of her jaw.

She nodded emphatically. 'Yes . . . Possibilities of direct action for good are so ludicrously few nowadays. You can work away at things – at causes – for years and years and never see any results. But just occasionally there's a chance to do something – something violent, probably – that will get results *quickly*. We've all got out of the habit of fighting for what we consider to be right.'

Angus had said the same thing. *Angus* . . . Angus and Margaret fighting for what they considered to be right. On opposing sides . . . Angus and Margaret *together* – fifteen, nearly twenty years ago . . . How intolerable that it should always be of Angus that he was obliged to be jealous . . .

'Have you ever fought?' Sleep had taken a sudden grip and his own voice came from a distance. He could hardly hear her unemphatic 'No.'

'Margaret? . . . Did you know – when you kissed me last night – that they were going to – ' He managed a half-gesture towards his head.

141

She said slowly, 'You mean that you were attacked *here*, outside this house?'

He listened with anxiety to the tone of her voice and then nodded, satisfied. She was saying urgently, 'Tell me what happened,' but he had dropped abruptly into a trough of sleep.

He woke into expectant silence, with no idea of how long he had slept. But she was still sitting beside him, still watching him – it couldn't have been more than minutes, perhaps not more than seconds. Margaret said gently, 'Wouldn't you like to go to bed? Sleep would really be the best thing for you.'

He wrestled with the idea. 'Here?'

'Why not? There's Luc's room – ' She paused, and her mouth twisted. 'He's gone, actually. For good . . .'

'When?'

'Last night. I told him I'd – had enough.'

'Last night after I'd gone?'

She nodded but didn't look at him, and Latimer felt a slow warmth spread out all through him from a new source. Slowly he raised a hand towards her with the palm flat – stopping traffic.

She said, 'What are you – ?'

'We talk too much.'

Gravely, humouring him, she lifted her hand in reply and touched it gently against his own – and at once the current sprang between the two palms. Startled, Margaret jerked her hand away. Her eyes widened.

Latimer said smugly, 'That's all right then.'

'What a lot you know . . .'

He listened with satisfaction to the amusement in her voice, forcing his eyelids up again for the second time. Margaret said, 'Bed for you.'

Sleep was washing over him in slow waves. He made an effort. 'Yes,' he said, 'I think I'd like that.'

Then he was unsteadily on his feet, and then in a white room with an oval gilt mirror and brightly coloured rugs, a big low bed . . . He sank down and noticed after a while that his shoes and socks had gone, and his clothes.

He lay under the cool sheet, floating. Margaret was moving

about in the room. He heard a drawer open and shut, a comb put down on a marble surface.

He said with difficulty, 'You?'

'Yes, I'm going to bed too.'

'No.' He made a final effort. 'Here. With me.'

He didn't think that she answered but he heard the shadow of a laugh, and then later on it was quite dark and he felt the bed behind him dip slightly under her weight.

He said, 'Margaret?'

'Yes . . . go to sleep.' There was a comforting warmth now behind his back.

He said, 'That's nice . . . that's friendly.'

13

Next morning there was no need for remembering. Even as he woke, Latimer was already aware of her warmth behind his back – and though he knew that many hours had passed their last words still floated in the air.

He said out loud, 'That's nice . . . that's friendly.'

There was no reply. He put a hand behind him to touch her – and the stiffness in his shoulder reminded him abruptly of his previous waking on the motorway to the airport. Worried – for no really valid reason – he rolled over. She wasn't there, but an impression in the rumpled bedclothes – a hare's form in the grass – reassured him. He nodded at it gratefully, climbed out of bed and tapped on the bathroom door. The bedroom shutters were still closed but little strips of sun had forced their way in through the cracks and motes of dust were sliding busily up and down the narrow beams. The big oval mirror showed him his own unshaven face with a fairly silly smile on it. But he was too content to mind even that.

There was no reply from the bathroom, so he opened the door and went in. Still no sign of her. He had a shower and shaved with a razor and shaving cream that he found on a shelf. Duquair must have left in a hurry.

143

When he was dressed he emerged cautiously into the daylight of the long hall. There was only silence and emptiness. He tiptoed about, reluctant to break the silence, and hoping futilely to catch a glimpse of Margaret before she knew he was there. But she wasn't in the *liwan*, or in the small sitting-room, or in the dining-room – where breakfast was laid for one. Latimer stood looking down at the single cup and saucer, and was suddenly aware that the maid, Leila, was observing him from the doorway leading to the kitchen. He enquired for the lady and she pointed to a sheet of paper on the breakfast table. He had never seen Margaret's writing before, and he looked at it curiously and with an immediate sense of familiarity.

Did you sleep well? – I think you did. Great things are going on – but they wouldn't interest you! I'll be in touch as soon as I can.

M.

Comforted, he ate scrambled eggs and drank three cups of coffee and then sat on the balcony and smoked a cigarette. At first he thought she might phone at any moment but then he remembered the list of journalistic chores that she had written down for Bill three nights before: 'Ministry of Foreign Affairs at ten, pop singer at one.' If that was an average day she mightn't be home for hours.

On another bit of paper he wrote:

I'm at the Criterion. Where are you? Phone me soon. Please.
S.

The air was slightly less steamy than it had been for the past few days and he walked back to the hotel, dropping down the hill by a series of steep flights of steps and then following the noisy cobbled road along the edge of the port. But it was farther than he had realised and it was nearly eleven o'clock and he was soaked with sweat before he got there.

The porter at the desk, busy sorting out mail, said absently that the key of room 509 was out – and with a slight shock Latimer realised that the whole elaborate charade must still be going on – Haider, Cordwainer, Angus . . . Angela. He suddenly found it hard even to believe in their existence.

He went up in the lift and turned to the right into the broad, silent corridor. As usual, there was nobody about and he padded silently round the first corner. Ten yards ahead of him a young man in khaki uniform was lounging against the wall. He was hardly more than a boy and he straightened up guiltily when he saw Latimer and came briefly to attention. But he relaxed as Latimer came nearer, and when it became apparent that Steven intended to go on round the second corner he even made a brief, indecisive attempt to stop him. But Latimer said, 'Good morning' and kept on walking – and the young man changed his mind, shrugged, and saluted instead.

Cordwainer, Haider, Angus . . . He wondered genially what had been happening to them all, what they'd all been doing . . . Much the same as before, probably. It occurred to him as he got to the door of his room that Angus might actually be there now. servicing his listening devices, or tuning them, or doing whatever one did to listening devices. Did one have to empty them from time to time, he wondered, like beehives, taking out the used tape and leaving the bees with a new empty wax container to work on? The door wasn't locked and he walked straight in.

Angus was there all right. He was lying peacefully on the bed with his eyes closed and his hands folded post-prandially across his stomach. He was wearing the same cotton trousers and yellow shirt but the college tie had been discarded. Instead, a scarf that Latimer recognised as his own had been tucked neatly – almost nattily – into the neck of his shirt. His face in repose was smooth, but with a choleric flush as though he'd been eating too many rich meals. A large white handkerchief had been passed under his jaw and knotted securely on the top of his head.

Angela was standing by the window. She was wearing a pale cotton raincoat, tightly belted, and her hands were thrust deep down into the pockets. She looked enormous and ungainly. Her hair, limp now and greasy-looking, had been scraped back behind her head and her face, bare of make-up, was as smooth and polished as a salad bowl, and as blank. She was wearing the green-rimmed spectacles and her eyes, much magnified, followed Latimer as he put out a hand to touch one of Angus's – and drew it sharply back again.

145

'How?' Latimer said at last, turning with difficulty away from Angus to look at her.

'I found him hanging from – that.' Her chin indicated the steel light-fitting above the writing-table. 'The upright chair was lying on its side, just below his feet, as though he'd kicked it away. I found him at four o'clock this morning. He'd been dead about five hours.' Her voice was level.

There was a considerable silence.

The idea of action came as a relief. Latimer said quickly, 'Shouldn't we – ' What did one do on these occasions? 'Shouldn't we send for the police?'

'Oh, I've done all that.' With a touch of impatience she turned her back on him and looked out of the window again.

'And what did they – ?'

'They just said it looked like suicide . . . but there'll have to be an inquest. They've been jolly nice, actually.'

She still had her back to him, and once she'd stopped talking there was nothing for him to do but to turn back again towards the tidy figure on the bed. He looked at the folded hands, the knotted handkerchief . . . 'Did the police do – all this?'

'No, I did that.'

'*You?*'

'Oh, it's a very comprehensive training . . . ' She turned round from the window and added conversationally, 'I'm not just the bloody amateur you made me look like yesterday evening.' The bitterness in her voice was the first sign of emotion that she'd shown.

'But why?' Latimer said. Loneliness seized him. As long as Angus had been alive – blamed and hated – Felicity had gone on living too. But now there would only be himself . . . and Nicholas. Abruptly he remembered Angus's urgent voice, only two days before, ' . . . *and when he is older I hope he will choose to make his home with me.*' Why should he kill himself? Aloud he said again, '*Why?*'

'Why what?'

'Why did he – ' An appalling thought struck him. 'Oh my God.'

'What?'

'We'd – we'd had a quarrel, really. Only two days ago. And

146

we'd always been – ' But even now he couldn't bring himself to tell her the whole thing.

'*You!*' Quite without warning she was blazing. 'You're too bloody self-centred to live.' Her face twitched. 'Don't you ever think of anything or anybody else?'

Latimer stared. She said wearily, 'Angus was murdered . . . Anybody but a cretin would have seen that right away. Why should he want to kill himself? Oh, I know – ' She raised her voice as Latimer tried to speak. 'I know all about your wife. And now you've got some idea about him impersonating you but – '

He shouted, 'I *know* it was him! He was using this room! – you said so yourself.'

She turned her back without a word and at once he thought tiredly, why bother? The impersonation was over . . . From now on there would be only one Steven Latimer.

He let a minute go by and said quietly, 'Why should anybody murder Angus?'

'I'm not sure . . . ' She walked past him and stood looking down at Angus.

And suddenly Latimer saw that she must have spent hours like that – after the police left and before he came – standing quite still beside the body, trying to work out what had happened.

'We knew that – *something* was going to happen last night. There were reports of fighting in Panjeh and the whole Haider group was in a state of excitement . . . and so were all the Front people. Angus was in here . . . Somebody must have come in – ' She looked up at him sharply, as though a thought had just struck her.

Latimer said dryly, 'It wasn't me. And I can prove it.'

'No – no, of course not.' Her tone was almost apologetic. She looked again at Angus. 'He must have discovered – something . . . Too much, anyway . . . '

'About what?'

She looked for a moment as though she couldn't understand what he was saying. Then she picked up a newspaper from a pile on the writing-desk and handed it to him.

'UNREST IN PANJEH' said the headline, and underneath, 'Leftist forces attempt coup.'

According to broadcasts monitored in Dubai, the Ruler of Panjeh was today driven from his palace by forces of the Popular Front for the Liberation of Panjeh The royal palace was surrounded shortly before dawn and the royal guards surrendered at once. The Ruler's fate is uncertain. The broadcasts, lasting only a few minutes each, are being transmitted every hour on the airport radio transmitter. But a private message denying the reports and purporting to come from the Ruler himself has been received in Dubai. The situation remains confused.

Guerrilla forces of the P.F.L.P. have been active in the interior of the island for several months. The sixty-eight-year-old Ruler, who attended the coronation of Her Majesty...

Latimer said, 'Well, well, well – ' Today it was marvellous news. He could see it only in terms of Margaret and how she would react. She would be jubilant, of course – and really, he thought, he could share in her jubilation. Saladin was no loss to anyone. He glanced at his watch. Would she be home again by now?

Angela said sarcastically, 'Don't let me keep you.'

He said, 'But can't I help in any way?' – and for the first time wondered about her hostility: only yesterday she had been notably friendly.

She shook her head wearily and then added, 'Just a minute.' She pulled an untidy mass of paper out of her pocket. 'There's a telegram about you somewhere.' She shuffled through them and handed him a piece of paper torn off a telex machine. He read the whole thing through four times – it was all about oranges. Then, belatedly, he realised that it must be in some fairly simple code, and in the same moment he discovered that he could read it. Then he remembered what the code was.

'From the *Department*?' he said incredulously.

She nodded.

'But why *on earth* should they think I'd be willing to work for them?'

148

'You worked for them once before.'

'And nothing on earth would ever induce me to work for them again.'

She nodded again. 'I told them you'd say that . . . They said they thought you'd feel differently now that Angus was dead.'

'It's nothing to do with Angus.'

She shrugged. 'The whole thing is Peter Arden's idea. He's coming out to take over but they can't get him on a plane before tonight. They want someone to go down on the Jumbo today.' She glanced at her watch. 'Now.'

'But why must anyone go? There's an Embassy in Dubai. They'll report anything that happens. What do the Embassy here say? Haven't they heard anything?'

'I don't know . . . ' After a moment she said reluctantly, 'They wouldn't tell me if they had.' For the first time since he arrived the rigidity of her face had slackened. She looked exhausted, and for a split second he wondered if she was going to cry.

As gently as he could he said, 'Why not?'

Her face tightened. '*Why not?*' she mimicked. 'Just *think* for a minute. By the time you'd finished at Jasmin Travel yesterday they were ringing all round Beirut to find out who I was. And I'm on the Embassy list under my own name.'

He said defensively, 'Well, I'm sorry, but it was a silly cover to use and Angus ought to be ashamed of – ' He stopped.

She said wearily, 'It wasn't ever meant to last more than overnight. Till the meeting with Angus at the St. Georges . . . But you were so unco-operative. He'd wanted to recruit you right away but – '

She added, 'London's furious too . . . '

The skin round her eyes was dirty-brown, the rest of her face was yellow. But this time he was more careful. He said levelly, 'But what I still don't understand is why anyone at all has got to go. There's a British Ambassador in Dubai. He'll report to London, and the Foreign Office will certainly tell the Department – even if the Embassy here won't tell you.'

She said quietly, 'It isn't only information. If the Popular Front has really taken over in Panjeh – with Chinese or Russian support – there'll be an uproar in London. The government's

149

already under fire for not doing more for the sheikhs – the oil people are always urging them to send troops in again. And of course the sheikhs *want* us back – they've all been simply terrified ever since the guerrillas started up in Panjeh. We helped Saladin to set up his Defence Force, but that wasn't enough to reassure the rest of them, and in the end our government gave Saladin and the other sheikhs a secret guarantee. They said that, if necessary, and in the last resort, they'd send in troops again . . . And we're the channel of communication – the Department are. Saladin still won't have a British consulate on the island and he doesn't like it known that he has anything much to do with the British these days, but in fact we've been advising him all along. Angus used to go down there secretly – the Ruler would fly him in his helicopter. He was there a week ago, just before that rig was blown up . . . He told Saladin not to worry, the guerrillas weren't strong enough for any kind of an attempt against Saladin himself.' Her mouth twisted. 'London will want to know why he said that. So will Saladin – if he's still alive.'

Latimer said incredulously, 'The British government are planning to send troops back into the Gulf?'

'Well – ' she made a curious sound, 'that's just the point. It's hardly the moment if they can possibly avoid it. The Canal talks are going quite well . . . *So*, someone from the Department has got to go down to Panjeh, quickly, and see what's happening, and report back and – so on and so on.'

Latimer saw the point, but it wasn't his problem. He said so. She nodded without surprise. Then a thought struck him. 'What about Haider? Does he know? Where is he?'

'Oh, he knows all right. He put out a press statement first thing this morning, welcoming the guerrillas' success . . . But he shows no signs of going down to join in the fighting. He's still shut up in his suite at the moment, seeing nobody. No . . .' She grinned suddenly, and with malice. 'Only the camp followers have gone.'

'Camp followers?'

'Well, one of them. The Wedderburn woman. She's a red-hot Front sympathiser. She went on the six a.m. plane to Baghdad – ' She stopped. '*Now* what's the matter?'

Latimer made an effort but it wasn't enough. His voice shook. 'Are you sure?'

Angela's registering of the truth was barely a flicker – as she'd said herself, she wasn't an amateur. She said lightly, turning away towards the window, 'Yes, I'm sure.'

'So she's in Baghdad?'

'Not now.' Angela glanced at her watch. 'She'll be in Dubai by now . . . in jail.' She was enjoying herself.

'*Jail?*'

She explained patiently, 'None of the sheikhs would dream of giving a visa to anybody from the Popular Front. So if she lands in Dubai she'll just be put straight into jail . . . Quite unpleasant, I should think.'

Past caring, Latimer said, 'Suppose I say I'm willing to go down to Panjeh today and talk to Saladin on behalf of the Department, would they pay my fare?'

Her head came round so fast that the tail of hair flicked like a whip. '*Fare?* Well, of course – and expenses, and – '

'What about visas?'

'The Embassy'd cope with that.'

Common sense reasserted itself abruptly. He said sadly, 'But Saladin would never agree . . . He doesn't like me much.'

With surprising energy Angela said, 'He'll agree to exactly whoever we choose to send . . . But you don't *want* – '

Latimer's hand closed round the folded note in his pocket. He said, 'Oh yes I do. I'd *like* to go.'

4
THE GULF

I

Angela slept, curled up like a large woolly dog with her hair all over her face, until the plane was over Basra. Then she woke abruptly and peered out of the window.

'What's *that*?'

She sounded cross, as though she'd caught Latimer concealing relevant information. 'It's the Shatt-el-Arab,' he told her meekly. 'When the Tigris and Euphrates join up they're called "the Arab River".' It looked like a strip of glass, grey and opaque, separated from the brown on either side by a narrow fringe of dark green. 'You'll see the Gulf in a minute.'

She nodded, accepting his story, and then, opening a small square suitcase, took out a vast tub of face cream and started to rub it into her face. The brown country below changed into naked shiny mud flats, mould-spotted with white salt, into which the waters of the Gulf thrust themselves in snaky creeks and inlets, looking from above like the trunks and branches of fleshy, leafless trees. The wide creeks were grey, shading to green in the narrower, shallower branches and to vivid turquoise at the extreme tips. It was a formal, scaleless, almost diagrammatic landscape.

Despite himself Latimer said, 'Oh *look* –'

She paused, leaving a dollop of cream unattended on either cheek, and looked. 'But there's nothing there,' she objected, and returned to her work.

Three minutes later the Gulf itself floated into view below them – pale, candid blue like the shell of a bird's egg, a different colour altogether from the rich superimposed blues of the Mediterranean. And to the right, abruptly, the land turned yellow. Arabia . . . Seen like that from the air, it is one of the most startling of transitions: Iran to the north is tawny and mountainous; Iraq is brown alluvial mud; and Arabia is sand – yellow sand emptiness. And there, at the head of the Gulf, they all meet.

But Latimer knew better this time than to draw the sight to Angela's attention. The plane idled out over the Gulf, heading south-east, and the land on either side sank into a blur on the horizon. Angela finished her make-up and started on her nails.

He will need an assistant, London had said when Angela rang them up to say that he'd agreed to take the job – for coding and liaison, and . . . Quite unnecessary, he'd said, seizing the phone out of her hand, I don't *need* an assistant. Oh yes you do. Oh no I don't . . . Miss Barrington *will go with you,* they had said, and in the end it had been an ultimatum: either Angela went with him or else – It was clear to Latimer by this time that her real job would be to keep an eye on him and really, he had reflected wearily, he could hardly blame them. He had turned briefly from the phone to look at her, standing by the bed. She had looked exhausted and defenceless . . . All right, he had shouted into the phone, all right.

B.O.A.C. had held the plane for them for twenty minutes and even so they had only just caught it.

Now she put away her nail file and turned to him kindly, with the shorthand for a smile. She said, 'I think we should run quickly through our plan of action . . . The first essential is information.'

She had found time somehow to get her contact lenses in and she was confident again, back in control, and Latimer saw with a sinking of the heart that this would be her tone for the whole

153

trip – businesslike and brisk. Two days ago he might have found himself impressed, albeit reluctantly, but now . . . He realised that he had never actually envisaged *doing* anything for the Department: he had taken the job on – had *pretended* to take the job on – solely so as to get to Dubai, and if necessary back to Panjeh. But now, saddled with Angela, he would be obliged to bustle about, collecting information, reporting to London . . . Paralysis seized him.

At Dubai a very young man with a pink, sweaty face was waiting outside the customs hall. He said, 'Robinson,' and grasped Latimer's hand. He must be new in the Embassy – Latimer hadn't seen him before. He was wearing cotton trousers and an open-necked shirt that stuck to his torso in large uneven patches. Latimer mumbled his own name, and disengaged his hand as quickly as he decently could. Robinson looked as though Latimer wasn't quite what he had been expecting but he led the way without further argument to a Land-Rover waiting outside the building. A driver in khaki uniform with a face like a brown hawk under his *kafir* held the door open, his right hand stiffly at the salute, and Latimer stood back to let Angela get in first. Robinson stared – and Latimer realised that he hadn't until now grasped that she was of the party.

'I didn't know – ' Robinson said stiffly, as though her arrival had been planned as an insult.

'I didn't know either,' Latimer said irritably, climbing up in front of them both.

Angela and Robinson joined him in the back, the hawk-faced driver climbed into the front and they drove off. The air came at them in a suffocating wave filled with flying grains of sand. Latimer had always disliked Dubai, finding it noisy and appallingly hot, and he wondered gloomily now how long he would have to stay.

Robinson leaned forward to nod civilly to him across Angela's solid form. 'Cooler today,' he said. Then, surprisingly, he gave a nervous little laugh. 'The Ambassador's only on tour so I shouldn't by rights have it up.'

Latimer said, 'Ah – '

'The flag,' Robinson explained, laughing again and waving

a hand at the small multicoloured oblong fluttering from a special rod on one of the Land-Rover's front mudguards. 'I mean, he's not really away. I'm not – ' he dropped his voice slightly, 'I'm not *in charge*.'

Latimer said, 'Ah,' again. Did Robinson think he was going to report him to London?

'But – ' Robinson's voice became noticeably firmer, 'I think it keeps up prestige.' The guards at the airport gate, impressive figures in the showy uniforms of the newly-formed Dubai Militia, crashed to attention as they passed and presented arms. The swags of braid at their shoulders jumped and all the tassels on their headdresses swung like bells. Robinson acknowledged the salute gravely. 'It gives pleasure all round,' he said, with evident truth.

Latimer had had about enough of the flag by this time and there were a lot of things that he wanted to know. 'I think you know why I'm here,' he said, sounding like a screen conspirator.

'Yes, yes,' Robinson said loudly, 'but – ' He lowered his voice, looking at Latimer with meaning, and they both leaned forward across Angela until Robinson judged that their heads were close enough together. Then he said, 'But – ah – *pas devant*.' He indicated the back of the driver's head, draped in its black and white *kafir*, and Latimer groaned inwardly: Robinson was going to be conscientious about security. He hunched his shoulders and Robinson started to talk loudly about 'casings' and 'cold rolled strips': he had constructed some elaborate fantasy, it appeared, and Latimer was to be the representative of a British steel company . . . He hadn't yet had time to write Angela into the script, of course, but in due time, no doubt, she would be turned into Latimer's secretary. Latimer gave an inward, ironic laugh.

Robinson seemed perfectly happy playing charades by himself so Latimer simply grunted from time to time and they drove towards the town across a flat stretch of desert that now, at three in the afternoon, was throwing up a dense, distorting shimmer of heat.

The town of Dubai rose slowly out of the desert to meet them – graceful, sand-coloured wind towers left over from an earlier prosperity and steel banks and stressed-concrete hotels from the more recent one. Modern Dubai is a boom town built on a single occupation – smuggling of the most sophisticated, twentieth-century kind. Two or three times a week the big jets from London fly in consignments of gold bars, addressed to this or that well-known and respectable merchant, all perfectly legal and above board. And even when the heavy bars are repacked into smaller boxes, and even when the boxes are loaded carefully into the graceful hulls of the little fishing-dhows anchored in the creek, no offence against exchange control or customs regulations has been committed. But the curving hulls conceal powerful engines, and the dhows' captains waste no time on fishing. The boxes of gold are landed quickly, in moonless nights, on the coasts of India or Pakistan, where gold commands so high a price that in two successful trips each member of a dhow's crew can earn more than in a whole season of blameless hard work with the fishing fleet. So Dubai flourishes, and every year another steel-and-glass bank or another hotel with an iced-water tap in every room rises out of the mud along the edge of the creek.

The Land-Rover swung over a long, arching bridge and they turned towards the town and drew up outside the British Embassy, a pleasant modern building with a huge royal crest and a flag outside. There were more salutings and then, with almost unbelievable relief, Latimer found himself inside a cool half-darkened office with the hum of air-conditioners all around him. Robinson sat down reverently behind what was clearly the Ambassador's desk and said, 'Here we can speak freely.'

He spoke freely. The Ambassador, he said, very much disliked being involved in any way with what he believed was called 'the Department'. The Ambassador was accredited to Panjeh as well as to Dubai and his function was to act, when necessary, as a channel of communication between Her Majesty's Government and the Ruler of Panjeh. If the Ruler had indeed been deposed – and there were a few unreliable rumours to that effect – then he, the Ambassador, would wait until London recognised the new regime (whatever it proved to be) and would then act as a channel of communication to it, the new regime. Any dealings that Her Majesty's Government might choose to have with the Ruler of Panjeh through the so-called Department were of no concern to the Ambassador or his Embassy and he didn't want to have anything to do with them, or even to know about them. Such dealings could only do harm to his, the Ambassador's, close and cordial relations with the Sheikh of Dubai and with the other Rulers to whom he was accredited. He had received instructions from London to give Dr. Latimer all reasonable help and intended to interpret this as the sort of help that they would normally give to a reasonably senior representative of a British business firm . . .

Latimer interrupted him to shout, 'All right! I don't exist!'

Robinson ignored him. 'The Ambassador's last words were – '

Latimer supplied them: ' "Tell the bastard I won't have him lousing up my position here, and if he gets into any trouble on Panjeh he's on his own." '

Astonishingly, Robinson giggled – and about fifteen years dropped off his age. 'That's almost *exactly* – ' he began with animation, but Angela's voice stopped him. They had both forgotten Angela for a moment and they looked at her with surprise, as though one of the air-conditioners had spoken.

She said softly and with a slight breathlessness, 'I wonder if I might make a suggestion?' It was the voice she had used at Beirut airport, when Latimer first encountered her. So much had happened in the past three days that Latimer had forgotten the impact that Angela had originally made on him. Now she smiled at Robinson and Latimer saw the poor wretch blink.

'There are certain items of information that Dr. Latimer needs, very urgently. If we are to telegraph to London today, perhaps – ?' She paused, and smiled again.

Robinson gabbled, 'Yes, of course. Yes.'

'What information do you have from Panjeh itself?'

Robinson's chest expanded and he flung himself back into the part of the Ambassador. 'Well, the rebels are firmly in control. That much is certain. They are still broadcasting every hour on the airfield transmitter. Here is a – ah – transcript.' He shuffled through the papers on the desk and handed her a typewritten sheet. She read it gravely and then, almost as an afterthought, handed it on to Latimer.

'Comrades! Fear nothing! Saladin the oppressor is dead!

The Popular Front for the Liberation of Panjeh is triumphant!
There is no longer need for concealment! Declare yourselves!
Long live the Popular Front for the Liberation of Panjeh!'

Latimer read it twice, and he still didn't like it. 'Isn't there anything more concrete?'

Robinson was hurt. 'What sort of thing do you want?'

'Hasn't anybody got into Panjeh yet?'

'No planes. Gulf tried again this morning, but they weren't allowed to land.'

'What about the press – why aren't they here in force, chartering helicopters?'

Robinson smiled. 'Not one *single* journalist has got in yet.' He spoke with the satisfaction of a good civil servant. 'Our own Sheikh here is refusing all visas to the press till he's had time to talk to his pals. They're meeting today – now, in fact.' He glanced at his watch. 'All the Rulers – Sharjah, Abu Dhabi, Ras-al-Khaimah – the lot. To decide if they're going to do anything about Panjeh . . . But he won't be able to keep the press out indefinitely.'

'There was an AP report yesterday from Dubai. We saw it in the Beirut papers.'

'Yes, but he's a local, and he's been told to shut up now, till further notice.'

There was silence.

Latimer said carefully, 'Do you know of any *other* travellers who've arrived here today, trying to get on into Panjeh?' His voice came out plummy and over-casual. 'Any – known supporters of the Front, for example? The person I have in mind is a – er – English woman who –'

But Robinson was shaking his head. '*Most* unlikely. The Ruler doesn't like supporters of the Front . . . '

There was silence again. Latimer said, 'Tell me about the Panjehi here in Dubai.' Angela glanced at him sharply: this wasn't in the script. 'Are they a – close group? Would they be easy to organise?'

Robinson frowned, puzzled.

Latimer said, 'Do you think it likely that they could be induced to join in an invasion of Panjeh organised by the Popular Front?'

Robinson said doubtfully, 'There's been a lot of interest in the Front, of course, ever since the guerrillas really got going in Panjeh. But I don't know if they'd be willing to fight . . . What's this about an invasion?'

'It's a – possibility.'

'An invasion of Panjeh by the Panjehi who live here, in Dubai?' He was getting excited.

'That sort of thing.'

Robinson stammered with eagerness, 'But – but – there *is* something. I hadn't known whether to mention it. You see, early this morning – *all the taxis disappeared.*'

Latimer stared, speechless, fighting a terrible urge to laugh. Angela's head was going like a metronome, flicking from one to the other.

And then Latimer remembered, and Robinson's remark was suddenly of enormous significance: all the taxi-drivers in Dubai were Panjehi exiles.

2

They drove north out of Dubai, through the town of Sharjah, out into the open empty desert. To their left was the sea, intensely blue, ahead and to their right was sand – dirty-yellow and featureless, stretching away to the horizon. In the extreme distance to the north and north-east the mountains of Oman pressed up over the rim of the desert, a jagged brown blue that rose slowly higher as they progressed. The road was broad and well tarmaced and there was virtually no other traffic, but they drove at a steady amble that made Latimer feel after a time as though they were standing still. The Ambassador's car could clearly not be used for his disreputable purposes, and there were no taxis. This was Robinson's own vehicle – an elderly Land-Rover that had seen long service with the Trucial Oman Scouts before he bought it cheap. He had lent it to Latimer eagerly, longing to take part himself in the expedition but concluding finally that duty required him to stay in the

Embassy. He said goodbye to them wistfully. 'Tell me all when you get back.'

It was about fifty miles to Ras-al-Khaimah, the little sheikhdom situated on the mainland immediately opposite Panjeh. The coast between Dubai and Ras-al-Khaimah was flat and sandy with no proper harbours or jetties, and it seemed probable to Latimer that the rendezvous for the invasion, which must have taken place that morning, would have been at Ras-al-Khaimah itself – and everything would be over and finished before they got there. He fumed and fidgeted, coaxing the elderly machine along at a steady thirty miles an hour. The sun was already losing its heat and a light wind blew steadily from the sea, flicking sand in through the cracks round the side windows and covering their hands and faces, the inside of their mouths and nostrils with a fine layer of grit.

After ten miles they passed Ajman, a square white fort a mile to their left on the very edge of the sea. But after that there was nothing – just the sky and the empty sand and the ribbon of tarmac leading north. After an hour Latimer touched Angela's arm and pointed ahead and slightly to their left, to a barely perceptible gap in the mountains that closed the northern horizon. The extreme left-hand end of the chain was Panjeh itself. And almost at once they met the first taxi, a powerful Mercedes – streaking south, back to Dubai. It was crammed: grinning faces under close-fitting white hats or intricately-knotted dull red turbans, bundles of what might have been curtain material, a length, apparently, of metal tubing – and rifles, masses of them, sticking out of all the windows at random angles so that the car seemed to bristle like a porcupine. As it flashed past white sleeves waved in greeting and a burst of shots exploded joyfully into the air.

'Panjehi,' said Latimer quietly. Then he slammed down his foot and the Land-Rover leapt forward, shuddering and banging. They were shaken like dice in a box.

'What on *earth* – ?' Angela yelled, but her voice was swallowed up. Latimer didn't bother to reply. He knew no more than she did.

Two more taxis passed them, dashing south, and Latimer craned round to see what it was they were carrying. The first was moving too fast for him to do more than glimpse the now familiar gallery of excited faces, but the second was going more slowly, veering wildly right and left across the road under the weight of an enormous metal chair fastened insecurely on to the roof. Latimer saw the wind catch it like a sail and press the car across the road and almost out on to the sand. The driver was dragging at the wheel and as they passed Latimer caught sight of his face, contorted with effort.

They looked, Latimer realised suddenly, exactly like a successful raiding party returning home . . . But there hadn't been time, surely, for them to have crossed by boat to Panjeh and to have returned already? In any case if the invasion had been successful the victorious forces would surely have stayed on the island. If the revolution had failed, of course . . . but the men in the taxi had certainly not been defeated.

And now, looking ahead, he could see the channel between Panjeh and the mainland and the familiar shape of the island itself. In the west the mountains were low and rounded but on the coast facing the mainland enormous deeply fissured cliffs sprang straight out of the sea. The island looked black and massive in the fading light, forbidding.

'Look!' Angela had seen them first.

A few miles ahead, close to the shore, Latimer suddenly caught a glimpse of two small fishing-boats. Then the road twisted, running up the side of a small ridge so that the island was hidden. But as the Land-Rover ground its way up over the crest of the ridge Latimer slammed on the brakes and reached down by the seat for Robinson's binoculars. They flung open the doors and jumped out and Latimer leaned against the bonnet carefully adjusting the glasses.

'Yes,' he said quietly, 'that's it . . . the invasion of Panjeh.' Three miles ahead of them a cluster of fishing-boats was anchored near the shore and on the shore itself – at this point close to the road – was a dense mass of people, their white clothes showing up clearly in the dusk. The rendezvous. Pay-Day . . . The invasion fleet ready, the liberating troops assembled for embarkation, the objective in sight, the short sea-crossing . . . But even from where they stood Latimer could see that the forces *weren't* embarking and that the mass of people

6 161

on the shore was static, like a swarm . . . a swarm *round* something. What? Vehicles, certainly. The taxis, of course . . . but
something else as well, larger – much larger. A bus? Several
buses? Latimer fiddled with the glasses but he couldn't get a
clearer view.

'Come on,' he said impatiently, 'let's go,' but he went on
fiddling.

Angela seized the binoculars. 'Let *me* – '

Only ten miles away to the north the mountains finally joined
the coast and there, though they couldn't yet see it, must be
Ras-al-Khaimah – a good anchorage, proper jetties . . . Why
weren't they using it? The Sheikh of Ras-al-Khaimah might
object – but where they were now was just as much Ras-al-
Khaimah territory . . .

Angela said impatiently, 'I can't *see* . . . Let's go,' but as they
turned towards the Land-Rover a fourth Mercedes came grinding up the ridge to meet them. This one was more crowded
than ever – there were even two small boys hanging on to the
outside – and the salute of rifle-fire was deafening. It was also
alarming: several of the shots kicked up the sand just beside
their feet. But the intention had been unmistakably friendly
and the small boys were still waving as the taxi disappeared
down the ridge in the direction of Dubai.

Angela and Latimer looked at each other.

'The invading army,' Latimer said doubtfully, 'but going
the wrong way – ' *The spoils of victory* . . . There was a joyful
burst of rifle-fire from the retreating Mercedes and at the same
moment, like a response, they heard the first faint sound of
firing from the beach three miles ahead.

Even though the cockpit had been stripped of its instruments
and the interior gutted the little plane still looked from the
outside neat and pretty – perched lightly on the road as though
it might take off again at any moment. Its wings and fuselage
were pink in the last of the sunset and the lettering on the side
was black and bold:

TRADE WINDS FOUNDATION FOR INTER-
NATIONAL UNDERSTANDING

But the road underneath it was littered with splintered planks from the packing cases and the sand for fifty yards in every direction was trampled as though a herd of buffalo had gone over it. It looked like a battlefield – which indeed it was. There were two dead bodies, both killed by rifle-fire, and four men badly wounded.

As the Land-Rover drew up and Latimer and Angela jumped out, the last of the crowd, still fighting over the spoils, broke and ran for the taxis: a Land-Rover and two Europeans had the look of authority and they didn't want to get involved. Out beyond the shore the last of the fishing-boats was already in motion, heading back to Dubai, black and graceful on the milky sea.

It was Angela who found the pilot, a fair-haired young Austrian, lying under the starboard wing. He wasn't badly hurt but he had been stunned and when he first came round he was tearful and confused. It was a trick, he kept saying, a trick . . . it wasn't *his* fault, he didn't know where the man was, he'd never heard of him . . .

Latimer fumed with impatience but Angela extracted the story patiently. They had set out from Beirut at 10 p.m. the previous night, and except for a refuelling stop at Baghdad, had flown directly to the rendezvous point. There had been two planes – this one and the other. This one had contained only the supplies, he said: the rifles, the ammunition and the money – ten thousand sterling in Maria Theresa dollars, wrapped like chocolates in silver paper and stacked in solid wooden boxes. He had been instructed to land first, and the second plane was to follow him down after two minutes – in accordance with the operation plan. But instead, the second plane had circled twice and had then headed off north-west, towards Panjeh, and had disappeared behind the island. The waiting crowd had been quite respectful at first. They had stood around, not even daring to touch the plane, just looking. But then they had started shouting, '*Haider bin Hassan, Haider bin Hassan,*' chanting the words over and over. '*Haider bin Hassan!*'

Angela said in astonishment, 'Haider's *with* you? Where?'

But even before the young pilot had shaken his head, puzzled and confused, Latimer realised that it simply wasn't possible in terms of time. Less than eight hours ago Haider had been in Beirut.

The pilot asked slowly, 'Who is – *Haider bin Hassan?*' Remembering the crowd, his voice was suddenly frightened. 'Is he Arab?'

It was obvious that the name meant nothing to him. Latimer said soothingly, 'Yes . . . an Arab.' But *why* had Haider stayed in Beirut when he was so eagerly expected here? Why? Pay-Day, Haider's own plan – and yet he had chose not to come ;.. Whom had he sent instead?

'The second plane – ?' Latimer said eagerly, but the young man had started to cry again. The crowd had been waiting and waiting, he said, for this *Haider bin Hassan,* and when at last they realised that he wasn't coming – that they had been tricked, that the invasion was off – then they had become angry. They had been determined at least to *see* what was inside the plane. They had forced their way in and had started to open the crates, and then . . . He had done what he could, the pilot said, but he was only one against two or three hundred and though he carried an old army pistol he had no ammunition. He had tried to defend the entrance to the plane, using the pistol as a club, but they had pulled him off the ladder like a leech off a rock and had hit him again and again . . . He was weeping uncontrollably.

'But the second plane,' Latimer insisted, 'who was in the second plane?'

The young man made an effort. The second plane, he said, had contained only the leaders.

'*Who?*' Angela and Latimer spoke together.

'The Frenchman and the two Englishmen.'

'Do you know their names?'

Without a moment's hesitation he said, 'Mr. Cordwainer, Mr. Duquair and Mr. Latimer.'

There was a moment of total silence and then Latimer cleared his throat.

'Who?' he asked again, more quietly.

'Mr. Cordwainer, Mr. Duquair and Mr. Latimer.'

Angela said impatiently, 'There's been a mistake,' but Latimer interrupted quickly, 'What was he like – this Latimer?'

'He was English . . . he wore glasses . . . not young, not old.'

Latimer felt suddenly dizzy. He had seen Angus dead, he had touched him . . .

'You're *sure* he was English?'

The pilot flung up a hand in irritation. Of course he was sure. Mr. Latimer had travelled with him, in his plane, from Beirut as far as the refuelling stop at Baghdad.

So he had been wholly, totally, criminally wrong about Angus . . . but – *who was it*?

Angela said impatiently, 'Well, it doesn't matter anyway. We'd better go,' and Latimer roused himself. They helped the pilot and the other wounded into the Land-Rover and set off back towards Dubai. At the top of the ridge they paused. The light had gone altogether now and they could see nothing, but they listened in the darkness to the soft spattering sound as the wind started to spread a fine layer of sand over the disorder. By morning the footmarks would be quite covered up, and if the police didn't come soon, so would the dead.

3

The Land-Rover turned in at the gate of the Embassy and Angela said, 'I must say that I think it's very odd – '

It was 11.30 p.m. and they had been to the hospital and to the police and now Latimer hoped that he was going to bed. He wondered gloomily whether Robinson would have thought of booking him a room at a hotel.

Angela repeated, '*Very* odd . . . You knew that Margaret Wedderburn was mixed up with the Popular Front, and you knew that Cordwainer was her brother-in-law, and yet when he turned up in Beirut with a couple of planes you simply didn't make the connection – '

Latimer said, 'Yes, but – ' He still found it difficult to connect Cordwainer with the Popular Front though that was certainly the way the evidence pointed . . . But what about the Austrian pilot's story? Why had the second plane – the plane carrying Cordwainer and Duquair and 'Latimer' – why had it suddenly abandoned the agreed plan and flown straight on to Panjeh . . . ? There were too many unknowns.

And where was Margaret? – stuck, presumably, in Baghdad . . . And he was stuck in Dubai.

The Land-Rover stopped and he climbed down wearily. A servant in uniform flung open the front door and they passed in, blinking, under the big coat of arms, into the delicious cool and the brilliant light.

Robinson came rushing out of the Ambassador's office to meet them. They had already rung him from the police station and his eyes were circular with pleasure and importance. 'I'm just dictating a telegram to London. Come in and tell me if – '

'Any news?' Latimer interrupted.

'What? No – oh, except that flights into Panjeh have started again. The first one went at six o'clock this evening.'

'But who's in control there?'

'The communists – at least, they're still broadcasting every hour that Saladin is dead and the Front's triumphant so I suppose they must be. Come on in – '

Latimer trailed wearily after him into the big office. Robinson riffled through the papers on the desk, handing over one or two for Latimer to look at. 'Another statement to the Beirut press by Haider bin Hassan, 8 p.m. today . . . *'triumphant struggle of progressive Panjeh forces against colonialist oppression'* . . . greetings to the new regime . . . Fairly routine stuff. Angry telegram from London asking for news . . . more transcripts of broadcasts from Panjeh. *'The Popular Front is triumphant'* . . . 7 p.m. this evening . . . 8 p.m. . . . I hope that woman knows what she's doing.' A note of worry had suddenly come in his voice.

Latimer flicking tiredly through the sheafs of paper, said, 'What woman?'

'A friend of the Ambassador's – of his wife's, actually. She only got here this morning but when she heard that there was a plane going on into Panjeh this evening she insisted on going with it. I wasn't sure what to do with the Ambassador away, but she was so determined that in the end I had to let her go.'

With a sudden clear premonition Latimer said, 'What's she – ?'

'Wedderburn, her name is, but – '

Angela burst in, 'But you *can't* have let her go! The woman's a communist – *and* a journalist. I thought you said no visas were being issued to the press.'

Robinson shook his head, unruffled. 'I told you, she's a friend of the Ambassador's wife – she can't be a communist. She's had a tourist visa in her passport for weeks, actually. She told me she'd been planning a visit here for ages but was never able to get away . . . Pity they're both on tour.'

Latimer laughed. He couldn't help it. He threw back his head and shouted with laughter.

Angela said furiously, 'You must arrange to have her thrown out first thing in the morning.'

Latimer said quietly, 'She's in Panjeh . . . and I suppose this means that I can't go there now. The guerrillas will hardly welcome a representative of H.M.G.'

Robinson said, surprised, 'Oh no . . . there's a telegram addressed to you from Panjeh – it doesn't say who from exactly. It just says "Latimer visit acceptable". That's funny . . . '

Angela said slowly, 'London will have telegraphed direct, proposing Dr. Latimer's name. This must be the reply . . . ' With an attempt at briskness she said, 'When's the next plane we can get to Panjeh?'

'Six o'clock tomorrow morning,' said Robinson.

'Well then,' Angela said, 'I think we should think in terms of catching that, but we should perhaps consult London first . . . '

With a small, unworthy sense of triumph Latimer said carefully, '*I* shall certainly catch that plane. But the Panjeh telegram doesn't mention you, Angela, and in all the uncertainties of the situation . . . I shall leave you in Mr. Robinson's capable hands.'

The door into the cockpit slammed open, its metallic crash audible even above the roar of the engines. The pilot's left arm made circular beckoning gestures and Latimer hoisted himself to his feet and staggered forward, steadying himself on the nets slung under the roof. The Dakota was adapted for freight and made no concessions to passenger comfort: for the last half-hour he had crouched on a metal bench tucked into the bulge of the fuselage, his head and shoulders thrust forward by the returning curve. He stood up with relief, glad to stretch, but the plane was banking steeply and he found himself hanging from the nets like an orang-outang, hauling himself hand over hand into the cockpit.

As he reached the cockpit he squatted down and the pilot glanced round quickly, giving a brief thumbs-up sign. The lower part of his face was hidden by the flap of his flying helmet but Latimer could tell from his eyes that he was grinning. The plane levelled out and he took a hand off the controls and pulled the microphone away from his mouth.

'Permission to land!' he yelled into Latimer's ear. 'They've just said Yes!' He was delighted. 'Here we go!' Without further warning he thrust the Dakota into a steep falling turn and Latimer grabbed at the back of the seat as a tilted mountain of bare rock theatrically lighted by the rising sun came dashing up towards them. The plane's angle increased, the sound of the engines rose to a shriller scream and the rock-face slipped past the cockpit – so close that Latimer was aware of individual erosion scratches on the mountainside. The plane levelled up and then leaned over the other way. This time the mountain came at them from above – or so it seemed – and he could have put a hand on to the rock-face as it passed. In just one moment, he realised suddenly, he was going to be extremely sick. He had always loathed this flight but this time it seemed worse than ever. He closed his eyes, but fear dragged them open again almost at once as the plane steadied itself for another turn.

'Tricky run-in, Panjeh!'

Latimer tried to speak but couldn't and the pilot turned his head right round and peered at him with concern. 'You all right?'

The inevitable mountainside was hurtling up towards them and Latimer moved a weak hand to draw it to the pilot's attention. The corners of the pilot's eyes crinkled with amusement as he swung the plane round. 'Nearly there!' he yelled reassuringly, and Latimer closed his eyes again.

When he opened them the miracle had occurred. They were through the pass and into an open saucer of darkness surrounded by further barriers of jagged mountains. Up at fifteen hundred feet it had been daylight, down here the dawn hadn't yet arrived. But there was light of a sort, a grey reflection from the sky. They were flying low over a shadowy plain dotted with darker tufts – vegetation perhaps, or rocks. Half a mile ahead the long streak of paler grey dashing to meet them defined itself as an airstrip, distorted by perspective into an elongated arrow head. The pilot put on his lights and set the Dakota down with a crash on to the black-and-white squares that marked the start of the runway. The scream of the engines reversing filled the cockpit, the plane slowed abruptly and the vibration lessened. The light was improving with every minute. At the far end of the runway Latimer could see now the small white airport building with its flagpole beside it. And standing in front of the building was a group of figures. The plane ran on, losing speed. There was a Land-Rover there too.

The pilot chuckled, enjoying the situation. 'Reception committee,' he said. 'Recognise anyone?'

Latimer didn't answer: the pilot didn't really expect an answer.

The plane slowed still further and Latimer caught sight of something that up till now had been hidden by the airport building: the second Trade Winds plane was standing just to one side of the runway. The pilot saw it at the same moment and grunted. 'Get out the red flag,' he said, 'I think we're going to need it.'

A Land-Rover came roaring out on to the tarmac even before the Dakota's engines had stopped, and though he could see nothing Latimer heard it draw up with a squeal of brakes under the starboard wing. The plane's engines slowed, roared briefly, missed a couple of times and stopped – but inside the metal hull the noise went on for quite a time. Gradually he became aware of voices outside, commands being shouted. The pilot unstrapped himself and came slowly back into the cabin. On the ground a Dakota's fuselage is tilted at an angle and he moved with caution. Methodically he started to undo the heavy metal bolts of the door. With his hand on the last one he made a visible effort, grinned over his shoulder and said, 'Fortunately I always carry a Party card.' But he was nervous. They were both nervous.

'Workers of the world,' said the pilot, 'unite.'

He tugged open the heavy door and they peered out together on to the tarmac.

'Dr. Latimer, good morning! Welcome back.' A tremendous salute. It was Dickens. 'His Highness is waiting for you.'

Dickens. *His Highness is waiting* . . . Then the guerrillas were most definitely not in control. The pilot said softly, 'Cor' stone the crows.'

Latimer said weakly, 'Oh . . . good morning, Dickens. How are you?'

Dickens lowered his right arm reluctantly. 'I'm well. And you?'

'Fine.' There was a pause. The pilot roused himself belatedly and unfastened a metal ladder from under the roof. He ran out its full length and slotted it into the bottom of the doorway.

Latimer clambered down and was met with another tremendous salute. Had Dickens always overdone it so blatantly?

'His Highness is anxious to see you as soon as possible,' Dickens said, and Latimer looked with surprise at the big Land-Rover crowded with privates of the Defence Force. It looked more like close arrest than a guard of honour.

The pilot said, 'You've got some cargo for me, Major.'

'I don't know about cargo,' Dickens said distantly. 'You'd better ask at the airport building . . . Latimer, will you get in the front? We've got a fairly tight schedule.'

Latimer climbed in slowly and nodded at a couple of the privates whose faces were familiar. They grinned back cheerfully, flashing white teeth under the shade of their *kafirs*.

The pilot said, 'But you radioed us only – ' he glanced at his watch, ' – only a few hours ago. *'Please arrange urgently for onward transport of wounded to London.'*' So what's it all about then?' The Australian accent had become stronger as he went on. He knew Dickens of old and didn't like him.

'I think you'll find,' Dickens said stiffly, 'that His Highness has made other arrangements.'

'What other arrangements?'

Reluctantly, Dickens jerked his head in the direction of the Trade Winds plane and all the tassels on his *kafir* swayed.

'That toy? It'll never make it . . . I'm off then.' He turned angrily towards his plane but Dickens made a sudden noise of distress, 'No, no! You're to stay and take Dr. Latimer back to Dubai, at your usual scheduled time . . . Eighteen hundred hours. That's right isn't it?'

The pilot hesitated, glancing at Latimer, and Latimer said quietly, 'I'd be grateful.'

The pilot nodded grudgingly. 'I'll give you till then.'

Dickens gave a little *tut* of annoyance and climbed in beside Latimer. As they set off the sun broke suddenly through a gap in the mountains and the white airport building was flooded in cool light. But the rest of the valley was still in shadow and the mountains to the east were black and flat, their outlines fuzzy with the intensity of the light behind. Latimer glanced at his watch. Six twenty-five.

They bowled across the tarmac at first, very fast, and then more slowly, bumping and lurching along the track leading towards the pass and the shore.

Dickens began at once, glancing at Latimer shyly and with obvious admiration, 'I say, Latimer, why ever didn't you tell me all those months that you were working for – ah – you-know-who? You should have done. I can keep a secret. I've been an undercover man myself, actually. Once in Hamburg we had to pass a message to some chap and I dressed up in civvies.' He laughed happily at the recollection.

Latimer said shortly, 'I wasn't,' and then at once, 'What happened to those two patients from the rig explosion – the day I left?'

171

For a few moments Dickens was silent, then he turned to Latimer a face expressing carefully the gravest puzzlement. 'Patients?' he said vaguely.

'Come off it, Dickens, it's only a week.'

The Land-Rover gave a lurch and Dickens said, 'Oh yes, I remember. An Irishman . . . I rather think he's dead.'

'You *rather* think? Where's he buried?'

'I expect the hospital took care of all that.'

Latimer said grimly, 'And the young Arab . . . the guerrilla?'

Dickens gazed straight ahead. 'He's dead, I believe. Died in prison.'

A surge of revulsion and loathing swept through Latimer. *Died in prison* . . . And he, Latimer, had gone away, knowing perfectly well what would happen . . . And if I'd stayed, he thought savagely, just what could I have done? But reasoned argument wasn't going to diminish guilt. He glanced wearily at Dickens' face. Did he never ask himself such questions?

'How's Rifai?' he asked.

Dickens said loftily, 'I haven't seen him.'

There was quite a good dirt road through the pass, and at the far end the sea appeared suddenly as a wedge of brilliant blue in the vee formed by the mountains. The hills here were black rock, gleaming in the sun as though the rain had just stopped. But there hadn't been rain for years. The only growing things were camel-thorn and a few vast dried-out thistles. They passed a flock of goats poking about in the dry riverbed, their ginger-brown hair so coated with sand and dust that they were almost invisible.

Once at the coast they were on to the pitted remains of the pre-war road and bumped and jolted across one of the rocky promontories into a small bay with a broad sandy beach and a cluster of mud houses with fishing nets spread out over the roofs to dry. The driver at once abandoned the road and the Land-Rover shot forward across the sand.

Latimer looked around him curiously. After only a week away the whole landscape seemed to have receded, like a memory.

'Quite a time we've had, these last forty-eight hours.' Dickens was clearly longing to talk, but he sounded uneasy.

Latimer said cautiously, 'So I imagine.'

'You know this part of the world so well that I don't suppose anything would surprise you now.'

He hadn't phrased it as a question and Latimer let it go.

'His Highness is quite a character actually ... marvellous old man in many ways. A bit out-of-date, mind you, but in this part of the world – well, really, you have to be a bit out-of-date don't you, if you want to keep up?' Dickens laughed heartily and Latimer tried to make out what he was after. 'His methods are a bit – medieval, of course ... '

What did he want? Indiscreet criticism of Saladin?

Latimer said cautiously, 'It's a medieval part of the world, of course.'

'*Exactly!*' Dickens was suddenly radiant. 'That's exactly what I've always said. After all, Saladin wouldn't have stayed in power for twenty years if he'd run the place like a girl guide camp, now would he? And I can tell you that he means to stay in power another twenty, if he can. I don't know what line London are taking – ' He lowered his voice confidentially. 'They've probably been taken in by all that political guff that the guerrillas have been putting out. Liberation Front and all that. And it's true that they've had some help from the Chinese in the past, and this last couple of months there have definitely been some Russian arms coming in, and some of the leaders are real proper commies, of course, but most of them aren't *politicians* at all, you know – they're just gangsters. They just want to break everything up and take over. It's a police job really, putting down gangsters ... One can't take them seriously as *more* than gangsters, really. And for that sort of thing police methods are the only solution – '

'Are you trying to defend His Highness' methods to me, Dickens?'

Dickens' face contorted. 'Well, they're not *our* police methods, of course ... but your Mr. Bailey, when he was down here last week, he said to the Ruler that if we caught any of the guerrillas we ought to keep 'em in prison and then he'd send somebody down to – interrogate them. Scientifically.'

Latimer could just hear Angus saying that.

Dickens shifted uncomfortably in his seat. He said tentatively, 'I imagine that's why you've come?'

They had reached the end of the beach now and the driver slowed down and eased the Land-Rover back on to the road. It was little more than a succession of pot-holes and the Land-Rover lurched and shook, but it was the only way across the next promontory.

Choosing his words carefully Latimer said, 'I've come because the Ruler asked the British Government to send somebody.'

Dickens turned to look at him with the beginnings of hope. 'But not specially for interrogation?'

A boulder scraped along the Land-Rover's underside. Latimer raised his voice and repeated, 'No.'

'So you're not expecting to talk to the prisoners?' The note of hope in Dickens' voice was now unmistakable.

The road was climbing sharply, twisting and turning through enormous boulders, and the Land-Rover's engine was grinding noisily but inside Latimer's mind there was a sudden silence.

He said, 'What prisoners?'

'Well, the commie leaders. We got the whole lot as they landed this morning, didn't you know? Cleared out the whole package.' For the first time he sounded thoroughly happy, pleased with himself. 'We didn't get the tip-off until just before midnight last night and by three o'clock this morning we'd got them. The whole lot.'

Latimer's tongue was suddenly too large. He said with difficulty, 'Who – ?'

The Land-Rover lurched into a pot-hole and Dickens shouted, 'What?'

Latimer tried again. 'How many?'

'Three.' There was a grinding crash and the Land-Rover tipped sideways and came to rest against the rock-face. Cordwainer, Duquair and – 'Latimer'. Just ahead the road had been blotted out by a fall of stones.

Dickens swore loudly and clambered out, and the privates scrambled out of the back, chattering cheerfully. Latimer climbed out too and lit a cigarette. It was clear from the way in which Dickens and the men went to work that this sort of thing had happened frequently before. The Land-Rover was lifted back on to the road and then, with the men shoving from behind, it ground its way, tipping and lurching, over the fallen stones.

Dickens and the men climbed back in. Latimer had been preparing his question but Dickens forestalled him. 'Look!' he said.

The road had taken another twist and there below them was the harbour. It was an enclosed bay, very like the one they had just left, but here the points of the two promontories guarding the entrance were so close together that it looked from above as though there was no way out to the sea at all. It was a view that had always filled Latimer with claustrophobia. Immediately below them was the town, still in deep early morning shadow, an untidy confusion of flat roofs and dusty open spaces, crammed in between the cliffs and the beach. It was surrounded by high walls and on the side nearest to them Latimer could see the impressive gateway with its stone pediment and the two brass cannon. But they were only for show. The real strength was elsewhere. High up on the rocks on the far side of the bay squatted the fort, dazzling now in the level light of the sun. It was all white, with towers and turrets and arrow-slits and a flagpole – just like a cardboard castle. But it wasn't cardboard, and even at that distance its weight was oppressive. It was low and massive, pressing down so closely on to the unevenness of the rock that it might have been poured into position.

The road twisted, beginning to run downhill, and the fort was hidden.

Latimer said casually, 'That woman who came over on the plane last night . . . Wedderburn, I think her name was. What happened to her?'

Dickens said, 'A woman? Really? Don't know anything about that, old boy,' and Latimer, listening carefully, thought that his surprise might have been genuine.

Latimer asked, 'Are the three prisoners . . . *in* the fort?' But Dickens didn't answer and after a moment Latimer turned to look at him.

Dickens' face was scarlet. He said angrily, 'No, of course not. I've just been telling you . . .'

He had told Latimer nothing, but it seemed foolhardy to insist. They jolted down the hill without speaking. Dickens looked at his watch.

At the bottom the road improved and the Land-Rover picked up speed and shot away towards the walls and the impressive gateway.

Dickens looked at his watch again. He said appealingly, 'You said yourself that it's a medieval sort of place . . . '

Latimer started to say something non-committal but the sentries had signalled to the Land-Rover to stop and as the driver switched the engine off he heard the crowd in the distance. Latimer's first ludicrous thought was that there must be a football match going on, but then he glanced at Dickens' face.

The sentries stepped back and saluted, waving the Land-Rover through, and Dickens said with suddenly renewed nervousness, 'You've got to understand the sort of people he's dealing with – the Ruler, I mean. They're very simple people – primitive, really. I didn't approve. Really I didn't. Not that he consulted me, actually, but if he wants to make his point, he's got to – '

The driver had swung the Land-Rover into a narrow street between high, white walls and was accelerating sharply. There was nobody about. Dickens, who had been looking intently at Latimer as he talked, glanced quickly out through the windscreen, realised abruptly where they were and started to shout at the driver to slow down, to wait a minute . . . But the driver pretended not to understand and the Land-Rover rocked on round two more corners. They could hear the crowd now even above the sound of the engine. Dickens leant across Latimer and grabbed at the wheel.

'I said "Slow down", you bloody fool.'

But they had turned the last corner and were there.

Considering that they must have had to run it up in quite a hurry the platform wasn't at all a bad job – about fifteen feet long and six feet high. It was made, as far as Latimer could see, entirely out of packing cases. Its superstructure was elementary – a ten-foot upright at either end of the platform joined at the

top by a solid beam. It had been set up in an open sandy space
surrounded by houses. Panjeh was so crammed in between the
cliffs and the beach that there wasn't room for a square, or
even for a parade ground, and this was simply the largest available space – a gap where three streets met. But it was large
enough. The entire male population of Panjeh must have managed to get themselves in there, shouting like banshees and
waving their arms about – contorted brown faces under red or
white turbans, boys with shaved heads and embroidered white
skull-caps, old men with wispy beards like skeins of flax – all of
them wearing long dirty-white shirts to the ankle and many
of them belted with festoons of rifle cartridges. It was a crowd
that didn't move much, though every individual in it was so
fiercely in motion. They were wedged against the high white
walls, pressed up under the base of the platform, or simply
held immobile by the weight of other bodies.

Close to, the sound was worse even than when they had first
heard it distantly from the gate. It was an animal noise, a howl
– and they were howling with pleasure, the terror that each one
of them felt as he looked at the platform commuted at once into
mere enjoyable alarm by the friendly pressures of the crowd.
They would have howled in much the same way if a ship had
gone down with all hands in sight of shore, or if the three
figures up on the platform had been unexpectedly struck by
lightning in the crowded centre of the *suq*.

The driver, wildly excited, had slammed the Land-Rover
straight into the outskirts of the crowd and there they stuck,
embedded. Latimer recognised one or two faces, but he had
never nourished illusions about the Panjehi and was unsurprised
now by their pleasure in the sight. But he had thought that
when he finally saw the prisoners (and from the moment that
Dickens first mentioned them he had known that it would
happen, somehow) he had thought that when he saw them he
would at least know – that one question at least would be
answered. But he had forgotten – though he knew it perfectly
well in theory from reading the newspapers and if he had been
asked how such things were done in Arab countries he would
certainly have remembered and said that it was likely to be so –
he had forgotten *how* they hang traitors. Dangling from the

cross-beam the big sacks rotated, anonymous, first in one direction and then the other.

Cordwainer, Duquair and – 'Latimer'. Would he ever know now who he was?

5

Latimer said harshly, 'All right, Dickens, I've seen that . . . Where do we go now? Or do your instructions specify that I've got to watch for a full five minutes?'

Dickens' face was already scarlet and now it turned crimson. He shouted at the driver at the pitch of his voice. 'Back out, you ape! Get this bloody Land-Rover out of here. Get into gear – '

Reluctantly the driver engaged the gears and started to ease the Land-Rover back out of the crowd. The soldiers, who had tumbled out of the back and climbed on to the roof to get a better view, clambered back in again, chattering with indignation.

Dickens and Latimer were silent. The Land-Rover was freed, finally, Dickens said curtly, 'To the fort,' and the driver started off, driving by the most circuitous route and at a footpace to express his resentment.

In the narrow lanes it was shadowy, still almost dark in places. But the cliffs hanging over the town were dazzling – a brilliant pale yellow in the early sun – and occasionally a high wall, catching the sun, reflected a yellow gleam down on to the sandy floor. There was nobody about. Once or twice in the distance a scrap of black drapery flicked into a doorway or round a corner, but by the time they got there the door would be shut or the next stretch of white-walled lane empty. The women, it seemed, were being cautious – and the men were all at the hanging. They jolted slowly through a section of the *suq*, but most of the shops were shut, secured with intricately-carved wooden shutters or rolling blinds of corrugated iron. Cautious faces looked out from the few shops that were open. In one of them an Indian tailor was sitting crosslegged behind his sewing-machine. He jumped up as he saw the Land-Rover go by and there was a loud rattle as he started to tug down the iron shutter of his shop.

Turning down an alley, a mere slit between two of the shops barely wide enough for the Land-Rover to get through, they emerged abruptly on to the beach and Latimer held his breath to avoid the stench. Where the beach met the houses there was a wide belt of rocks and pebbles mingled with bones, scraps of decaying food, broken plastic bowls and sandals, a few tins and bottles, filth of every kind – the whole rubbish of the town. One or two dogs were picking about, and a whole flock of big crows were busily at work. But beyond this area a wide expanse of perfectly smooth and clean yellow sand sloped gently to the sea. The water was deep blue and flat, with only the narrowest frill of white where the shallow waves broke twenty yards out from the shore. There were three or four white dhows at anchor, outlined against the dark rocks that curved round on the seaward side – and straight ahead of them, hanging above the harbour and its dhows, was the fort. From this angle it looked as though it must have grown there, must have sprouted from the rock on hard roots.

The beach stretched away, level and empty, for a mile in either direction. The sand was hard and smooth, sprinkled with millions of minute shells as clean and shiny as the whites of boiled eggs, forming themselves into intricate, random designs – sprays and ferns, feathers, leaves and exploding galaxies. Thankfully Latimer breathed in the clean smell from the sea. All through his years in Panjeh the seashore had always represented an escape into freedom, solitude and cleanliness.

The Land-Rover bowled along across the hard sand, leaving the town behind, and a rough track snaked its way out from the last of the houses to join them. They were heading now straight for another giant barrier of cliffs, but Latimer knew that at the last moment the track would dodge past the foot of the rocks and turn left, climbing up on to the promontory, out towards the sea – out towards the fort, that evil-looking molar.

He said, 'Why's His Highness using the fort?' Saladin generally lived in a modern palace in the town.

179

Dickens said, 'Well, we're still a fairly operational footing. There's been a revolution here, you know – unsuccessful admittedly, but nasty.'

Latimer saw the dogs before he remembered what the place was. There were five or six of them, big soft-haired sandy-coloured animals with mournful eyes. One or two of them were sniffing about or scratching without great hope at the newly turned sand, but the rest were just standing around looking in different directions like guests at a party who haven't yet been told what's expected of them. To a casual view the place looked just like the rest of the stony strip between the beach and the cliff, but if one looked closer one saw that some of the stones had a sort of organisation about them. It was the town's burial ground. There were a certain number of gravestones, but few Panjehi could afford them and the vast majority of graves were marked simply by a line of flat stones with an upright stone at either end. There were two men at work beside a parked Land-Rover. They were wild-looking figures, both wearing the dull red Panjehi turban and festooned with cartridge belts over their long white robes. They looked like members of Saladin's personal guard – and the Land-Rover must be Saladin's because no one else in Panjeh owned one. Latimer looked at them curiously. They had just finished making a grave and were beating the flat stones down into position with their bony dark brown feet. Their heads turned briefly towards the Land-Rover as it bumped past and for a moment they paused in their stamping, but they didn't wave or shout a greeting. Dickens too leaned sideways and peered at them anxiously, but Latimer noticed that he didn't ask any questions.

'Was that on our sightseeing programme?' Latimer asked.

Dickens said angrily, 'I don't know what you mean.'

'Who was it?'

'Quite a number of people were killed in the fighting, it could have been any of them.' But Latimer could hear the uncertainty in his voice.

He said automatically, 'You're hushing something up, Dickens' – but his mind had already moved on, to the fort, to the coming interview with Saladin . . .

The Land-Rover was climbing steeply now, lurching and

rocking up the stony track on to the headland. There was a view out to the open sea and, beyond, to the mainland, with the mountains of Oman black against the morning sun.

At close quarters the fort was more massive and threatening than ever. It hung over them, the great white walls spreading out towards the ground like the trunks of trees, and the black iron gate uncompromisingly shut. There were a dozen or so soldiers in front of the gate and Dickens recovered his good humour abruptly as they recognised him and came crashing to attention under their swinging *kafirs*. There was a lot of shouting of orders and a small door in the black gate opened cautiously.

Dickens said, 'We walk from here.' Latimer was conscious of rifles in the arrow-slits above their heads, and out of the darkness inside the narrow doorway two more pairs of eyes inspected them before they were allowed through.

He said, 'This seems a bit exaggerated,' but Dickens was back on his own ground and ignored him altogether. There was a long narrow passage and then they were out into the courtyard, a jumble of single-storey mud buildings round a much-trodden patch of sand. A sentry leaning against the wall came sharply to attention, and a huddle of dark brown and white sheep and goats scattered in front of them, bleating. Some women squatted round a doorway, amorphous in black draperies, their faces sinister and repellent in the bronzed leather masks. Above the low mud buildings the white walls hung protectively.

Dickens strode ahead across the courtyard. Latimer dawdled, reluctant now and apprehensive, scuffing at the sand with the toe of his shoe. But Dickens paused in an open doorway and looked back with impatience. 'This way!' he called, and Latimer followed him.

He had only been in the fort once before, but he knew that Dickens wasn't heading for the audience chamber. Instead they passed through two dark rooms, down a narrow open passage, through another doorway, and Latimer found himself in a bare white-washed room that might have been a guardhouse. A sentry at the door stepped aside to let Dickens through, and then Dickens in his turn stood still to let Latimer go forward alone. His gesture as he did so was familiar and Latimer's attention was for a moment distracted. Who else had waved him forward like that?

Then he found himself standing by the table. When he made no move the sentry came forward politely and lifted the dirty white sheets off the three bodies. Latimer looked. Then he turned away, fighting down the vomit in his throat.

Dickens said his piece. 'Those were three law-abiding shopkeepers from the town. They all had stalls in the *suq*, but they also had houses on the outskirts of the town. The guerrillas wanted to use those houses to store arms and explosives ready for their attack on the town the night before last. These men refused and that's what the guerrillas did to them . . . they did it *before* killing them and – '

Latimer shouted, 'I can see!'

Satisfied, Dickens nodded. 'Now,' he said, 'we will go and see His Highness.' When things were going well he was even prepared to give Saladin his title.

The floor of the audience chamber was covered with thick carpet in an overpowering design of red and orange on a dark blue ground. The walls were lined with mirrors incised with designs of flowers and birds. From the intricately-mirrored ceiling hung a dozen vast electric chandeliers of pink glass, full on. Saladin had recently been talked into employing a firm of interior decorators from Paris and the effect was dazzling. It was a vast square room and running all the way round the outside was a shallow step about four feet wide. On this, pushed right back against the walls, was a continuous row of heavily padded dark blue velvet armchairs. There was no other furniture, but a large stainless steel apparatus of faintly surgical appearance stood incongruously in the centre of the room under a plastic cover. It was a room that could have seated over a hundred people without difficulty. There were perhaps thirty in it.

Jalis . . . the Sheikh sits. The Ruler was sitting in the exact centre of the wall facing the door. The *kafir* over his head was made of the finest white cotton and when he moved the narrow silver hilt of a dagger showed briefly on the belt at his left side.

His feet were tucked up under him, hidden by the voluminous skirts of his dazzling white robe. Latimer recognised sourly that this must be an important occasion: Saladin normally wore ancient and very worn garments, none too clean.

Two chairs away from Saladin to his left an uneasy, deferential figure in a badly-fitting tropical suit was crouching forward on the edge of his chair, a pad balanced on his knees and a pencil in his hand, ready to take dictation – Bahpoori, the Ruler's Indian private secretary. In other chairs round the room, deferentially distant from the Ruler, were twenty or thirty other men. They wore the red Panjehi turban and festoons of cartridges, just like the two figures that Latimer had seen in the graveyard. Two of them carried hooded falcons on their right wrist. On the step in front of Saladin's chair squatted a negro, barefoot, in voluminous white trousers and shirt and a white skull-cap. In his left hand, deftly wedged between the fingers, he carried four little cups, and as Latimer entered he was pouring into them a stream of black coffee from the pot held in his right hand, high above his head. The Ruler, his secretary, his entourage, his coffee-bearer . . . So far all was as might have been expected. But there were two other men sitting with the Ruler, in the places of honour immediately to his right and his left. Cordwainer and Duquair.

6

Saladin said, 'Panjeh is the firm friend of Great Britain.'

It was the third time he'd said it. Latimer was sick of the whole conversation – if you can call it a conversation when only one person speaks, dropping individual sentences into the silence and failing to hear if anyone else tries to join in.

But in any case it wasn't a conversation at all, of course, it was an audience.

Cordwainer was smiling, but he looked as though he were covering up a great deal of uncertainty, and when Saladin spoke he frowned with concentration as though the meaning of the words was beyond him. He was as unrumpled as ever, in a pale tropical suit and suede desert boots. His mere appearance exacted respect. Duquair was less well-pressed but still, by comparison with Latimer, immaculate. He sat quite still in the big chair, his eyes on the floor, one square fist supporting his cheek so forcefully that the whole right-hand side of his face was pushed upwards and his eye was half closed. It was the first time that Latimer had actually seen him in the flesh and he studied him cautiously. He looked older than in the photograph, and nastier.

'I would like you to tell the British government that as a result of the operations of the last two days I feel myself in a stronger position militarily than at any time in the last three years.' Saladin's English, though slow, was really very good. 'The Defence Force did excellent work – ' Dickens half unfolded like a dog hearing the rustle of chocolate paper, ' – excellent work. It is due to their prompt action in putting down the guerrillas' attack from the interior that I am not obliged to request immediate military aid from the British government.'

Missing the point, Dickens sat forward in his chair and glowed.

Latimer said loudly, 'If the hangings I witnessed this morning were carried out by members of the Defence Force there will certainly be questions asked in the British House of Commons... Your Highness.'

Dickens crumpled like a paper bag and Cordwainer looked worried, but Saladin might not have heard him.

One of the falcons moved suddenly, stretching out its enormous wings and uttering sharp little cries of distress. Its head, scarlet and gold in the leather hood, turned blindly from side to side. Its handler spoke to it reassuringly, and the big wings folded back and down again. There was silence.

Still crouching, the coffee-bearer came crab-like along the step to refill Latimer's cup. He was grinning and Latimer wondered, not for the first time, how much English he understood.

The Ruler changed suddenly into Arabic. He asked quietly, 'Where is Bailey?'

'He is dead.'

'How?'

'He hanged himself.'

'Why?'

'I do not know.'

Cordwainer's smile had slipped altogether. He sat forward in his chair, looking sharply from the ruler to Latimer and back again. It was clear that he understood no Arabic.

Saladin said, 'Was he not murdered?'

'Who would murder him?'

There was silence again.

Saladin reverted to English. He said distinctly, 'Acting on information received from a loyal son of Panjeh the Defence Force was also able to capture three Russian agents in the early hours of this morning as they landed on the coast of Panjeh to join the rebels in the interior. In accordance with the traditions of justice in Panjeh they were at once executed ... as you have seen. I have documents and equipment taken from these Russian agents that I shall ask you to pass to the British government.' He must have learnt it all by heart.

'The presence of Russian saboteurs in the Arabian Gulf is now proved beyond any possibility of doubt, and Panjeh is clearly a prime target. As an outpost of the free world Panjeh will need both military and economic assistance to counter this double threat – internal and external. I would like to have urgent discussions with the British government on this question. I am glad to welcome you today as an envoy of the British government, Dr. Latimer, because your knowledge of the island will enable you to judge accurately what you see.' Looking at the thin, clever face Latimer felt all the old loathing. 'I should like you to tell the British government what you have seen here today. I would like you to draw their attention in particular to the brutal acts of terrorism committed by the guerrillas against innocent, law-abiding citizens, and to the loyal enthusiasm of the ordinary Panjehi at the capture and execution of the Russian saboteurs ... The ordinary Panjehi has no sympathy whatsoever for the guerrillas, there is no support among the people for their ideas. That has now been demonstrated beyond all possibility of doubt.'

Latimer said carefully, 'Her Majesty's government will wish to know exactly what has happened. I should be glad of an account of what happened yesterday and the day before . . . I would like an account of the guerrillas' attack on the town.'

Saladin's face didn't move.

After a moment's silence he said, 'The fighting was confused.'

Latimer leaned forward. 'The British government will have to know in detail what has happened . . . What about the broadcasts from the airfield transmitter?'

Saladin said, 'These are details . . . The broadcasts were made by the guerrillas, and later the airfield was recaptured.'

'I have a number of other queries, Your Highness.'

Cordwainer said, 'Now what on earth was all that about? Do please explain to me. I find all this political stuff confusing beyond belief.'

The end of the audience had come abruptly. Saladin had stood up and swept from the room, all in one movement, leaving Latimer's questions unanswered. His entire entourage had risen and gone after him, Dickens and the Indian secretary had followed, and the coffee-bearer had brought up the rear – pausing only to collect the little cups.

Latimer said rudely, 'What are *you* doing here?'

Cordwainer looked surprised. 'We're here on business – ' a graceful movement of his head included Duquair, 'and we seem to have got ourselves slap into the aftermath of a revolution or something. I must say I'm quite in the dark.' He took out a flat gold cigarette case, opened it, and held it towards Latimer – a gesture from the 'thirties. As an afterthought he added, 'I had no idea when I saw you in Beirut that you were coming here. I could have offered you a lift in my plane.'

'What sort of business?'

'What? Oh, oil. The *only* business in the Gulf.' He smiled, drawing Latimer into the joke. 'We've just signed a contract with the – ah – with His Highness. He's been getting a bit fed up with Shell, you know. They're too *big* for him. They make somebody like Saladin – ' he lowered his voice with exaggerated mock-caution, 'they make him feel pretty small. He'd got the impression they were grinding him for every last penny on the contract for the exploration rights, so for the actual extraction of the oil – ' he paused and smiled again, 'he's coming to us. Anglo-French.'

He added modestly, 'I don't expect you've heard of us. We're quite a small firm . . . I'm a director, and Mr. Duquair here – have you two actually *met*, by the way? – he's our Beirut representative. Luc, this is Mr. – ah – Dr. Latimer.'

They nodded. Latimer said feebly, 'I didn't know you were in oil.'

'No? Well, I have a lot of interests, actually.'

Duquair leaned towards him and muttered into his ear. Cordwainer nodded. He said apologetically, 'So – will you excuse us? We've got to get going. I'm off back to Dubai to give a press conference. I'd like to offer you a lift now but I've agreed to take two of the palace guards who were wounded in the fighting . . . Yes, well – ' moving towards the door he laid a hand familiarly on the surgical contrivance in the middle of the room. He said to Duquair, glancing up at the chandeliers, 'The current looks all right.' To Latimer he explained, 'We couldn't think what on earth to bring – as a present, you know. But then we heard that His Highness suffers from rheumatism, so we bought him one of those lamps – infra-red and ultra-violet, all that sort of – '

'Were the rifles for him too?'

Latimer had their attention now. Cordwainer said cautiously, 'Rifles – ?'

'He didn't get them, did he, and I can't believe that it was an accident. What else did you bring him? Where's the other man who was in your plane? – the one who called himself "Latimer".'

Cordwainer said, 'I really haven't the faintest idea what you're – '

Latimer said, 'Where's Margaret?'

'Margaret?'

'Margaret Wedderburn, your sister-in-law. She arrived here in a plane last night. Where is she?'

Astonishingly, Cordwainer laughed. 'I rather hope she *isn't* here, you know. She's a red-hot commie, didn't you know that?

Tough as they come. She'd probably be in the mountains with the guerrillas by now.'

'The first time we met you described her as gentle and sensitive and deeply wronged.'

'Oh – well.' For just a moment Cordwainer seemed less than entirely at ease.

But then Saladin was back. They heard a command in the ante-chamber, the carpet-muffled crash of sentries coming to attention – and he was there. Cordwainer bowed gracefully, miraculously obliterating his cigarette, and Duquair and Latimer bobbed their heads.

This time there was no entourage, only the Indian secretary, and Dickens trailing along behind. Dickens looked like a small boy who has been told to come in at once and apologise, but Saladin made no reference to him.

'It has occurred to me,' he said, ignoring the others and addressing himself directly to Latimer, 'that as a representative of the British government you will wish to visit the grave of that poor man before you leave.' Latimer looked blank and he went on at once. 'Your patient. The driller, from the rig that was blown up last week. He was, I understand, an Irishman. We have just buried him this morning. The company have of course been informed.'

He lifted a hand and the secretary jumped forward. 'Mr. Bahpoori and Major Dickens will take you, and then you can go straight on to the airport. Goodbye, Dr. Latimer.'

He inclined his head, they all bowed again, and then he was gone.

Mr. Bahpoori wasted no time. He started at once, waddling towards the ante-chamber. Cordwainer said thankfully, 'Goodbye, goodbye,' and in a moment Latimer found himself out in the glare of the courtyard with Dickens at his shoulder. The heat had built up and the air came at them in a damp cloud: Mr. Bahpoori was sweating before they'd even got as far as the Land-Rover. To Latimer's surprise they went without a driver, Mr. Bahpoori himself struggling with the unfamiliar controls. Dickens followed alone in another Land-Rover without any of his men.

Nothing was said about their destination but Latimer wasn't

kept long in uncertainty. The Land-Rovers lurched down the steep track away from the fort, bumping and sliding, and finally after about ten minutes came to rest in the burial ground at the foot of the cliff.

The dogs had lost heart long ago. One or two of them were still about but they were lying idly on the ground, more for lack of anywhere better to go than with particular interest in the grave. Latimer and Mr. Bahpoori had travelled in absolute silence. Now, with evident relief, Mr. Bahpoori scrambled down and took out of the back of the Land-Rover a small Union Jack and three plastic delphiniums on long green plastic stalks. Latimer gazed at them – astonished, and full of admiration for Saladin's thoroughness. Dickens was already impressively at attention and Mr. Bahpoori now marched briskly to the foot of the grave and drew himself up into a fair imitation of Dickens' wooden immobility. There was a pause.

The slippery plastic stems lolled in Latimer's left hand, the little square of hairy patchwork (where on earth had he got it from?) hung limp in his right. It was all absurd ... However, there was nothing for it. Latimer too drew himself up and marched forward. He bent down and laid the Union Jack neatly, four-square, on the Irishman's grave – hoping that he'd known enough about Panjeh while he was alive to understand, and forgive. He fixed it in position with four small pebbles, which, like all the other stones of the grave, were now unpleasantly hot to the touch, and he put the plastic delphiniums down beside the flag. Then he stepped back two paces and stood for a moment with the sun scorching on to the back of his neck. You poor devil, he thought.

Mr. Bahpoori was sweating more profusely than ever – but mostly, Latimer thought, with relief. He shook Latimer warmly by the hand – up and down, up and down. 'Goodbye, goodbye, good journey, good luck – '

'Goodbye,' said Latimer, disengaging his hand.

Mr. Bahpoori sprang into his Land-Rover and reversed it ineptly in a spatter of sand. Then it lurched off up the hill with Mr. Bahpoori waving a jolly hand above his head.

Latimer sat down on the flat stones of the grave, beside the delphiniums. He said, 'So the revolution was a fake.'

Dickens said, '*What?*'

'There was no atttack on the town and the broadcasts on the airfield transmitter were made by Saladin's own people. That's right, isn't it?'

Dickens' astonishment was so great that there was no need to press him further.

Latimer nodded, satisfied. 'It was a good charade, very nicely done. But a pity they sent you the wrong audience. Angus would have lapped it up. Now, next question. Who were the three people who were hanged this morning?'

But Dickens was still struggling. 'I can't imagine how you knew – about the revolution, I mean. He didn't want to tell you, actually. I don't know why. I think it was a jolly sharp idea myself. It's easy to underrate old Saladin, but he dreamed that all up by himself. They broadcast every hour on the hour all through yesterday, saying that Saladin was dead and the guerrillas were in charge, and a whole lot of their chaps from the mountains came down into the town and started shouting slogans. We bagged about twenty of them.'

'Are they in jail?'

Dickens face twisted slightly. 'No. They were shot at once.'

'So who's this "loyal son of Panjeh"?'

'Loyal son – ?'

'Who gave you the information about the landing of the three Russian agents . . . I assume his loyalty was stimulated by interrogation?'

'Oh . . . yes . . . well, that was – that was that young chap I brought to the hospital the day you left. You remember? The one who'd blown up the rig and had a wounded shoulder . . . *He* told us. Now look, Latimer – ' he glanced at his watch.

Latimer said expressionlessly, 'Saladin had that boy under interrogation for a whole week and he only produced the information about the Russian agents just before midnight last night?'

'Yes . . . yes, that's right. Look, we ought to go now. I've got to get you to the airport.'

'I don't believe it . . . Dickens, there are still two people I want to be able to account for. The man who was in Cordwainer's plane with him and Duquair, and a girl called Margaret Wedderburn. Where are they?'

'Latimer, I've simply *no idea*. You asked me about the girl before, you know, but I've never heard of her. Now – '

Latimer got to his feet abruptly. 'Yes,' he said, 'we'd better go. You drive.'

Annoyed by his tone but unable to argue Dickens climbed into the Land-Rover and started the engine. Latimer got in beside him and the Land-Rover bumped off slowly towards the beach. Latimer said conversationally, 'We'll go first and take those three bodies down off the gibbet.'

Dickens opened his mouth so slowly that he might have been testing the mechanism. He said, 'But – ', and then it occurred to him that Latimer was being humorous. He laughed appreciatively, 'Ha, ha, ha,' and accelerated slightly.

'And after that I want to go to the hospital.' Dickens was sure now that he was joking, so he only said, 'Can't you sit a bit further over, Latimer? You're making it impossible to steer.'

Latimer didn't move, and after a moment Dickens glanced down irritably and the Land-Rover slowed as his accelerator foot froze in astonishment. 'Where did you get *that* from?'

'I borrowed it yesterday, from an Austrian. A pilot. He'd been beaten up by a crowd of Panjehi who wanted what was in his plane . . . Go on driving.'

'But – ' Dickens struggled to define his sense of outrage. 'But doctors don't shoot.'

'In normal circumstances, no.' Latimer leaned over, unhooked the cover of the holster on Dickens' belt and removed the pistol.

Dickens said incredulously, 'You're behaving like a gangster.'

Latimer laughed with real pleasure. 'No, I'm behaving like an arm of government. Like the Post Office Savings Bank.'

Dickens glanced at him doubtfully and drove on for a few minutes in silence. 'What do you actually want?' he said finally. They were nearly opposite the town now, isolated on the broad emptiness of the beach. Before Latimer could answer, Dickens said plaintively, 'Sod it, Latimer. You're treating me like some shifty old Arab. I'm a British subject and a British – *was* a British officer, and that's where my first loyalty lies. Of course. And my first duty. But I'm on contract to Saladin now and I have to do my job. You must see that. And my job is to help him put down these bloody commies.'

'I, on the other hand, am here on a purely private mission.'

Dickens said slowly, 'I think we'd better go back and talk to Saladin.'

7

This time there was no entourage, no private secretary and no huge audience chamber. Dickens had sent in a message by one of Saladin's guards and now led the way through a series of dark shabby halls separated by locked doors, stopping at last in a tiny silent room with no windows and very little light. The floor was padded with carpets and cushions, and there were heavy rugs hung round the walls. The air was stuffy and full of incense and the flame in the one brass lamp flickered. Latimer peered round him with curiosity. In all his years on the island he had never been in one of these secret, claustrophobic rooms – though he had known that they must exist.

Saladin himself, when he arrived, seemed by contrast modern and matter-of-fact. He came in quickly, lifting a curtain to one side, and the negro coffee-bearer with his little cups came clinking in behind. Saladin nodded to Latimer and sat down on a pile of cushions against the wall. The negro folded himself silently into a corner and Dickens and Latimer sat down cross-legged on the carpet.

Saladin said at once, as Dickens had done, 'What is it that you want?' Negotiations had started.

Latimer had in fact only one card to play, and he played it quickly. 'The British Government,' he said – they were talking Arabic this time – 'in considering Your Highness's request for military and economic assistance to counter the communist threat to Panjeh, will wish to be assured that yesterday's events occurred exactly as your Highness has described them to me. For example, I must see with my own eyes the bodies, clothes and equipment of the three Russian agents who were hanged this morning.'

Saladin waited for a minute and then nodded, 'I agree.'

Latimer said carefully, 'Mr. Cordwainer and Mr. Duquair arrived here last night in Mr. Cordwainer's plane. There was another man with them, an Englishman calling himself Steven Latimer – my name.'

He paused but Saladin said nothing. Latimer went on, 'And an Englishwoman, Margaret Wedderburn, arrived here by the regular Gulf Airlines flight last night . . . Where are these two people?' When Saladin still didn't speak, Latimer took a chance. 'They are both British subjects,' he said, and saw one corner of Saladin's mouth twitch.

So Saladin knew something about the man . . . But when he spoke it was about Margaret.

'This Wedderburn,' Saladin said. 'She has written against me,' he glanced briefly at Dickens, who nodded, ' – and if she came to Panjeh it would be to give help to the rebels. She would think they had been successful . . . She would be stupid.' Listening to the note of satisfaction in Saladin's voice, it occurred to Latimer with a stab of distress that Margaret too had been a victim of the fake broadcasts: she had taken them at their face value and flown in at once to Panjeh, confident that she would find the guerrillas in control, a commune set up . . . But it was absurd to blame her for her credulity, he thought angrily. They had all been taken in.

He said, too quickly, 'Where is she?' and Saladin looked at him sharply. He said slowly and with pleasure, 'You have seen how we in Panjeh treat foreigners who come to our island to give help to the rebels.'

But it wasn't a simple statement of fact. His voice held the questioning tone of a man proposing a very slight alteration in the terms of a deal . . . Latimer's heart rose. Saladin couldn't have spoken in that way if she *had* been one of those three figures . . . He said coldly, 'Miss Wedderburn is a British subject. The British government will hold Your Highness responsible for her safety.'

But Saladin couldn't be browbeaten in that way. He said, 'If this Wedderburn makes illegal rebellion against me, the British government will not stop me from putting her in prison.'

Latimer swallowed. Prison. That at least was one better than – 'Miss Wedderburn is in prison here?'

Saladin shrugged. 'I know nothing of this Wedderburn.'

'As a representative of Her Majesty's Government, I would wish to see her at once if she is in prison. Her Majesty's Government will require a full report on the conditions in which she is being held and on –'

Saladin brushed him aside. 'That would be done. If she were in prison I would send at once for the Consul from Dubai. She could have a lawyer . . . ' He knew it all, far too well. 'But I must remind you, Dr. Latimer, that in Panjeh the penalty for assisting rebels is death.'

'Miss Wedderburn comes from a very ancient English family. The British government would not wish her to be in a Panjeh prison.'

It sounded pretty weak and Saladin didn't bother to answer. There was a long silence. Latimer began to wonder whether he would have to say anything more before Saladin suggested terms.

Then Saladin spoke, very softly. 'I did not want to accept you today, Dr. Latimer, as a representative of the British government. You know that. When you were here at the hospital you talked often to the rebels, you encouraged them . . . ' These were old accusations and Latimer let them go: Saladin would come to the point in a minute. 'I want you to leave the island at once now and never attempt to return. I want you to write me a letter now admitting that you broke the terms of your contract while you were here, that you encouraged the rebels. I want you to say in your letter that you will never come back to the island. Never. And that today you will not attempt to visit the hospital.'

Latimer nodded slowly. He said, 'I agree . . . ' It was a fair exchange. A letter like that in Saladin's hands would discredit totally any public criticism of the Panjeh regime that Latimer might choose to make, now or in the future. He said, 'And Miss Wedderburn?'

Saladin said impatiently, 'I know nothing of her,' and stood up, a single fluid motion. Latimer and Dickens scrambled hastily to their feet.

As though as an afterthought Saladin said to Dickens in English, 'If any trace of this Wedderburn is found on the island before Dr. Latimer's plane takes off, put her on board . . . '

He glanced again at Latimer, who nodded. 'Very well. Mr. Bahpoori will bring you paper and ink.'

'And the other man?' Latimer said loudly. 'The man on Cordwainer's plane?' The sense of relief and triumph was so great that he could hardly control his limbs or his voice.

Saladin, astonishingly, smiled. Still in English he said 'He was nothing . . . The coolie for Mr. Cordwainer's plane. The mick – ' he glanced at Dickens who supplied the word doubtfully. 'Yes, the mechanic.'

Latimer said stupidly, 'And his name was Latimer?'

Saladin's lips drew back still further. 'No, I don't know what it was, but Cordwainer always called him by your name. He wore spectacles like yours and looked . . . He was a man of the people, you understand.'

Absurdly, Latimer felt himself go red. He had thought he was near to a solution of the mystery – and it turned out that there had been no mystery at all. It was characteristic of Cordwainer, now that he thought of it, to have brought a special mechanic for his planes, and characteristic too to have made this silly, elaborate joke – snobbish, harmless and hurtful.

'The mechanic stayed at the airfield, of course, with the plane. They have gone back now, to Dubai . . . and this Wedderburn,' he looked again at Dickens, '*if* she is found she will be put on Dr. Latimer's plane.'

Latimer said 'Yes – ' and then with excitement thought, *Margaret will be on the plane.*

Saladin nodded his head decisively and the negro scrambled forward to lift back the curtain. An instinct of caution struck at Latimer – a sensation like fear. He said, 'And the three Russian agents? You have not forgotten?'

'No . . . ' Displeased, Saladin glanced at the enormous modern gold watch on his wrist. 'They will be cut down at noon, and you can see them then.' Had Saladin really hoped to distract him by fixing his attention on Margaret . . . ? He would have to be more careful.

Then Saladin had gone and Dickens said heartily, 'Satisfied?'

Latimer nodded slowly. 'Yes . . . so far,' and then Mr. Bahpoori arrived with the paper and ink and Latimer settled down to write his letter to Saladin.

8

As the Land-Rover bumped back through the pass towards the airfield Latimer was suddenly depressed. He was also shaking all over . . . from fatigue and anti-climax, and with disgust. The bodies of the Russian agents, cut down and thrown into a small hut at the edge of the town, had been revolting – but he had examined them meticulously, and their clothes and equipment, needled all the time by the fear that even now Saladin had something important to hide, one more trick in reserve . . . Latimer didn't doubt that Margaret would be on the plane, because that had been the central point of the negotiation. But somewhere along the line he had missed a clue – he was almost sure of it, and the anonymous Russian agents had always seemed to him likely to provide at least a lead. But in the end he had been forced to admit that he was satisfied, and Dickens and he had climbed back into the Land-Rover. Dickens was taking no chances this time and the back of the vehicle was again crowded with soldiers of the Defence Force. He had lost no time in relieving Latimer of the useless pistol but he wanted, clearly, to be ready for any future monkey business.

And now he was *going to see Margaret* . . . but in his exhaustion he could feel no more than a sort of hopeless nostalgia.

Dickens said, 'There's the plane,' pointing – and Latimer, who had seen it several minutes earlier, nodded. It was parked just in front of the airport building, and there were a couple of soldiers on guard at the foot of the iron ladder. The pilot was walking up and down beside the plane, smoking. The Land-Rover bumped forward across the scrub and camel-thorn at an agonising foot pace, and then in a final spurt swept out on to the tarmac at speed and drew up with the inevitable squeal of brakes.

The pilot said flatly, 'There's a sheila on board. They're deporting her.'

Latimer said hollowly, 'Oh . . .'

'I don't know if we'll get off the ground at all in this heat but Saladin's itching to see the last of us. We're starting now . . . Right with you?'

'Fine.' He started up the ladder like an automaton and behind him Dickens said loudly, 'Well, goodbye then, Latimer.'

Latimer half-turned, raising a hand and Dickens, mollified, saluted impressively. 'Goodbye, Dickens.'

It was quite dark inside the plane – or seemed so after the glare outside, and it was also stifling: the plane had been parked in the sun all morning. Latimer stopped just by the door and groped for something non-metallic to hold on to. He said doubtfully into the darkness, 'Margaret?'

There was no reply, and he took a couple of hesitant steps forward. The darkness began to define itself in different shades of grey – squares of pale grey where the windows were, black in the spaces between, darker grey where . . . and suddenly he saw her. The floor of the plane sloped sharply up towards the cockpit door and she was sitting at the extreme top of the cabin, folded down on to the metal bench. She looked forgotten and insignificant, like a piece of luggage that someone has left behind.

Latimer said again, '*Margaret?*' blundering eagerly up the metal slope towards her.

She said, 'I gather that I owe all this to you,' and he barely recognised the angry voice as hers.

'Owe? Well –'

'To be deported, under armed guard, like a criminal – '

'But Margaret – '

' – presumably to face charges in the United Kingdom – I can't think what else would justify such behaviour. I was foolishly unaware in Beirut that you were an *agent* of the

197

British government, a member of the *Department*.' She spat the words.

Latimer winced. He said, 'For Christ's sake, Margaret — '

'Don't swear at me . . . '

'And don't be so bloody schoolmistressy . . . ' He took a deep breath and started again. 'I wanted to come and find you. They offered me the fare if I would come and see Saladin for them.'

'Why should they ask *you*?'

He said reluctantly, 'I worked for them once before . . . a long time ago.'

It was clear from Margaret's silence that she regarded her point as proved.

Latimer said deliberately, 'I worked for them in September 1956. In Egypt.' Margaret looked up at him sharply. 'It was a shambles. The Egyptians I'd recruited were all caught. Four of them were shot. The rest went to prison for ten years. And I killed one man myself, in cold blood, in order to get away. He was an Egyptian soldier.'

There was a moment's silence and then she said, defiantly, 'And you're proud of it, I suppose.'

'Oh, don't be childish.'

The metal ladder clattered under a man's weight and the pilot appeared in the doorway. 'Set to go?'

Latimer nodded and then, with an effort, said aloud, 'Yes . . . sure. Let's go.'

The pilot pulled in the ladder and stowed it under the roof. He bolted the door and walked up through the cabin to the cockpit, glancing curiously at them as he passed. He said, 'Strap yourselves in.' The door of the cockpit slammed behind him and Margaret said at once, 'I apologise.'

Latimer sat down wearily on the bench opposite her and groped for the straps. 'That's all right.'

She went on pacifically, 'It just seemed rather unnecessary, that's all . . . All those soldiers — loaded rifles and so on.'

He said slowly, 'What *exactly* do you mean?'

'They said it was all your orders.'

'*What* was?'

Controlling herself, she said carefully, 'I was at the hospital,

198

waiting till this evening's plane, and suddenly two Land-Rovers came screeching up, full of soldiers brandishing rifles. They bundled me into the back of one of the Land-Rovers and drove me across the pass at about a hundred miles an hour and shoved me in here in this appalling heat and left me to roast . . .' Her voice had become progressively angrier, but now again she controlled it and said politely, 'So you see, I was cross when they said that you had ordered it. I thought you might have come and found me yourself if you had wanted to.'

The pilot had started the engines and the plane was vibrating. Latimer shouted, 'You were at the *hospital*?'

'Yes. They refused me a visa when I arrived last night and rather than make me wait at the airport for twenty-four hours they quite decently said I could sleep at the hospital, if I promised not to attempt to go into the town. And I must say it was fascinating. Dr. Rifai is so nice, isn't he? and I gave some blood and –'

But Latimer had started to laugh. Crouched painfully on the bench, he rocked backwards and forwards, contorted with laughter. Margaret stopped talking and watched him. She looked hurt. Latimer made an effort. Saladin, it seemed, had a far more developed sense of humour than he had realised.

The plane jolted and started to move forward slowly. Latimer took out a handkerchief and dried his eyes. Out of a side window he could see that Dickens had backed his Land-Rover off the tarmac and was standing beside it, waiting to see them take off. It was as though they were looking at the surface of another planet. Dickens, ripping off a final salute, was weightless, and when Latimer waved back it was across light years. For all practical purposes he had left Panjeh for ever. Latimer's heart rose.

Margaret looked at her watch. She said sadly, 'I wonder if he's died yet.'

'Who?'

'There's a man dying at the hospital.'

Latimer said harshly, 'It happens all the time.' He had no wish to be reminded of the hospital.

'But he was in such terrible pain . . . And he was English –' She added hastily, 'I know it shouldn't make any difference.'

'*English?*'

'Well, he spoke English . . . There's something odd about him actually. Nobody would talk about him and I wasn't allowed in to see him. They just said he was an Arab from the town, but you could hear him all over the hospital. "Holy Saint Patrick", he kept saying, "Holy Saint Patrick".'

9

For the first half mile Latimer ran as fast as he could go, taking the tufts of camel-thorn like a hurdler and scattering sand and pebbles with a noise that sounded deafening to him even above the roar of the plane's engines. Then, sooner than he had dared to hope, he was behind a small hillock, pressed flat to the burning ground and gasping.

Behind him the scream of the plane's engines rose still higher as the pilot, having seen him safely into cover, put his plane into its run towards take-off. The scream receded down the runway and, cautiously, Latimer raised his head. Now he would know whether Dickens had seen him drop from the plane as it waited, revving its engines, at the extreme end of the runway. But the Land-Rover was still parked on the edge of the runway, nearly a mile away, and there were two or three figures there too . . . Latimer lowered his head again and lay still.

Saladin was a clever man – a psychologist. He had explained the extra man on Cordwainer's plane with a story that wouldn't stand up for five minutes once you looked at it, but Latimer had swallowed it at once, whole – because it hinged on mockery of himself. But now he knew that the Irishman was still alive, and everything followed from that.

He had not in fact, he remembered with surprise, been made in the least suspicious by the sight of that early morning burial – and his insistent questioning of Dickens had been no more than a general protest at the charade that was being mounted for his benefit. But Saladin had felt obliged at once to provide a satisfactory explanation . . . How do you hide a death?

thought Latimer. In a grave. How do you hide a grave? In a graveyard. If the Land-Rover hadn't passed at the moment it did the fact of that extra death would simply have evaporated.

The plane had at last hoisted itself off the ground and now circled back over the airfield, gaining height. Latimer saw the pilot's face peer down from the cockpit, looking for him, but he didn't move. He hoped the pilot was as reliable as he seemed, and would pass his message rapidly to someone in the Embassy in Dubai. Because if he didn't . . . The plane was receding, lifting itself up slowly over the mountains, heading towards the sea, towards Dubai. The sound of its engines faded to a drone.

And Margaret – where would she go now? Would she wait in Dubai? . . . wait for *him*? Put like that, the idea was at once improbable. And yet he had come to Dubai, to Panjeh, only for her.

From the direction of the airport building Latimer heard faintly the sound of the Land-Rover's engine, and then it too receded and ceased: it must have gone back through the pass towards the town. For five more minutes he watched the airport building, but there was no sign of life and finally, climbing stiffly to his feet, he set off up the valley immediately behind him. There was a rough track here that would bring him down eventually on to the shore on the far side of the town – on the far side of the promontory on which the fort was built.

It was rough going and the heat was appalling but the first part was the worst and when he had scrambled over the first line of rocky hills he found himself on easier ground, a dusty track leading down a dry riverbed to the sea. He jogged along, sweating, looking up at the line of hills on his left, over which he would have to climb to reach the burial ground. There were a few places where he could have clambered up, but then he would have been as exposed as a lizard on a whitewashed wall and he preferred to go on down the full length of the dry valley to the sea and then climb over the neck of the promontory. Occasionally he paused, his heart beating, thinking he had heard the beat of the helicopter's engine, but it was always a false alarm and he jogged on slowly.

It was more than two hours before he reached the shore, a

tiny strip of white sand where the valley's dry riverbed met the sea. The hills on his left flung themselves into the sea in a jumble of enormous boulders and rubble that thrust itself out into the blue water for half a mile and then rose up again, solidified, to support the oppressive weight of the fort. Immediately on the far side of the rocks – if his memory was right – was the graveyard. He poked about among the massive bits of stone until he found what he was looking for – the inevitable goat track, and clambered up thankfully.

It took him no more than twenty minutes to cross the neck of the promontory, picking his way, avoiding the crevices and the shale, placing his feet with caution on the sloping rocks. And then, for the third time that day, he was looking down at the stones and the newly-turned sand of the grave – at the Union Jack and the plastic delphiniums.

In the distance the white roofs of the town quivered under the impact of the sun. It was three o'clock and the hottest moment of the day. Even the sea had been crushed by the pressure of the heat. The surface of the harbour still threw off points of brightness but its blue had darkened to purple and there was no longer a line of white on the shore to suggest movement or coolness. It looked like a pool of lava.

The dogs had taken themselves off long ago, so there were no spectators as Latimer bent down to remove the flag and the plastic flowers and started one by one to shift the stones. They were heavier than they looked. His clothes were already wet through and now each time he leaned over to take hold of one of the stones big drops of sweat fell out of his hair and on to the ground.

He had no tools except a spanner, borrowed from the plane. He shifted three stones from one end of the grave and started to gouge with the spanner at the ground underneath. But the sand had been heavily and effectively stamped down and the spanner made little impression. He tried digging with his hands, but that was even less effective – and painful. In the end he found that the only way was to loosen the sand with the spanner and then shift it afterwards with his hands. But it took a long time. It was nearly an hour before he reached something hard.

He cleared the sand gently away from the face and even then, for a moment, he was puzzled. It is a curious experience to look down into a grave and to see a face so like one's own. They had even buried Haider in the horn-rimmed spectacles that he had chosen because they were just like the ones that Latimer had worn when they were both together at Oxford.

Latimer shovelled the sand back with his hands and stamped it down. He replaced the stones and tidied up as best he could. After a moment's hesitation he even replaced the Union Jack: he reckoned that with at any rate one part of his personality Haider would have been amused.

10

At Dubai airport there was pandemonium: the press had arrived. A sweating television team was trying to get its equipment through the Customs.

'For? What's it *for*? Godalmighty, it's a television camera, can't you see? . . . Merv, you try.'

Tossing back his beautiful hair, Merv leaned gently on the piled-up equipment. His earrings glittered. 'Telly? . . . telly?' he said softly to the dazzled Customs man, 'whatever d'you *do* in the evenings then?'

It was clearly going to take hours – and Latimer started to get impatient. The pilot had put the Ruler's helicopter down in a obscure corner of the airfield but it couldn't be long before the press found out that it was there – and then all hell would be let loose. The unpleasant two hours during which he had been in the hands of Saladin's guards, followed by his abrupt and still unexplained release, had left him dazed and exhausted. But he was holding on to one idea: Cordwainer. He signalled at the Customs man over the heads of the television team that he had no luggage and started to sidle past. Merv's friend glanced at him sharply but he let him go.

Immediately outside the Customs hall Peter Arden grabbed his arm. 'Steven! What in the name – ' Faces turned from all sides and he hustled Latimer on towards the exit. In a sagging tropical suit Arden was fatter than ever, and his hair and moustache were straggling wildly as though they'd shot up suddenly in recent rain and hadn't yet been trimmed.

This time there was no Land-Rover, no Robinson. Angela was waiting for them in a taxi. She looked depressed and more than a little frightened and gazed appealingly at Latimer as he clambered in. Arden must have been giving her hell.

Arden gave rapid instructions to the driver and the taxi shot forward. '*What* have you been doing?' he hissed into Latimer's ear. '*What's* been going on? The most *disgraceful* behaviour. I – ' Angela he ignored entirely.

The taxi-driver was wearing the dull red Panjehi turban. He drove with exuberance, and Latimer wondered how much he, personally, had got out of yesterday's bonanza. A rifle? Twenty pounds in Maria Teresa dollars?

'*Answer* me, Steven.'

Latimer said, 'We've got to find Cordwainer. I know he's here somewhere, giving a press conference.'

'Cordwainer? The industrialist? Yes, he's here. Or he was this afternoon. But Steven, do you *realise* what you've done? You've been expelled from Panjeh. Deported. A representative of – ' He checked himself, glancing at the red turban, ' – of *us, deported.* There'll be an appalling row, questions. Saladin is *furious.*'

Latimer said, '*I'm* furious.'

In the main street a rival television team, better organised, was using the last of the sunset to get some introductory footage on to film. They had tethered a camel to a parking meter and a familiar-looking paunchy man with a microphone strung round his neck was talking earnestly into the camera. He was wearing his political upheavals expression.

Latimer said, 'Saladin's firmly in power again. The Popular Front is finished – for the moment. What more do you want?'

'Desecrating a graveyard . . . have you gone mad?'

Angela said timidly, 'There may be reasons,' and they both turned to stare. Peter said, 'I'm coming to *you* later.'

Five minutes later the taxi drew up. Latimer said, 'But aren't we going to the Embassy?'

Arden laughed bitterly, paying off the taxi. 'No, we are not. The Ambassador takes the dimmest possible view of your recent activities . . . and he says you were specifically warned.'

He hustled them into the hotel with a painful grip on Latimer's elbow and collected a key from the desk. Then they all went up in the lift and Arden had unlocked the door and got them both through it and into the anonymous little bedroom before he let go.

Latimer said, 'All right. Drop all this nonsense. Cordwainer's your man, and the sooner you arrest him the better.'

Arden sat down with a bump on the low bed. ' "*My man*"? "*My man*?" You've seen too many movies. What on earth are you talking about?'

Latimer felt himself go red. He said carefully, 'Haider is dead and I believe that Cordwainer was primarily responsible for his death.'

'Haider's in Beirut.'

Latimer said patiently, 'No . . . He's in a grave in Panjeh . . . I've just seen his body.'

Arden said irritably, 'He's made three statements to the Beirut press in the last twenty-four hours. Of *course* he's in Beirut.' Then seeing Latimer's face, he said more slowly, 'Start at the beginning.'

Latimer said carefully, 'Cordwainer is a director of Anglo-French, a small oil company that's trying to get itself a foothold in the Middle East. But all the lucrative concessions are held by the big companies.'

Peter said angrily, 'I know all that.'

'Somehow or other – probably through Duquair – Cordwainer heard about Haider. Haider had joined up with the Popular Front people out of sheer desperation. Britain and Egypt had let him down, and no one else was even interested in the Gulf. I don't think he ever believed at all in the Front's politics but he'd have joined any movement – whatever it was – that held out a prospect of getting rid of Saladin.

'The Front were putting a lot of time and money into propaganda among the exiled Panjehi in Dubai and I think they probably found that Haider's position as son of Hassan, and his claim to be the legitimate Ruler of Panjeh, cut far more ice in the Gulf than they would really have wished. Ideologically it was all wrong, but he was certainly very useful to them and I think this accounts for the really quite important position he got into. He was never really a leader but he was certainly allowed to behave like one.'

Angela said, 'His official title was Secretary of the Agit-Prop section.' She was lying flat on the second bed, her long legs crossed, and even with his mind on Haider Latimer was forced to register how decorative she looked.

Arden snapped, 'Don't interrupt.'

It was the first sign of interest he had shown in what Latimer was saying.

'Well, then Cordwainer appeared on the scene and offered Haider an infinitely better deal than he would ever have got out of the Front. He said he was prepared to finance an invasion of Panjeh to put Haider back in as Ruler. He, Cordwainer, would provide the money and the arms – and Haider, through the Front organisation, would provide the manpower. In return, of course, Anglo-French would get the contract to exploit the new oil.

'Haider's been taken for a ride quite a number of times by potential backers and I suspect he drove a hard bargain. For one thing he didn't want to mess up his position with the Front till he was sure of the other deal. And I'm quite certain that he didn't give his final agreement until he'd actually *seen* the rifles and the money. And that made the timing a bit tight.

'Because the Russians really had started at last to send help to the guerrillas. For them, of course, it was mainly a question of containing the Chinese advance in the Gulf. They were cautious about arms but they agreed as a start to send three agents, officially to strengthen the guerrillas' leadership but also of course to report back on whether the prospects for a communist revolution in Panjeh were really strong enough to justify the international rumpus that would certainly follow.

'I suspect that the Cordwainer-Haider affair was timed for some time next week, certainly not sooner. But then the guerrillas jumped the gun. They blew up the rig. They may have wanted to show the Russians what they could do even without a strengthened leadership. Or perhaps they were just trigger-happy. Anyway, they did it. And the Front People in Beirut started at once to mobilise the Panjehi in Dubai in case the guerrillas pulled off a coup. Cordwainer had to do something quickly. He got himself – and the arms, and the money – out to Beirut as fast as he possibly could, he finalised his deal with Haider, and the same night they set off.'

Arden said sharply, 'Who?' He had his familiar, sceptical, tutorial face on.

Latimer said, 'Cordwainer, Duquair and Haider.'

'But Haider remained in Beirut –'

'*No*. He went too. He was in one plane, with Cordwainer and Duquair. And the rifles and the money were in the other. The plan that Haider had sold to his Front pals called for a rendezvous at a spot in the mainland coast opposite Panjeh, and an immediate sea-crossing.

'But Cordwainer, of course – ' Latimer stopped. He still found it so difficult to believe.

Peter said worriedly, 'Cordwainer's an M.B.E., you know.'

'Yes . . . that's exactly it. He's the director of an oil firm and of a whole lot of other companies and he hadn't the slightest wish to foment a revolution – let alone to get involved with a Popular Front movement, however indirectly. And of course it's just the sort of thing that M.I.5. gets very excited about if you happen to come originally from eastern Europe. So – ' Latimer stopped again. He said slowly, 'I think what must have happened is this . . . Cordwainer ordered the plane containing the rifles and the money to land first at the rendezvous point. Then, instead of putting his own plane – in which he also had Duquair and Haider – down too, as arranged, he flew straight on to Panjeh, and it must have been then, while the plane was actually in the air flying towards Panjeh that they . . . overpowered him, I suppose. Tied Haider up. It must have been as crude as that . . . And delivered him to Saladin, like a parcel, as soon as they arrived . . . I think that until that moment Haider genuinely believed that Cordwainer would let him use the Panjehi exiles to overthrow Saladin and put himself into power – with Cordwainer's rifles. But Cordwainer didn't mind in the slightest who was Ruler of Panjeh so long as he got his contract. And Haider could be used to better effect as a bargaining counter . . . Cordwainer must have been in contact with Saladin for quite some time. He wanted that oil contract very much indeed – and Haider was his entrance fee. For Saladin, of course, it was cheap at the price. He probably *was* fed up with Shell and quite ready for a change – and this way he got Haider as well . . . '

Latimer stopped but Arden didn't comment, and after a moment Steven forced himself to finish the story. He recited quickly, as though reading aloud from a document of little importance, 'Haider was killed with a bullet through the head. Before that he had been tortured. It seems almost certain that Saladin succeeded in extracting from him all the information he needed about the Front's plans, and the guerrillas, and, in particular, the details of the three Russians' arrival. And no doubt he got quite a lot, too, about the Front's organisation on the coast. Which Saladin will now pass on, as a gesture of friendship and co-operation, to the Sheikh of Dubai.'

After a moment Arden said grudgingly, 'I suppose it's all possible . . . but you know, if Haider had been on that plane we'd have known. I've seen the cables and – '

'I've seen his body.'

Arden looked at him thoughtfully. 'Is that what you were – digging up?'

Latimer nodded. He smiled diffidently, 'Haider was – disguised.'

'As – ?'

'As me.'

Arden was amused, and showed it. Angela said slowly, 'Mr. Arden, please let Dr. Latimer explain . . . I think I understand.' Latimer said, 'Haider had a room booked in my name next to his own suite in the hotel, and when he wanted to get away from the hotel without his entourage knowing he simply went in there and changed into European clothes. And he put on spectacles. His beard must have been a false one. He would have been recognised close to, of course, but at a distance it would be okay.'

Arden said suspiciously, 'But why?' He still thought the whole story might be a joke.

Latimer said, 'So as to be able to go and see Duquair, who

was Cordwainer's Beirut agent. Duquair had a special back entrance to his house. They were negotiating the terms of the deal.'

Arden said, 'But what I still don't understand, Steven, is why he chose to use *your* name. I know he knew you at Oxford, and you were friends, but he could so easily have called himself John Smith.'

Latimer said slowly, 'He'd used my name once before.'

Arden looked at him shrewdly. 'That story you told me in Oxford last week, about the girl . . . Was that Haider?'

Latimer nodded. 'Yes. He must have been at Barton all through September '56. The Department were – *you* were training him for a possible coup against his uncle.'

Arden nodded without embarrassment. 'That's right . . . I'd forgotten. But I say, Steven – ' his expression was crafty, 'why did he use your name *then*? To get *you* into trouble?'

Latimer shook his head. 'At that time it was the main dream of Haider's life to be able to pass as an Englishman. He wanted to *be* an Englishman, really . . . I doubt if he thought at all about the implications for me. The whole thing was a fantasy, and when it was over he simply went back to being Haider bin Hassan again – and forgot all about the girl, probably. But when the need arose, twenty years later, to pass as a European he used the same name . . . But then I happened to come to Beirut and the balloon went up . . . '

Arden thought about it for several minutes. Then he nodded, satisfied. 'And you were all he thought an Englishman should be – ' He laughed loudly, delighted. 'Half Irishman, half Jew. Good old Steven, the perfect Englishman . . . Well, I must say, that's all extraordinarily interesting and thank you for telling me, but I'm afraid, Steven, I've got to come back to your behaviour in Panjeh. You went as *our* representative, you know, a representative of the *Department*, of Her Majesty's Government – '

Latimer said, 'For heaven's *sake*, Peter – '

Arden stopped, genuinely surprised. 'What?'

'Well – what I said earlier. We oughtn't to waste any time. Cordwainer probably won't stay long.'

Peter said slowly, 'You want to talk to him?'

'Talk! – no, but we ought to arrest him.'

Peter's voice was suddenly languid. 'I'm not a policeman – and anyway, this is Dubai.'

'There must be extradition arrangements.'

'Oh, I dare say . . . ' He sounded vague.

'Peter, are you or aren't you going to arrest Cordwainer – or at least arrange to have him arrested?'

'What for?'

'*What for?* Well, for a start, for bringing about Haider's death. For planning a revolution. For – '

'For cancelling your contract with Barbizon?'

Latimer said angrily, 'Don't be flippant. Of course I have a personal grievance against him, but the man's a criminal.'

Arden shook his head slowly. 'Forget it, Steven. Anything he did, he did in Panjeh, and that's Saladin's look-out. And Saladin's his pal. As far as the U.K.'s concerned he's far more likely to get a knighthood – or a special award for exports. I don't think you understand even now what's happened. Shell's half Dutch, Anglo-French is ninety per cent British. The new contract is a breakthrough for the U.K. in the Gulf. The Board of Trade will be jubilant.'

Latimer said slowly, 'Are you serious?'

'Entirely . . . of course I am.'

'And if he also killed Angus?'

Arden's face shut tight. 'Angus committed suicide. The Beirut authorities held their inquest this morning, and we accept their verdict. Never mind what we in the Department really think. We never make a stink when this happens to one of our agents – far too much is liable to come out. Angus committed suicide.'

With sudden panic Latimer said, 'But *you* realise – you yourself – that Cordwainer's a criminal?'

Arden hesitated fractionally and then he shrugged. 'All right. Angus was murdered by some local Beirut thugs. We're not sure yet who was paying, but we're assuming it was someone connected with the plans for a coup in Panjeh. Angus had been Saladin's political adviser for years, and he was known to be in Beirut *in order* to penetrate Puff-lop and any other groups with designs on Panjeh. Perhaps they thought he'd discovered something . . . I'd been thinking it must have been Haider who arranged it all, though it's not really his style, but now from what you tell me about Cordwainer − ' He thought about it for a moment and then shook his head. 'I don't think it'll work, though, time-wise. Cordwainer had only just arrived in Beirut − not more than a few hours − and in any case he had no reason to think that Angus had discovered anything about his plans, certainly nothing about him personally. And nothing about Duquair either. We had nothing at all to connect Cordwainer with Panjeh, even. If Angus had discovered anything he'd have let us know.'

Latimer felt as though his throat were closing up. He said with difficulty, 'I told him.'

'*You? Told him what?*'

'I told Cordwainer that Angus wanted to see him . . . and that he was in my room.' It had been when he met Cordwainer in the foyer of the Criterion, just after he left Angela. He heard his own voice again, half-drunk, giggling at his own stupid, non-existent joke . . . '*I've lent it to a friend of mine. Angus Bailey . . . I'm sure he'd like to meet you.*'

Arden said, 'Well . . . ' looking at Latimer with interest, 'in that case that's probably the answer.'

'So you'll arrest him now?'

Arden controlled himself with obvious difficulty. 'Will you *stop* it, Steven. *Stop* playing policemen. I've told you twenty times already why I'm not going to do anything more about Cordwainer . . . What you've told me simply tidies up the case, and thank you.'

Latimer thought for a moment he was going to say something more, but instead he stood up briskly and took a black briefcase out of the bottom of the wardrobe. He clicked it open, took out some large sheets of blank paper and spread them out on the dressing-table.

Latimer said, '*Peter* − '

Arden shrugged again, irritably, sitting down on the dressing-table stool and uncapping his fountain pen. 'What's the use? He's not a criminal in any sense that I'm obliged to take notice of . . . What's the date?'

'But don't you care about Haider?'

211

'Frankly, no. He's been an embarrassment to us for years . . .
Here – ' he'd had another idea. 'Angela, you must know
shorthand.'

Angela came up off the bed like a fish on a line and took
the pen out of his hand.

Peter moved to one side to let her sit down. 'I don't see
why you're taking Haider's cause so much to heart, Steven.
He caused *you* enough trouble, heaven knows, and he treated
that wretched girl disgracefully.'

It was true, of course, and Latimer realised that it would be
no use trying to explain to Peter. He couldn't explain it to
himself. Were Haider still alive he wouldn't have stopped until
he'd caught up with him, and then – but his mind didn't go
any further than that. But Haider, murdered, was still, in spite
of everything – Haider. The injury he had done to Margaret
wasn't relevant: it wasn't for *that* that Cordwainer had delivered him to Saladin tied up like a parcel, to be tortured and
shot. And Cordwainer was responsible for Angus's death too.
Angus . . . he would have to tell Nicholas.

Peter had started to dictate a telegram to London, striding
up and down in the narrow space. ' . . . I was able to persuade
His Highness the Sheikh of Dubai to use his good offices with
the Ruler of Panjeh to secure Dr. Latimer's immediate release.
As instructed, I . . .'

Arden was refusing to involve himself with the problem of
Cordwainer – or to involve his Department, or the government. So that left him, Latimer . . . Which was the most
expensive hotel in Dubai, he wondered. That would be the
place to start looking for Cordwainer.

' . . . On the morning of September . . . ' Arden halted,
throwing up his arms theatrically. 'I really *must* know what
the date is. I can't keep saying "last Friday" . . . and Steven,
you stay here. You're only not under arrest because you're with
me.'

Taking his hand off the door-knob, Latimer said soothingly,
'Okay, okay,' and sank down on to a bed. The key was still on
the outside of the lock and that ought to give him the five
minutes that he needed . . . Arden was watching him suspiciously. Latimer rummaged submissively in his trouser pockets

and pulled out his diary. 'It's the twelfth, or something. What's today? Thursday?' He flicked over the pages, and stopped abruptly.

Angela said, 'Friday.' She thought for a moment and then nodded, 'Yes, Friday.'

Latimer said, 'Then I've got to get on a plane.'

Arden's suspicion turned to irritation. He said, 'You can do whatever you bloody well like once I've finished this telegram. But you can't leave now.'

'I've got to be in England tomorrow afternoon.'

'For heaven's sake, Steven, what are you trying to pull now?'

Latimer thrust the diary at him. 'Look,' he said, ' "Nicholas. International Day, 3 p.m." Could anything be clearer?'

11

Robinson and Angela took him out to the airport. Now that he was actually leaving, the Ambassador's displeasure had abated and he'd sent Robinson to see Latimer off on his behalf. Or perhaps he just wanted to be absolutely certain that Latimer got on the plane.

Angela was silent and inclined to be snappy but Robinson was as equable as ever.

'Keep an eye on Cordwainer,' Latimer said urgently. 'Let me know everything he says and does, and when he leaves if you can possibly let me know where he's going . . . ' He had been speaking to Angela but Robinson answered. 'Yes, yes of course.' But he really wanted some details about the events on Panjeh. 'Is it really true that you desecrated a *graveyard*?'

'I'd love a drink,' Angela said abruptly.

Robinson shook his head, unoffended. 'You're forgetting,' he said, 'Dubai's dry.'

'No, I mean a *drink*, something wet.' She sounded tense and irritable.

'Oh I see, a *drink*. Oh yes, well, nothing easier. Coke? Seven

213

Up? . . . Right. You, Steve? Right . . . ' He ambled off.

Latimer said at once, 'What happened to Margaret Wedder-burn?'

Angela shrugged. Irritably she said, 'She went back to Beirut . . . Steven – shall I see you in London?' It came out in a sort of jerk.

'Oh, I expect so –'

'*No* . . . ' Her irritation erupted again. 'You know perfectly well what I mean.'

Latimer wasn't at all sure that he did and he looked at her warily.

In a careful voice she said, 'Does – *us* go on?'

Latimer said helplessly, 'But Angela . . . ' There was a moment's silence.

He said, 'I'm over *forty*, Angela.'

'And I'm twenty-three.'

Her meaning was plain but he ignored it. '*Exactly*, you're young, and beautiful, and – and you ought to have somebody young and jolly, like – like –'

'Like Robinson, I suppose.'

He seized the suggestion gratefully, not thinking, 'Yes! Why not? He's –'

'He's an ass – ' Abruptly she was in tears. ' – and you're a bloody fool.'

'Here! Oi!' Robinson – and three insecurely balanced Cokes. 'They've called your flight, you know. Not that we want to lose you or anything, but –'

Latimer hadn't any luggage so the three of them just walked over to the gate and by the time they got there Latimer's empty hands felt as conspicuous as a pair of boxing gloves. Should he kiss her? – pat her shoulder? – shake hands? 'Well –' The enormous paws swung.

'Goodbye –' Too late he realised that he didn't even know Robinson's Christian name. 'Ah – goodbye. And thank you for everything.'

Robinson held out a hand and Latimer shook it energetically. Robinson said, 'Don't you worry, I'll look after her,' and dropped an arm round Angela's shoulders. Latimer saw her go white for a second, and then red – and only then remembered that Robinson must still believe that she was Latimer's secretary.

She realised it too in the same moment and grinned weakly.

She said, 'Steven . . . That subject we were discussing just now – I'm glad to know finally what your views really are . . . But I must tell you something. I wasn't quite candid with you on one point. That – parcel that you asked about . . . it isn't in Beirut, it's in London.'

Slower, as always, he said, '*Parcel?*'

She grinned again, briefly. 'Well – baggage.'

12

It was raining in Oxford and there were no taxis at the station. Latimer set out to walk and his shoes were soaked through before he'd even crossed the canal. He caught a bus, eventually, from St. Giles, but then had to walk again from the Banbury Road down to the school. In Arabia an hour of such rain would have been a never-forgotten miracle, a happening from which to date events for years to come. Here, it had clearly lasted for days and would last for several more, pounding the gardens to a damp pulp, blurring the transition from summer to autumn. In Arabia . . . in Arabia Haider lay in a sandy grave and the evening paper in Latimer's pocket reported his unexplained disappearance from his Beirut hotel: it seemed probable, the report added, that he had been drowned while bathing . . . Drowned certainly, in a tideless, polluted sea.

A white car went past him, almost without a sound, flinging out a fine spray of dirty water like – like the soiled outer petals of some exquisite flower . . . It was years since the sight of a car had aroused such emotion in him, and five minutes later he paused to admire it again, parked in the rain beside the front door of the school.

Nicholas was waiting just inside. Behind him a solid door was clearly marked 'Headmaster'. There were small boys everywhere, fizzing about like rockets out of control, and the

215

noise was grotesque. Nicholas's greeting was more constrained even than usual and when they had shaken hands he made no move to lead Latimer off to the international delights that were doubtless waiting. Instead, they stood awkwardly in silence until it became gradually clear that both his constraint and his reluctance to move were connected with the small boy standing beside him – small, but perhaps, on closer inspection, just marginally larger than Nicholas . . . and Latimer perceived abruptly that Nicholas was in fact speechless with the glory of the elder boy's mere propinquity. Nevertheless the general silence became, after a time, embarrassing. Finally, Latimer spoke.

'Have you seen the white car? The one outside?' He muttered it out of the side of his mouth, jerking his head briefly in the direction of the front door. He had no idea how Nicholas really expected him to behave. 'It looks super but I don't know what – '

'It's a Borghini-Kraus *Chimera*.' It was the larger boy who had spoken, but Nicholas had to repeat the words twice before Latimer understood.

Nicholas added reverently, 'It's got a *turbo-engine*,' and then whispering, 'It's Wayno's *father's*,' and with a look of great meaning and varied noddings of the head he succeeded in indicating that *this* was Wayno, and that the father was in with the headmaster.

Latimer looked with respect at the youngest there had ever been in the Under Elevens – and that legendary figure nodded back kindly. Then he spoke. He said, 'It's the Mark Two. Nought to sixty in five seconds, top speed two-fifty, sensor-controlled disc brakes, four-wheel drive, radar . . . '

Latimer said feebly, 'Are you going to be a mechanic – ?' He would have added ' – when you grow up', but the tolerance in Wayno's eyes prevented him.

Wayno shook his head slowly. 'Follow me,' he said. But he made no move.

Latimer said, 'Ah – ' After a moment he glanced sideways for help. Nicholas was gazing at him with concentration, *willing* him to understand.

Recognising the difficulty (but more, Latimer thought, to

216

relieve Nicholas's embarrassment than his own) Wayno said kindly, 'When a plane lands at a big airport it's led into its proper place by a car with 'Follow me' written on the back. I'm going to drive one of those.'

Latimer said again, 'Ah – '

A bell rang, an electric jangle that shifted every boy in sight as though the current had passed directly through his body. In one moment they had all disappeared, totally, as if by magic.

A young master with a pink face very like Robinson's then appeared and rounded up the loose parents and coralled them politely in the school hall. Latimer sat down near the back on a folding chair of peculiar discomfort, and waited. There was a long pause and then, abruptly, all the lights in the hall went out and the grey curtains on the stage were illuminated from below. They parted in the middle and the headmaster stepped through. He was lean, with a colossal chin that he carried well up, and Latimer remembered with discomfort the missionary spirit (we - are - the - people - to - do - something - about - a - boy – from – so – unsatisfactory – a – home) with which Nicholas had originally been accepted.

Pointing his chin at the ceiling the headmaster welcomed the assembled parents and announced a programme of dances from many lands. It would be followed, he said, by tea. There was also an exhibition of the boys' paintings . . .

Latimer's mind slipped out from under the words. Had it really been worth it? – coming all this way in order not to disappoint Nicholas. He had abandoned his chance of dealing once and for all with Cordwainer, and he might never have another.

The headmaster disappeared. A disembodied voice said loudly 'Greece!' and the grey curtains jerked apart. Taped music of a faintly oriental nature began abruptly. The *dabké* – powerful, monotonous, intricate steps designed to test the concentration of a hundred generations of drunken Greeks . . . The gym-shoes stepped, crossed, stamped, stepped again, and the line snaked uncertainly across the stage. These must be the juniors.

He could wait, of course, until Cordwainer came back to England and then seek him out. 'You have left me no *choice*,' he would say, as Cordwainer had done. But he wouldn't use only a fist. He would ring the doorbell of Cordwainer's house – it was in South Eaton Place, he remembered suddenly, with a butler probably . . .

The music rose to a frenzy and the line shuffled off into the wings. The final, smallest boy agitated a red handkerchief, the curtains drew together and everybody clapped. A slight buzz of conversation started and two parents, arriving late, came clambering apologetically along Latimer's row of chairs, silhouetted dimly against the light on the stage curtains. Latimer hoisted himself to his feet, the wife murmured, 'Thank you', and for the split second after he recognised Anna the implication escaped him. But then he looked over her shoulder and saw him – Cordwainer.

The grey curtains jerked open again and parents at the back hissed at once 'Sit down'. Latimer and the Cordwainers folded abruptly on to the nearest chairs and Anna whispered with obvious pleasure, 'Dr. Latimer! I didn't recognise you. Oh – ' and her attention had gone, up on to the stage.

It was Wayno now, doing something by himself. What was it Nicholas had said? A sword dance – that was it. For Scotland. It looked more like rapid back-pedalling on a bicycle, Latimer thought, and it went on for far too long . . . His mind was frozen, immobile, unable even to approach the problems posed by Cordwainer's unbelievable irruption into Nicholas's International Day.

Wayno leaped wildly upwards for a last time and landed heavily on one knee, both arms spread out. The music stopped and everyone applauded, but none so loud . . . Beside him the Cordwainers were almost apoplectic with enthusiasm. Cordwainer – Wayno – 'His father comes and goes so much' . . . Loudly, uncaring, Latimer groaned.

Anna said, still clapping, 'They really teach them wonderfully, don't they?' Her eyes were shining.

'Margaret's here too,' she added vaguely. 'Somewhere . . . '

They stood awkwardly side by side, in silence, holding cups of tea. The Cordwainers had gone to see the art exhibition,

Nicholas and Wayno hadn't yet reappeared and no one else seemed inclined to talk to them.

For the twentieth time Margaret rattled the spoon nervously in her saucer. She said, 'What will you do, now?'

'I haven't thought really . . . ' He couldn't even begin to explain the shipwreck that had struck all his plans, and his ideas, in the last half-hour. With a wariness equal to her own he added, 'And you – ?'

She shrugged. 'Nothing's settled . . . ' Then, with a rush, 'Steven, what *did* happen? – yesterday, I mean. I haven't been able to think about anything else. I was so – so *ungracious* when you got on to the plane and – heaven knows I don't understand yet what *was* happening but I do so want to know.'

Latimer said helplessly, 'It's still going on.' He would have to decide somehow – soon – just how much or how little to tell her about Haider and about the man who had arranged to have him murdered, Cordwainer – her brother-in-law, Wayno's father . . . Incautiously he added, 'I don't know how much to say.'

'The whole truth. Naturally.'

He said violently, 'You may think differently about that once you've got the whole picture.'

She corrected herself immediately. 'I *believe* that I would always prefer to know everything, but I may be wrong.'

Latimer stirred his tea with concentration. 'Perhaps we could talk about it all when – if we both get back to Beirut.'

'So you're still going to Beirut?' Her disappointment was clear.

Hurt, Latimer said stiffly, 'Yes, certainly.'

'And after that? Will you practise in London again?'

Latimer said slowly, 'I've finished with doctoring.'

'Oh *no*! That's ridiculous.' She turned right round to look at him. 'You can't do that.'

'Why ever not?' Her vehemence annoyed him.

'Because – well, because it's a socially valuable skill and if you possess it you have an obligation to – you have a debt to pay, to society.'

'All right, but in my case *either* the debt is already paid *or* it never will be, and I prefer to think the former.'

219

'*You*! Whatever do *you* matter? That's a thoroughly selfish point of view.'

Latimer was appalled: Angela had said the same thing, in almost the same words. He said anxiously, 'Do you really think I'm so selfish?' and at once Margaret laughed.

'No, of course not, and anyway – ' Her voice had dropped abruptly into its lowest register, gruff and full of amusement, ' – anyway, why should you care what I think?'

Latimer said carefully, gripping his teaspoon with unconscious violence, 'I – value your opinion . . .'

A number of small boys had come sidling into the room, impelled from behind, and were now re-attaching themselves cautiously to their relatives, drifting obliquely across the room so as to make it clear that they merely happened to be passing.

Margaret said, 'You're going to break that spoon.'

Latimer said urgently, 'Everything I said that night in Beirut was true. *Is* true. Margaret –'

Observing Nicholas's crab-like approach she said, 'Is this one yours?'

'He is now.'

In exactly the same conversational tone she said, 'Do you think that you and I would always bicker so dreadfully?'

'Oh *yes*!' Latimer was suddenly light-headed with relief and excitement. 'Oh yes, I'm *sure* we would!'

Nicholas greeted them sombrely. 'Hi,' he said.

MEMORIAL TO THE DUCHESS

Jocelyn Kettle

Alice Chaucer is the heroine of this fascinating and lively novel set in the fifteenth century.

As the wife of William de la Pole, Duke of Suffolk, she became second only to the Queen of England. From Agincourt right through to the final Wars of the Roses she held sway in and around the Court. Widowed at the height of her husband's power, accused of treason by the Yorkists, always under strain – she used her cunning and her wit to face the turbulent events that washed round her and always succeeded in survival.

'Carefully constructed and researched ... she really does pass on the enjoyment she feels in her subject' – *Books & Bookmen*

'An historical novel of unusual merit' –
New Zealand Press

CORONET BOOKS

THE CAMERON STORY

Morton Cooper

Cameron pretended to be a sleepy town. But underneath its coy façade rumbled a feeling for vice that was all too ready to erupt.

When two people came to Cameron, the eruption was dramatic. One was Monica Spencer – *the* Monica Spencer of stage and screen – a living legend of ageless beauty and unending scandal whose sins were closing in on her.

The other was Tom Jara – a wild man from everywhere, a guitar on his back and blood on his hands, a man filled with lust for power and fury for his fellow humans.

These two came to Cameron like sharks into a goldfish tank and Cameron's sleepiness was soon propelled into a hideous nightmare.

CORONET BOOKS

TO LOOK AND PASS

Taylor Caldwell

Dan Hendricks was one of those people whose talent far exceeded his wealth. One of those people, in fact, who would always know resentment in social circles and praise in those worlds where drive and ambition were the currency of success.

Laboriously he clawed his way to the top. He was given his share of luck and took it. Took it to make a studied marriage to someone he was unable to love, to cling closely to the few friends he had made. But the town tried to run him out . . .

And that was when Dan Hendricks' inability to merely look and pass really paid off.

CORONET BOOKS

ALSO AVAILABLE IN CORONET BOOKS

TAYLOR CALDWELL

☐	02407 0	Maggie Her Marriage	35p
☐	01939 5	The Wicked Angel	35p
☐	18801 4	To Look and Pass	40p
☐	18800 6	Your Sins and Mine	35p

MORTON COOPER

☐	16531 6	The Cameron Story	40p

JOCELYN KETTLE

☐	18635 6	The Athelsons	40p
☐	18813 8	Memorial to the Duchess	50p

All these books are available at your bookshop or newsagent, or can be ordered direct from the publisher. Just tick the titles you want and fill in the form below.

CORONET BOOKS, P.O. Box 11, Falmouth, Cornwall.

Please send cheque or postal order. No currency, and allow the following for postage and packing:

1 book—10p, 2 books—15p, 3 books—20p, 4–5 books—25p, 6–9 books—4p per copy, 10–15 books—2½p per copy, 16–30 books—2p per copy, over 30 books free within the U.K.

Overseas—please allow 10p for the first book and 5p per copy for each additional book.

Name ....

Address ....

....